P

The Cl

"Amusing . . . Enjoyable." —*The Mystery Reader*

"We all should have a Charlotte Adams in our lives."
—ReviewingTheEvidence.com

"Talented author Mary Jane Maffini has crafted a clever and fun tale . . . Red herrings and surprises await the reader [and] complexities of the plot make for a worthwhile read . . . Enjoy. I did." —*The New Mystery Reader*

"Charlotte is feisty, funny, and determined to help people, whether it's organizing their mud room or clearing them of a murder charge . . . Delightful." —*I Love A Mystery*

"A sense of humor and Charlotte's misadventures enliven the narrative." —*Gumshoe Reviews*

Organize Your Corpses

"A comedic, murderous romp . . . Maffini is a relaxed, accomplished, and wickedly funny writer."
The Montreal Gazette

"Mary Jane Maffini provides a first-rate, well-organized whodunit . . . A new series that is fun to read."
—*Midwest Book Review*

"A fast-moving story." —*Contra Costa Times*

"Maffini's new series . . . is off to a brilliant start with this fast-paced mystery." —*Romantic Times*

Berkley Prime Crime titles by Mary Jane Maffini

ORGANIZE YOUR CORPSES
THE CLUTTERED CORPSE
DEATH LOVES A MESSY DESK

Death Loves a Messy Desk

Mary Jane Maffini

BERKLEY PRIME CRIME, NEW YORK

THE BERKLEY PUBLISHING GROUP
Published by the Penguin Group
Penguin Group (USA) Inc.
375 Hudson Street, New York, New York 10014, USA
Penguin Group (Canada), 90 Eglinton Avenue East, Suite 700, Toronto, Ontario M4P 2Y3, Canada
(a division of Pearson Penguin Canada Inc.)
Penguin Books Ltd., 80 Strand, London WC2R 0RL, England
Penguin Group Ireland, 25 St. Stephen's Green, Dublin 2, Ireland (a division of Penguin Books Ltd.)
Penguin Group (Australia), 250 Camberwell Road, Camberwell, Victoria 3124, Australia
(a division of Pearson Australia Group Pty. Ltd.)
Penguin Books India Pvt. Ltd., 11 Community Centre, Panchsheel Park, New Delhi—110 017, India
Penguin Group (NZ), 67 Apollo Drive, Rosedale, North Shore 0632, New Zealand
(a division of Pearson New Zealand Ltd.)
Penguin Books (South Africa) (Pty.) Ltd., 24 Sturdee Avenue, Rosebank, Johannesburg 2196,
South Africa

Penguin Books Ltd., Registered Offices: 80 Strand, London WC2R 0RL, England

DEATH LOVES A MESSY DESK

A Berkley Prime Crime Book / published by arrangement with the author

PRINTING HISTORY
Berkley Prime Crime mass-market edition / May 2009

Cover illustration by Stephen Cardner.
Cover design by Edwin Tse.
Interior text design by Laura K. Corless.

For information, address: The Berkley Publishing Group,
a division of Penguin Group (USA) Inc.,
375 Hudson Street, New York, New York 10014.

ISBN: 978-0-425-22809-8

BERKLEY® PRIME CRIME
Berkley Prime Crime Books are published by The Berkley Publishing Group,
a division of Penguin Group (USA) Inc.,
375 Hudson Street, New York, New York 10014.

PRINTED IN THE UNITED STATES OF AMERICA

10 9 8 7 6 5 4 3 2 1

Acknowledgments

I am grateful to the many people who contributed time, expertise, and moral support in the writing of this book. As always I appreciate the warm friendship and insightful comments of Lyn Hamilton and Mary MacKay-Smith. Victoria Maffini once again brought her unique sense of humor as well as advice on this project. Christopher Myers of Troy, New York, continued to be a gold mine of information and I continue to be grateful. Thanks also to Geoff Zeiss and Howard Gervais for elusive technical details and speedy response, and to Stephan Dirnberger for his usual cheerful assistance.

My long-suffering husband, Giulio, ensures that I have a happy environment for the making of mysteries and the princess dachshunds, Daisy and Lily, provide ideas every time they emerge from their blankies. I owe a great debt to the community of professional organizers who do so much to help clients triumph over clutter and bring order to their lives. Special thanks are due to my friend Helen Gilman of Organize-U, as well as to Connie Faith Shanti of the National Association of Professional Organizers, San Francisco Bay Area Chapter, and her colleagues Debra Baida, Margaret Luckens, Danelle McDermott, and Lisa Mark for fabulous background information, delivered with style and humor.

Thomas Colgan and Niti Bagchi of Berkley Prime

Crime are always upbeat, helpful, and unflappable. I'd be lost without them. Thanks to production editor Stacy Edwards and copyeditor Amy Schneider for their diligence and eagle eyes. Naturally, all errors are my own.

Position your desk so your back is never to the door. This aids concentration, and it just might save your life.

1

As the flash went off in my face, I yelped and dove for cover. Even before I landed chin first on the grassy lawn of Memorial Park, I knew it was yet another mistake in a long month of negatives.

A worried-looking woman bent over me as I raised my head. A digital camera dangled from a strap on her wrist. "Are you all right? I was just taking pictures of the fair. I didn't mean to startle you."

Truffle and Sweet Marie, my miniature wiener dogs, compounded the problem by leaping at her, teeth bared. I hooked my fingers into their tiny jeweled collars, gathered them in my arms, and scrambled to my feet. She backed away at high speed.

With a dog tucked under each arm, probably not the most normal look in the world, I did my best to reassure her. "The flash startled me, that's all."

"Totally my fault. I should have checked with you first before snapping your picture." She stopped, gasped, and moved closer. "Oh! Aren't you Charlotte Adams?"

Oh crap.

"No wonder you're so jumpy! After all that happened to you. And are these Truffle and Sweet Marie? They're adorable."

"You know them?" I said, holding tight as Truffle made a less-than-adorable lunge toward her.

"Know them? Everybody in the county knows them."

"Watch your hand," I said. "They're a bit overprotective."

"They're little heroes. How about a treat, cuties?" Unless I was wrong, she was offering the homemade brown sugar oatmeal cookies that were being sold at the baking stand.

"Oh, I don't think—" The snap of tiny jaws cut that short. Of course, they can be bought off with special treats because they've been spoiled rotten after all the attention that's been showered on them. That was the reason I was spending my Sunday afternoon at Woodbridge's Second Annual Volunteer Awareness Fair. When September stole into Woodbridge, I still felt the effects of too much murder, too close to home. I found myself shrieking and spinning at sudden noises. An unexpected plate of baked goods could reduce me to a puddle on the floor. As my throbbing grass-stained knees showed, I was a mess. And I hate anything messy.

The dogs wolfed two cookies each before I escaped to check out the booths set up in my favorite uptown park, near the Old Dutch Church. As a way of enticing people, the Central Volunteer Committee was dishing out ice cream cones. Dogs were welcome, kids were squealing, and even the faint wail of sirens in the distance didn't bother me.

"Thanks for coming," said the huge grinning man wearing a baseball cap with the Central Volunteer Committee logo. He handed me an ice cream. "Woodbridge needs you!"

That was good news because I needed to spend some time with people who had worse things to deal with than being afraid. And Truffle and Sweet Marie needed to get over themselves.

I savored the double-chocolate cone as I trotted along the path, stopping at each booth. Truffle and Sweet Marie sniffed toes. I had already picked up brochures and information from the Restoration Committee for the Waterfront, the Friendly Visitors of Woodbridge, and Habitat for Humanity when I spotted the perfect solution.

Woodbridge League of Therapy Dogs.

My heart fluttered. I skipped a couple of deserving booths and hustled closer. I waved back at the cheerful volunteer in a black T-shirt with a pair of huge white paws on it. She slid a brochure into my hand. "Hi there. Do you know about our wonderful program?"

"A bit," I breathed.

"Do you have a dog?"

"Well, just these two," I said pointing down.

"Ooh. Two. Then you know how much joy they bring you."

Truffle chose that moment to bare his teeth.

I nipped that in the bud and nodded. Not always joy, but why muddy the waters? "He doesn't mean that."

She ignored Truffle's behavior. "Then you can imagine the difference a dog visitor makes to a stroke victim or a lonely senior citizen or a . . ."

Perhaps she was nearsighted.

"Count me in," I said.

". . . troubled reader."

"Where do I sign up?"

"Here's our info package." She reached for a folder. "There are registration forms and information inside. Pay close attention to the forms. We need ID for a police check and a health certificate from your vet. Vaccinations, all that. We'll need a check to cover registration for the dog or dogs. All that's in your kit."

"This is great. We've been hoping to find something like this. When can we start?"

"We have an orientation session scheduled in the Woodbridge Library auditorium this coming Friday. Don't miss it. The next one's not until the spring."

"An orientation session?" I liked the sound of that: well planned and organized.

"Oh sure, there's lots to learn. We have to make sure you and your dogs are ready before you begin." She raised an eyebrow at Truffle. "Especially you, young man."

Obviously, she knew a challenge when she saw one. "We'll be there."

"Excellent. You can fill out the forms and drop them off here with your check today or at the front desk of the library before Thursday. And I almost forgot. No dogs at that session," she said.

"No dogs? Because he barked? He's just being—"

"They'll get their turns. But the doggie evaluation will be scheduled later. First we get you owners up to speed."

"Doggie evaluation?"

"It's all in the kit. Training schedule. Evaluation criteria. Everything they have to know." She glanced over my shoulder and said, "Oh boy."

I turned and saw a glowering woman tapping her toes impatiently. Behind her, a man glanced at his watch. I never like to be the person holding up everyone else. I waved the folder and said, "Thanks. I don't have my checkbook. I'll fill out the form and drop it by the library."

The frazzled volunteer wiped her hair out of her eyes. "I'm by myself. It was so quiet before my colleagues stepped away to snag some iced tea. We should have known."

As she beckoned to the next person, a gentle voice behind me said, "Woodbridge Therapy Dogs is such a wonderful organization."

I found myself facing a soft-faced woman with silver curls. A doggie pin sparkled on her pink sweater. The sweater matched her nail polish and her cheeks. Although she was wearing jeans and silver sneakers with pink stripes, she didn't seem casual. Maybe it was the precise crease down each leg of the well-pressed jeans. If she'd had a bit more sparkle and been hovering in the air, I might have mistaken her for a fairy godmother.

I smiled back at her. "It does sound wonderful. I plan to sign up."

I swear she sparkled more than her doggie pin. "You'll bring something special to the group, and your sweet little dogs, too."

"Sweet? Don't be so sure."

She produced a silvery laugh and pointed at them. "Of course they're sweet. Everyone knows Truffle and Sweet Marie. They were all over the papers. They're very photogenic."

For sure, *they're* photogenic. Unlike me. This woman had such a kind face that I knew she wouldn't mention what I'd looked like being hauled into an ambulance after my last brush with death. Just as well, I'd heard enough about that.

"I'm sorry," she said. "I should have introduced myself. My name is Fredelle Newhouse, and I'm convinced they'll be excellent therapy dogs." She held out her small, perfectly manicured hand.

"Charlotte Adams," I said, shaking it. She had a remarkably firm handshake for someone so soft and pillowy looking.

"Everyone knows you, too!" she warbled on. "I got one of your organizing brochures in my mailbox, then I saw you on television, oh, I don't know how many times."

That wasn't such a good thing.

I said, "But . . ."

She patted my arm. "Oh dear, I realize that this isn't really the place to ask you about this when you're enjoying your weekend, but I have an office organization problem. I hope you'll be willing to find a solution. It won't take long. Just a few hours at most. It really would help so much to have someone with your reputation and skills and perspective on the situation."

"I don't have a perspective on the situation."

"My point exactly! You're not involved with anyone in the office and that would be so useful."

I was about to say that my organizing business was booked solid for three months, which was true, and in fact one of the unintended benefits of being all over the news. You win some, you lose some. For every client who canceled, another two were eager to get in line. At this rate, I'd soon know every closet in town. On the other hand, at lunchtime I'd received a call from the worried husband of a client who'd been rushed in for an emergency appendectomy. I'd scheduled most of the week for her downsizing project and would be rebooking her appointments.

"For once, I'm available. I can look at your office and estimate the time involved. I'll see if I can take care of it this week. I do charge for consultations."

"Of course you do! That's just good business. I'm so happy that you'll do it. I'd like to fill you in on the background to the project first. Shall we have iced tea? Or a latte?"

I glanced at my watch. My friend Sally and I had an excellent plan to spend the evening stuffing our faces with pizza and making big-girl talk once we'd read her children to sleep. I had a little time to kill before Sally got all four kids through bath time, a process not enhanced by Auntie Charlotte and dogs. My job was to arrive in time to mop up the puddles on the bathroom floor.

"Sounds good."

Seconds later, Fredelle and I were seated in the hospitality area and another toothy volunteer was serving us iced lattes with chocolate sprinkles and making sure we knew that Woodbridge needed us. Fredelle and I chatted a bit about the event and the crowd and the wonderful weather. I thought what a good choice I'd made moving back to Woodbridge from New York City. What Woodbridge lacked in excitement, fashion, and vile cheating ex fiancés, it made up for in ice cream, specialty coffee, and smiling community-minded people. Not to leave out childhood friends, in my case, the misfits who had stuck together with me for twenty of our thirty years: Sally, Margaret, and Jack.

So I was feeling well disposed when I asked, "So what kind of office organization problem?"

Fredelle said, "Messy desk."

I grinned. I love a messy-desk challenge. "There are lots of those around. I've seen my share."

"Not like this, I don't think."

I let a chuckle slip out, although perhaps I shouldn't have. Fredelle didn't seem to think there was anything funny about it. I reminded myself that she was probably quite embarrassed and might be hurt by my reaction. I straightened my face. "How bad is it?"

She took a deep breath. "Really, Charlotte, you'd have to see it to believe it. Could you come tomorrow?"

"I can check it out at least. I hope I can help. This is one problem that I always love dealing with. There are so many useful techniques that can help people feel less overwhelmed."

I flinched at my own words. I try not to sound preachy when I talk, but I don't always succeed. Apparently Fredelle didn't mind.

"Thank you!" She got out of her chair and gave me a

pillowy hug. I swear there were tears in her pale blue eyes. "What a relief. I'll give you the background. That way, tomorrow, you'll have a heads-up. I wouldn't want her to feel offended. The atmosphere is poisoned enough as it is."

I finally clued in that the messy desk was not Fredelle's own. Of course, she looked quite well groomed and precise, but you couldn't always go with that. Many people with messy work areas are quite careful about themselves and their grooming. "Sure. Tell me about it, including the strained atmosphere."

"Not strained. Poisoned. I am the office manager of a company called Quovadicon, and the desk in question belongs to one of the IT people, a fairly new employee named Barb Douglas. She's very good at what she does, but some people in the office are wasting a lot of time fussing about her work area. Fact is, Barb never has trouble finding anything that anyone asks for. She's helpful and does lots of extra things for people."

"Hmm." I'd met enough brilliant and creative people to know that a neat desk didn't necessarily mean a superior employee and vice versa. "Have you spoken to her about it?"

Her hand flew to her rosebud mouth. "I'd never humiliate her in front of everyone."

"I meant privately."

Fredelle leaned over to give Truffle a little scratch behind the ears. Sweet Marie got the same. "Of course, silly me. It's just that I'm under a lot of pressure about this touchy situation. But I feel for her. She's started a new job and people seem to have it in for her. Believe me, it's costing me peace in the office."

I bet. "Is that awkward with your other direct reports?"

"Oh. Barb doesn't report to me. I do rely on her for lots of equipment troubleshooting and that kind of thing. She's very good at explaining things and showing people what to do. Our regular guy is . . ."

"A techie."

"Exactly. Even though I've known him all his life, he's sweet, but incomprehensible." Truffle and Sweet Marie rolled on their backs for belly rubs. Fredelle didn't miss a beat as we chatted.

"Is he bothered by the desk? Is he the source of the discord?"

"Oh no. He thinks Barb is, well, magnificent. Anyway, he would never worry about something like her desk. He's just a bit socially awkward and he gets upset easily. He'll hate having us in his office and he'll probably be defensive about his new friend, Barb. That's another reason I wanted to be so careful about this."

"We'll do a walk-through and we won't make a big deal out of it. Unless you want me to go after work hours, you could tell your staff you want me to recommend efficiencies. Everyone can improve work with a few small changes. That way Barb doesn't feel targeted, and your techie doesn't need to get upset. Of course, you should be prepared for fallout from one side or the other."

"I suppose. But I have plenty of fallout anyway."

"I'll do my best. No guarantees."

She sighed deeply. "Thank you so much. You know, I almost didn't approach you. I understand that you are very good at this type of thing, but you look much more, um, oh I don't know, on television. But in person you seem so kind and friendly. Of course, I should have realized you were a nice person when you decided to sign up for Therapy Dogs."

I let the second television reference slide without a comment. I didn't want to speculate as to what *um, oh I don't know* might mean. Our local station, WINY, has a hate-on for me—one look at the stock footage of me would convince you I was a serial killer. Sally says there's no such thing as bad publicity, but I'm not so sure.

"Where can I find you?"

"Oh, of course! Quovadicon is in the Patterson Business Park out near the I-87. We're at 120 Valley Drive. We have a beautiful new building. State of the art. We're very proud of it." She fished into her small pink leather handbag. "Here's a business card."

Fredelle was very pleased, and I was happy for her. I would have liked to stay and get some background on the company, but it was time to head out to Sally's.

Two o'clock on Monday afternoon turned out to be good for Fredelle and for me, too, as it would be my last appointment of the day and I'd be able to avoid what passes for rush hour in Woodbridge.

"Quovadicon sounds familiar."

Fredelle said, "Because of the owner."

I must have looked blank because she added, "Reg Van Zandt."

"Van Zandt. Isn't there a Van Zandt Avenue?"

"Yes, and a Van Zandt Crescent and a Van Zandt Circle."

"Really?"

"Yes, and they're all named after him!" A slight red flush bloomed just above the Peter Pan collar. "Reg Van Zandt? War hero? Entrepreneur?" The flush headed rapidly toward her ears.

"Oh, right. So he's the owner?" Sometimes you just have to fake it.

"You haven't met?"

I shook my head.

"I wondered because you're both heroes in a way. But if you do meet him when you're there . . ." She hesitated. "Please don't mention it's because of Barb's desk. I wouldn't want him to think ill of her. She's new so it would be a shame if he got the wrong impression."

Ah, office politics. Something I didn't miss.

Out of nowhere Fredelle said, "I suspect Barb is getting over a bad relationship and that's why she's starting over in a new town at her age. She needs kindness and support, not—"

"Bitchy carping complainers?" I suggested.

Fredelle clasped her small white hands together prayerfully. "Oh Charlotte, you'll be perfect for this job. You'll fix everything in no time. It will be a piece of cake for you."

I smiled. "Hope so."

It did sound like a piece of cake. Much as I love making over a disastrous closet, you can have too much of a good thing. An office situation would make a nice change. And if we could avoid the office politics, harmless, too.

Label a fresh file folder every time
you start a project at home or work.
Attach clear pockets for related business cards
and miscellaneous small pieces of paper and receipts.
Note key contacts and numbers inside the front of the folder.

2

Todd Tyrell's gelled hair and supersize ultrawhite chompers filled the television screen. He babbled on about a threat to our community and the public's need to know. I've learned from personal experience how easily WINY can get things wrong. I thought the public had a right to peace and quiet.

The camera caught the fluttering yellow crime scene tape that marked off the spot. A close shot of a blue car filled the screen. A slender man with red hair and pale skin juggled his keys as he surveyed the scene and narrowed his eyes at Todd. Even though he wore that suit well, I decided he had to be a detective. Maybe it was his air of natural authority. He turned icy blue eyes toward the camera and gestured to the operator to move away. The scene switched back to Todd's teeth where it belonged.

And in other news, Woodbridge police continue to be tight-lipped about the body of a man found in the trunk of a car. The body was found by hikers in a secluded area on the outskirts of Woodbridge this morning. WINY news has received unconfirmed reports that the victim had been shot. Continue to watch WINY for updates on this breaking news.

My slice of double-cheese and anchovy pizza paused halfway to my mouth. "Do we absolutely have to watch this, Sally? It's horrible. Aren't we just trying to relax and have a bit of fun? And why is Todd the Tooth on during the weekend anyway? Is he their twenty-four-seven guy or something? Now that's scary. I definitely think the viewers could use a break."

Sally didn't take her eyes off the screen. "He's covering this because it's big news. Come on. I find Todd's program relaxing. Remember, I'm stuck here in the house with this adorable pack of rugrats. It's like being marooned on a wonderful desert island where you go slightly crazy. I have to stay in touch with what's going on in the world. Do you want my brain to shrivel?"

I glanced around at Sally's three curly-haired toddlers. After bath, jammies, and story, they wanted to join the party. Sally and I had made them a tent from a blanket spread over the dining room table. Now they were sleeping soundly, smelling of apple juice and baby shampoo. Sally had the baby, Shenandoah, snoozing on her lap. Until she'd clicked on the news, we'd been indulging in girl talk. Such a lovely moment.

I said, "Speaking of shriveled brains, it's unseemly for a mother of four to have a crush for fifteen years on a man with such a big head and so little in it."

Sally said, "Unseemly? What are you, my grandmother?"

"Allow me to point out that we're not still in ninth grade at St. Jude's when Todd was hot stuff. I mean look at him. All that fake tan. Ew."

"My grandmother's grandmother? I think Todd looks hot. Always has. Always will."

"Well, I think he looks like some kind of . . . carrot. Plus I'm pretty sure he gets his eyebrows plucked and shaped. That's just plain creepy. And since it's a 'back to high school' moment, doesn't his voice remind you of fingernails on a chalkboard?"

"Don't mute the sound, Charlotte. Give me that remote."

I hung on to the remote and clicked off the television. "Sorry, Sally. I don't want to hear about someone being killed."

"But it's the news. We have to stay on top of things. And we don't know this person. It's sad, but anonymous."

"Doesn't matter. What a terrible way to end your life. Imagine his family when they learn about this. Gives me the shivers just thinking about it."

Sally said, gently, with no hint of her usual carefree grin, "It's not about you, Charlotte. It's not like those awful things could ever happen again. You don't need to worry."

I grumbled, "I know it's not about me. But I still wake up in a panic almost every night."

"I thought you'd decided on volunteer work to take your mind off all that."

"Yes. That's the great news. I'm signing on for the Woodbridge League of Therapy Dogs with Truffle and Sweet Marie. The orientation is Friday. But don't try to change the subject."

"I'm not actually changing—"

"Read my lips: My new policy is: no more murder."

Sally conked out early for some reason. So there was plenty of evening left when I arrived home. I enjoyed padding around my own apartment in my frog pajamas and bunny slippers. Add the dogs to the mix and I was a one-woman petting zoo. I set up a new file for the Therapy Dogs project. I read the background material and finished filling out my forms.

It wasn't hard for people to get in: You needed two personal references and a clear police check. I hoped I'd pass that, as I had never actually been charged with anything despite a few high-profile trips to the slammer. Then I ruined the mood by studying the tasks for the evaluation. Truffle and Sweet Marie were going to present a challenge. Perhaps I should have read the criteria before getting quite so excited. Of the eighteen tasks on the list, there was one I was confident my dogs would manage. And only if there was a food reward. I bit my lip. Was it even worth going to the orientation session?

SIT?

Only when it's their idea.

STAY?

Hardly.

DOWN?

Out of the question unless they wanted to sleep on a cashmere sweater freshly retrieved from the cleaners.

LEAVE IT?

You must be joking.

Loose leash walking?

In a parallel universe.

Truffle and Sweet Marie had people to do things like that for them. The commands they might recognize were *Drop that shoe! Where are my keys?!* And *Get out of the fridge!*

These did not appear on the list.

I should have used more discipline with them in the early days, but it was tough to be tough with two tiny creatures who'd been through hell before they came to me. Well, now I had a new problem. What were the chances I could get them on an accelerated training program? How would I even go about it, as training dogs was obviously not my best thing?

Jack Reilly would know. My landlord and best friend since elementary school knew everything there was to know about dogs, including how to rescue them. Jack had talked me into taking on two scrawny, flea-bitten miniature dachshunds found on the median of the interstate. Did I mention this is a breed that's known for being stubborn? My life had never been the same. He'd have to help, because he got me into it.

Luckily, Jack was born to help. In the year and a half since I'd moved back, he'd always been available. Sometimes annoyingly so. But tonight he was at a meeting to plan a fund-raising bike race for the local dog rescue group, Welcome All Good Dogs, better known as WAG'D. Never mind. How long could that last? Sooner or later, he'd bang open the outside door and then make a racket getting into his apartment and then find a pretext to thunder upstairs and eat all my Ben & Jerry's New York Super Fudge Chunk. If there was one person in the world I could count on, it was Jack.

I contented myself with reading over some articles on office techniques to prepare for the next day and my visit to Quovadicon. I did a little research on the Web to see what was new in the world of messy desks. Of course, there are two schools of thought on this desk business. Some people think that not everyone benefits from the appearance of order. Others are horrified by that idea. I incline to the different-strokes-for-different-folks view, but that didn't mean I couldn't help.

Ten o'clock. Still no Jack.

The dogs and I worked on the SIT command. I learned that they were willing to sit on command provided suitable treats were offered, but only if they could sit on the carpeted area.

I set out an ambitious training schedule for us and tucked away the materials in the folder.

I tidied up the apartment so it would look serene in the morning. I tossed a load of laundry into my tiny stacking washer/dryer. I made my prioritized To Do list for the next day and laid out my clothes, shoes, and jewelry for the morning. I picked out a sleek charcoal pencil skirt, my favorite crisp white blouse, and a wide metallic belt. I jazzed that up with a pair of red and pink suede wedge heels that could stop traffic. I like to be businesslike, but not boring. I started a new file for the Quovadicon project and printed out a few relevant articles, plus directions and a map to Fredelle's office. I stapled her card to the inside flap of the file and packed up my briefcase ready to go, with the files in the order I'd need them.

I woke up the dogs for their last walk of the day, and we practiced SIT a few more times. After that, I brushed my teeth and all that good stuff. I checked my watch and gave it a shake, but no, it matched the time on the clock radio. Eleven thirty.

Finally I dug into the New York Super Fudge Chunk and ate it in solitary splendor. That meant I also had to brush my teeth again. I stayed awake until one in the morning waiting for the door to squeak open to Jack's apartment, but all I heard was silence.

—

On Monday, I had a client consultation before I hit Quovadicon to see the legendary desk in the early afternoon. We practiced SIT until I thought SCREAM might be more like it, but never mind. Before I left home, Fredelle called just to make sure I was still coming at two p.m. to see Barb's desk. She asked me not to let on to anyone. As if I would.

After a quick consultation just past nine o'clock, I

swung by the library before I met my second client at eleven. I enjoyed the drive through town on a crisp and sunny September morning. With a burst of undeserved optimism, I dropped my completed Therapy Dogs application form at the front desk. I did my best to look like the kind of person whose dogs would pass any evaluation.

I spotted my friend Ramona's silver brush cut across the library in the reference department.

"Quovadicon?" she said in answer to my question. "Sure. I know the company and the family. Everyone does. They're a serious deal locally. Good employers. Very community spirited and all that."

One of Ramona's many strengths is that she grew up in Woodbridge and she never forgets a face or a fact. "Great, because I didn't find that much about them on the Web. Some kind of shipping and logistics company. I understand half the new streets in Woodbridge are named after the owner."

"Quite a few for sure," Ramona said.

"Was he some kind of war hero? Vietnam?"

"No, more like World War II. I think he flew spitfires or something. Survived a lot of dogfights."

"World War II? He must be—"

"Getting on a bit? Early eighties. I think the story was that he lied about his age and enlisted at sixteen. Fudged his birth certificate. Every now and then, there's an interview with him in the paper. Icon in the community, human interest, that kind of thing. But don't rely on my memory; let's find the facts."

Ramona headed for the Woodbridge Room, her silver earrings swaying as she walked.

"Nice cowboy boots," I said, hurrying to keep up with her. "The blue is unusual." In fact, I thought I liked them as much as my hot-pink and red suede wedge heels.

"Hand-tooled leather, because I'm worth it," she said,

reaching for a clipping file and passing it to me. "You said the company, too? That's in a different place. Natch."

"Before you go, Ramona. I thought I heard a little subtext when you mentioned this Reg Van Zandt. Was that my imagination?"

She raised an eyebrow. "Must have been, because it would have been extremely unprofessional of me to suggest, even in subtext, that our local hero was anything but perfect."

"Oh."

"Hang on, I'll get you the info on Quovadicon."

I made myself comfortable at one of the solid wooden tables in the Woodbridge Room. I love the mood in there: all dark wood, leaded glass, old leather bindings. Very lovely, and a gold mine for anyone seeking any info on anything to do with Woodbridge, its history, and its inhabitants.

As I flipped through clippings on Reg Van Zandt, I got a sense of a man who'd been an impulsive daredevil. Signed up at sixteen. Flew more than a hundred missions. Shot down twice, escaped from behind enemy lines. He'd been a local hero when he got back. Despite the brittle, yellowed paper, the face of a bright eyed boy stared out triumphantly from the photos. Reg Van Zandt had been cocky and full of spirit, for sure. Full of the devil. Whatever had happened to him behind enemy lines hadn't dimmed his mischievous spirit one bit.

I flipped pages and followed the career of a man who'd set up a small shipping business that seemed to grow and grow. From a tiny brick building in the now fashionable downtown area on the banks of the Hudson River, the business had bloomed. The most recent clippings had shots of the ribbon-cutting ceremony for a new building in the Patterson Business Park. Twelve acres in a wooded setting near rail, water, and highway. A forty-thousand-square-foot building with nearly one hundred employees. Impressive. Of course, in the sixty-plus years that had passed since Reg Van Zandt had returned from the war, a lot had changed. Including the bright-eyed boy. Now he gazed up at the mayor as he shook his hand in the photo. Reg Van Zandt was in a wheelchair and well into his eighties. But unless I was wrong, he was still very much in charge.

And speaking of *in charge*, Ramona rumbled through the door, looking mad as hell, or as mad as Ramona ever gets.

"Bizarre," she said, "our file on Quovadicon is not where it should be in the business section. I hate it when people move things or reshelve them in the wrong place. I'll have to get in touch with you when I figure out where it's gone. And we're up to our patooties in people who all seem to have information emergencies. So many drama queens, so little time. Is your request urgent, Charlotte?"

"No," I said, not wishing to make the week's list of drama queens in the Woodbridge Library.

"Good."

"In fact, this file gave me quite a background. Thanks." I smiled gratefully. "I might see you on Friday. There's an orientation meeting for Therapy Dogs here in the library."

"No dogs in the library, Charlotte. You know that. Try to stay out of trouble. Although it does give my colleagues quite a thrill when you make the evening news."

"It's just the owners at the session. It's to fill us in on what's expected. We'll try not to bark or pee on the floor."

"The mind boggles." Ramona vanished with a click of the heels on her blue cowboy boots. I was hoping that she really was up to her patootie in information drama queens and not avoiding my question about her opinion of Reg Van Zandt, local hero.

My closet consultation gave me great pleasure. At a glance during my reconnaissance, I estimated that the client had more clothing than Macy's, much of it with the tags still on. It was straightforward, easy, and she was eager to do whatever she needed to transform her jammed clothing storage areas into results that would be magazine quality.

"Anything you say," she squealed.

You could practically spread the gratitude on a slice of bread. She had a check ready, too, and pressed it into my hand the second the contract was signed.

Afterward, I had my work plan agreed on and an appointment for the next week to set the stage for "the purge." It's important for the client to buy into this process, so I always block off enough time to make sure it gets off to a good start. It's hard to believe I get paid to do this, but I do, and I get paid well, too. In fact, well enough to buy lunch for my friends.

I dashed by Ciao! Ciao! picked up three focaccia sandwiches, and had my thermos filled with coffee. I headed over to see Jack at his bike shop, CYCotics. For some reason, Jack had picked a tedious strip mall on Long March Road to set up his dream operation. I would have suggested something a bit more upscale or at least trendy, but I wasn't asked when he took out a three-year lease.

He called it a destination business.

I called it empty.

Jack looked up and blinked at me from behind his wire-rimmed glasses. As usual, he was wearing baggy shorts with a million pockets. The Hawaiin shirt *du jour* featured perky pineapples, which had apparently made him extra hungry.

"Wow," he said, peering at the sandwiches. "Four cheeses."

I cleared my throat.

He said, "*And* prosciutto. I love that. This is great. You didn't have to do this, Charlotte."

"Two sandwiches for you, and tiramisu for after."

Jack said, "Tiramisu? You're a bud." He frowned, concentrating. "But then I'm not sure, I might have to eat that first."

Jack has always been a beanpole. He never puts on an ounce. Since I hit thirty, I have to work a bit to keep the waistbands of my pencil skirts fitting. I like him anyway. But sometimes at lunch, that's a challenge.

"I have some news for you. You've been gone so early in the morning lately and you're getting home so late, we have to catch up."

I looked at him in the expectation that he might tell me why he hadn't been home after one a.m. that morning. But that turned out to be a waste of a raised eyebrow.

Jack picked up his two sandwiches. "Yeah, I know. It's crazy lately. I wish I could stop and socialize, Charlotte, but with business picking up so much, I'm so far behind on stuff for the bike race that I can't slack off at all. In fact, I have to go. Can you lock up behind yourself? Gotta run."

I glanced around. I had yet to see a customer in CYCotics, although Jack swears he has plenty. "I can see that you're run off your feet."

"If my mouth weren't full," Jack said, "I'd have a snappy comeback to that nasty crack."

"Hey, just calling 'em as I don't see 'em."

I wasn't worried about my digs. We've been ribbing each other since grade school. It was better to tease him than to whine about how much I missed his company lately. I didn't want to seem needy and clinging, even in my needier and clingier moments.

As a rule, Jack pays no attention to any remarks. But this time, he narrowed his eyes at me. I'd never seen that before.

"Very funny. I'm busy with planning the bike race. You know that. We have lots to do. Race weekend's creeping up on us. The future of WAG'D depends on it. They need support."

As long as Jack Reilly was breathing, WAG'D would never lack support.

I said, "I know what a great cause this is, and I'd really like to help you with the race."

"Um, right. I do have to go. Thanks for the lunch. And, Charlotte? Please don't touch anything on the desk. Drop the spare key off at my place." A playful punch on the arm and he was halfway out the door.

"Wait a minute. I'm volunteering to help you with the race, Jack. And not for the first time."

"Um."

"What do you mean, *um*?"

Jack swallowed and paused, his hand on the front door. "You know."

"I don't know."

"Yeah, you do."

It's possible that I stamped my pink-and-red wedge heels at this point. "I do not. But one thing I do know is that people who are almost finished with their Ph.D. in philosophy should be able to express themselves better and not take refuge behind an *um*. That's what I think."

"Okay, fine. Bossy."

"What?"

"Are you aware that when you get your teeth into other people's business, you can be just the tiniest bit . . . ?"

"Helpful. I am a helpful person. I am not bossy. I make an effort not to be bossy. My job depends on it."

"Well, under some circumstances, you can be a bit too intensely helpful. It gets on some people's nerves. As your friend, I'm just saying."

"That's not true." I sniffed.

He shrugged.

"Whose nerves?"

"Don't push it, Charlotte. Just take the hint."

"That's not a hint. It's a kick in the backside."

"Sorry. Honest. But right now at this stage, there's really nothing I can do about it. I've suggested that you help, and some people told me why that wouldn't work. I'm used to you and I like you just the way you are, but maybe you should give some thought to how you are with other people."

"What people?"

"No people in particular, just people in general."

"People in general like me just fine."

"Okay," he said. "Later."

Jack was not just my friend; he'd been my best friend since we were kids. We shared banter and ice cream and even separate floors in his house. We shared dogs and jokes and political opinions. We shared so much of our lives. Something was happening to change that. This past month, I'd hardly seen him.

He fastened his helmet and wheeled his custom racing bike out the door. With one fluid movement he was on the road. As I watched, another long lean cyclist pulled up beside him, waved, and pulled out ahead of him, laughing.

Female, unless I was mistaken.

Alpha, apparently.

"Well, I never got on your nerves before," I protested to the empty shop. I made a superhuman effort not to reach out and straighten up the random stacks of receipts, chewing gum wrappers, empty coffee cups, orders, and catalogs piled in front of Jack's empty cash box.

Exactly which people was Jack listening to?

Woodbridge has a lot to recommend it, including being nestled in the Hudson Valley. The roads are good and swoop through lushly wooded areas. Despite the threat of rain, it was a lovely early fall day with the subtle switch to September gold in the trees. But I wasn't really watching as I drove out to meet Fredelle. I tried to adjust my thoughts from Jack's weird behavior to Fredelle's messy-desk problem.

It's always important to concentrate on the client you're meeting. You have to be totally present or you can miss a lot of cues and anxieties. Who knows why I was still stewing about Jack as I steered my Miata off Valley Drive and onto the long driveway leading to the Quovadicon headquarters. The two lanes were separated by a manicured median, with low concrete planters set into the grass at intervals. The war hero had invested heavily in the driveway leading to his business, I thought. He'd sunk a ton of money into the landscaping. I could imagine that a messy desk might send a bad message to the kind of man who cared so deeply about appearances. No wonder Fredelle didn't want her heroic boss to know about Barb Douglas's problem.

I wanted to do the best I could for this kindly silvery woman who cared so much about the well-being of her staff. I suppose I should have been thinking less about her and paying more attention to the road.

An image filled my view. A vehicle? Wasn't it supposed to be on the other side of the median? Had I made a mistake? I squeaked in alarm as I realized that the speeding green SUV was aiming straight for me on the wrong side of the road.

Avoid surprises and a soggy outfit.
Always keep a small umbrella in your briefcase
as well as a clear plastic bag to store it after use.

3

I froze. The vehicle was weaving wildly, leaving me no place to go. The white-faced woman driving seemed totally unaware of me. Seconds from a head-on collision, I unfroze long enough to whip the steering wheel to the right. As the Miata skidded toward the SUV, I yanked the wheel left and slid around. I managed to gun the engine and propel the car onto the grassy median. I slammed on my brakes, and my beloved Miata repaid me by jumping the low concrete planter in the middle. I heard the crunch as the undercarriage met the concrete. I scrambled out of the car and dashed across the median to the other lane to get the license plate number before the SUV was out of sight. But it had already rocketed around the corner.

As I stood openmouthed, a black-and-silver eighteen-wheeler shuddered to a stop in back of me with a loud whoosh of air brakes. That was something: first, being driven off the road and now standing in the path of a truck. Big rigs have always made me nervous. Stupid, I know, but my heart just hammers if I get too close to one. I dashed quickly to the side of the road. To add to the moment, it started to rain.

A burly middle-aged man with a baseball cap and an oversize mustache jumped down from the cab and stomped toward me, gesticulating. He was followed shortly by a younger guy with white-blond hair buzzed almost to the scalp. He was also tan. And very buff. I wasn't sure how I felt about the Celtic tattoos decorating both his arms.

The first guy said, "Are you nuts? Do you know how long it takes to stop one of these rigs?"

The young guy pointed to the Miata. "What the hell? How did you get a freakin' license?"

I react badly to that kind of comment. "I'm sorry, but you should ask the idiot who just shot down the wrong side of the road." I pointed to the other side before I snapped open my cell phone to call Tony's Towing. I'd sorted out Tony's office and he's always been grateful.

The older guy got the point. "How did you get stuck on that?"

"Not my fault," I said.

"No, miss. Ah'm sure," he said, dropping the grin, or maybe just hiding it behind that seventies mustache.

The second one still glowered.

I looked up at them from my full height of four foot eleven and said, "The wild woman I mentioned? That speeding SUV forced me off the road."

The first man scratched his baseball cap and opened his mouth. He said, "I think that was . . ."

The second one shook his head slightly. Some secret trucker code perhaps.

"Well, hell, I'm Mel," the mustache man said. "And he's Del. And you must be?"

Were they yanking my chain? I narrowed my eyes at them. "Just swell."

He snorted. "Can't help our names, now, can we? Let's

get you off that bit of concrete, little lady," Mel, if that was really his name, said. "Get back behind the wheel of that rice-burning toy and we'll get you on the road. Won't we, Del?"

"That Miss Swell or Mrs. Swell?" Del said.

"I'll just call my towing company," I said snootily.

"Now, now, little lady, don't mind Del. He can't help flirting with pretty gals. But he's harmless. Save your money."

With every bit of dignity I had, considering that my so-called toy car was practically impaled, I got behind the wheel and revved the engine. A bit of strained muscle from Del and Mel and the Miata shot forward onto the road, spewing grass. I waved good-bye as I headed for the building and the semi slowly rumbled off toward the highway.

I would have been suitably impressed when I pulled into the parking lot at Quovadicon if my knees hadn't been like jelly after my two near misses. Not only was the building on the end of a scenic drive, but the grounds were gorgeous. I hadn't really expected grounds, let alone this lovely wooded site. Whoever had done the site plan had left the woods pristine, and the building was set into the surroundings looking like it belonged there, the trees reflected on the glass cladding, a riot of fall flowers spilling out of cement planters near the front. I tucked the Miata in between a yellow Volkswagen "Bug" convertible and a shiny red Ford Focus and hustled up the front stairs to the wide glass entrance, set in tawny granite panels. I noticed that the wheelchair ramp had been nicely integrated into the building's approach and lent it a lovely curved flow. Definitely not an afterthought.

If Fredelle Newhouse hadn't told me the company was logistics, shipping, and storage, I wouldn't have picked up a single clue from the surroundings.

Fredelle was waiting for me by the door as I stepped through and snapped my umbrella closed. I always carry a clear plastic bag in my briefcase to keep damp umbrellas from ruining my papers. I smiled at her.

This time her sweater was candy pink and had a tiny black Scottie dog appliquéd over her heart. I hoped that the drizzle hadn't entirely wrecked my hairdo. If so, it was too late to do anything about it.

"I'm so glad you made it," she gushed. Her small hands fluttered, in a blur of matching pink nail polish. "Shame about the rain."

I couldn't think of a single reason why I wouldn't have made it under normal circumstances. No point in talking about the rain or even less about the weird events on my drive in. If you tell people you got stuck on a planter, they might be less inclined to take your advice.

She burbled on, "And right on time, too. Let's go ahead."

I smiled and glanced around the entrance. Elegant and classy. Silver-gray Berber carpet. Deep aubergine accent wall. For some reason I was expecting a wall-sized photo of the founder or at the very least a framed portrait, but there was only the crisp aluminum lettering of the company name mounted on the wall. *Proud to be in Woodbridge* was painted under it in flowing script.

Fredelle led. I followed. The espresso wood reception desk was discreetly set back and angled away from the door. As we passed it, she stopped to introduce me to a young woman who was gazing at her computer screen with an uncomprehending expression.

Fredelle cleared her throat. "Autumn?" she said.

"Mmm?" Autumn answered without actually turning. She had glowing skin and rich chestnut hair cascading in a shiny waterfall down her back.

"This is Charlotte Adams. Charlotte, this is Autumn Halliday. Autumn, Charlotte is going to be helping me find some more efficient ways to lay out our office." Fredelle twisted her hands as she introduced me. She might as well have been wearing a bright yellow T-shirt that screamed I AM A BIG FAT LIAR in glossy black letters. Not that it mattered, as Autumn had continued staring at the screen and fiddling with a lock of her hair.

She did however manage to say, "Awesome," but I was pretty sure she didn't mean it.

Fredelle cleared her throat, and Autumn tore her attention from the screen.

"Nice to meet you," I said, extending my hand to Autumn, who swiveled to stare at it before reaching out to give it a boneless shake.

"Autumn Halliday," she said, in case I had missed that before. "Nice to meet you too, Caroline."

She was back at the screen before we moved past the reception area. Fredelle said in a low voice, "Autumn's father is a very good friend of Mr. Van Zandt's. She's just finished first year college. I think she found it really difficult and she's taking a year off, and she asked Mr. Van Zee if she could have a job. Her father's not too happy that she's taking time off from her education, but he agreed to let her work here. Autumn and her father both chat with Mr. Van Zee, so I don't want her to catch on to what we're really doing."

Not much chance of that, I thought, as we hurried through a door and into a large square office area.

"Boardroom's over there," Fredelle said, pointing a pink fingernail at a glass double door leading into a glass-walled room with an impressive rosewood conference table. "There's a smaller meeting room here. And this is our main office area. We have salespeople, too, but most of them are out of the office today. Of course, most of the building is given over to warehousing and fulfillment. If you want you can get a tour there, too, but this is where the problem is."

"Perhaps another time," I said. I suspected there might

be forklifts and pallets and trucks and other machinery that was not my thing there.

A cluster of a half-dozen desks filled the central area. "My office is over here."

"I see you have a door," I said. "And walls, even if they are glass."

Fredelle stiffened. "But I keep the door open and the blinds up. We have to be available to our employees. Mr. Van Zandt believes in an open-door policy."

Hmm. Defensive.

I glanced around but saw no sign of the legendary leader. I did spot a middle-aged woman in towering heels who turned to sneer at us from the photocopier. I mention those heels not only because I am a shoe lover, but also because she would have been six feet tall even without them. She didn't really need the shoes to attract attention. Her leopard-print miniskirt would have done that on its own, or perhaps the tank top barely containing a surgically enhanced bosom could have carried the day. I wouldn't have wanted to foot the bill for her tanning sessions, let alone those hair extensions. She'd definitely dug herself a trench to stop the march of time.

She checked out my outfit and seemed to barely suppress a snicker.

As we stood there for an awkward moment, a slight, pale-haired man with vintage eyeglasses skittered past us, carefully avoiding eye contact. Wonder Woman rolled her eyes. Not usually what people do before being introduced, especially if a few of those spiky eyelashes might get dislodged. Never mind, I was secure in my opinion that the tanning, the hair extensions, and even the unlikely jauntiness of her breasts wouldn't make her a day less than fifty.

"Now what?" she said.

Her name was Dyan George, it seemed. Fredelle introduced me, and as I held out my hand, Dyan regarded it the way you'd look at gum under a movie seat.

"Charlotte is going to help us find some, um, more efficient ways to set up the office."

Dyan raised a precisely penciled eyebrow. "Start with the receptionist. I hear that in other offices they actually greet visitors and answer the phone."

Fredelle snapped back, "Autumn is coming along just fine. She's young and she's pleasant and she's willing to learn."

Dyan managed an exaggerated and insulting shrug. "Anything to hang on to your job, I suppose. Good luck with that."

Whoa. Usually it takes more than two minutes before the knives come out in a visit to an office. But even I could see that Dyan George was special.

Fredelle said, "I don't have to worry about *my* job."

I liked the fact that a steely edge crept in under the sweet worried tones. No one loves a pushover, not even me.

"I'll show you around, Charlotte," Fredelle continued as we abandoned the photocopier to Dyan. "Let's start with my office."

A pair of peace lilies on stands flanked the door to Fredelle's office. Somehow I wasn't surprised that Fredelle's workspace had a row of African violets in the large east-facing window that looked over the parking lot. I turned to the motivational posters over the filing cabinet (*Follow Your Dream*, *Climb Every Mountain*, and *Believe in Yourself*). Underneath the posters, a collection of porcelain puppies nudged a framed photo of Fredelle and what had to be Quovadicon employees taken at a staff picnic. Reg Van Zandt was front and center in his wheelchair. Fredelle beamed behind him. To the right Dyan had simpered at the camera. There was no sign of Autumn, but she was new. A very pregnant lady, blond and beaming, stood waving. A few dozen men in shorts and baseball caps grinned sheepishly in the background. I didn't see Mel or Del, but the girl seemed familiar.

"Who's this?"

"Oh dear, that's our Missy," Fredelle said. "Missy Manderly. She was on staff for ten years, ever since she finished high school. She knew everyone and everything about Quovadicon. She married one of the office supply sales reps who used to drop in a bit more often than was absolutely necessary. This was taken the week before she went on maternity leave. She's just had twins."

"That's dramatic."

"If anybody could ever manage twins with ease, it's Missy."

"I've seen her before."

"Well, Woodbridge isn't all that big, as you know. They bought an old house off Long March Road and fixed it up."

"My friend Jack has a business in that area. Perhaps I've seen her around there. Some people are more memorable than others. That smile makes a real impression."

"It hasn't been the same since she left. Dyan George may think she's efficient, but she can't hold a candle to Missy. Missy was perfectly organized and sensible and levelheaded." Fredelle lowered her voice. "Dyan's all about control, not really about how to get the job done. I'm just lucky that the whole office hasn't quit since she came on."

"Yes, I noticed that she makes digs about people to their faces and behind their backs."

"You mean Autumn? She doesn't even notice. She's very sweet, and even though I find myself defending her from Dyan, she's not the brightest bulb in the chandelier."

I coughed, surprised at the usually gentle Fredelle's comment.

She shrugged. "Don't tell me you haven't noticed. But she's one of the usual cases."

"What do you mean?"

"Mr. Van Zandt wanted her hired. Mr. Halliday, that's Autumn's dad, is a really good friend and a business associate of his. He wanted his daughter to have a safe place to work and not end up in a bigger city where bad things can happen. You may have noticed, she's kind of, um, naïve. So she'll stay until she decides to move on or finds another college to go to, if she can get accepted. That's the way it works here. Family firm. People first."

"And this person?" I pointed to the second row and the shy fellow who'd avoided eye contact with us earlier. He hadn't hung around for an intro.

Her face softened. "Oh dear. Poor Robbie."

"Poor Robbie?"

She smiled as though her imaginary puppy had made a puddle on my carpet. "He's so shy."

"Oh. And 'poor Robbie' is . . . ?"

"Robert Van Zandt. The owner's son."

I wasn't sure what the subtext to this was. "And he works here, too?"

"Mmm," she said. "Well, of course he does. As I said, family and friends first with Mr. Van Zandt, you know."

"What does Robbie do?" I made sure I didn't say *poor Robbie*. Chances were I'd meet this person, and I didn't want to have any prejudices toward him. Or worse, blurt out, *You must be poor Robbie*.

"He's not under me, here in administration. He does some kind of *liaison* with clients and backup for client service. He's actually quite gifted technically. He's also in the IT area with Barb. Reports directly to Mr. Van Zee."

I interpreted that to mean Robbie didn't do very much of anything, but that Fredelle obviously liked him a lot.

"Is Barb in the picture?"

"Sure, right there." Fredelle pointed to a woman in jeans. Her back was turned to Dyan. I couldn't make out her face clearly, but she appeared to be talking to Robbie Van Zandt in the second row. Somehow this didn't surprise me. Photos can reveal a lot about the dynamic of a group. Barb and Dyan wouldn't have been a good mix.

"And Dyan George?"

"Admin support. Accounts receivable mostly. Other accounting duties. Payroll. She's been here for a few months and she thinks she can take over as office manager, push me out the door into an early retirement. But I've been here since Quovadicon was founded, and she won't get this job without a fight."

Well.

I glanced at my watch. "And where is the desk you want me to see? I should keep moving."

"It's in the next area. We call it the IT section, but really there are just a few computers and things, lots of wires, monitors, and printers and extra drives. It's not pretty, though, so it's better to keep it out of sight. But there's no way we can keep people from noticing Barb's desk. They have to walk right past it to get to the staff room. It's causing all kinds of friction, as I said. Dyan's using the whole situation to undermine my authority."

That was interesting. Fredelle seemed more like the office mom than an administrator. It was hard to imagine her having any authority to undermine. But I knew enough about office moms to realize that they have their strengths and their supporters, and sometimes the ambitious newcomers learn that the hard way. With luck, this Dyan would, too.

Fredelle said, "No point in putting it off, I suppose. Let's go."

We strolled around the office, with Fredelle describing who sat where and what they did while I pretended to take notes. Quovadicon's offices contained solid, good-quality furnishings in pale wood veneers. The new-looking baffles dividing workstations were in a soothing shade of sand. There was nothing much to note: Dyan had a heavy vase with tiger lilies on her desk and an animal-print cover on her ergonomic chair. Not a scrap of paper anywhere in the office. Aside from an oversize photo of herself sunbathing poolside in a minuscule bikini, there was nothing on the wall. I figured she couldn't resist a chance to display her enhanced pectorals. Other than that, the Quovadicon offices presented a sea of neutrals—smooth, well-functioning, and just a bit boring. I found myself anticipating the drama of the messy desk in the IT area.

As we entered an enclosed area with two workstations, Robbie Van Zandt glanced up and dropped the paper he'd been staring at. From where I stood, it looked like a photo. He snatched it up and pushed it into a file folder. He flushed beet red and thrust himself out of his chair. Before Fredelle could say a word, he barreled past us down the corridor and through a door. Fredelle uttered a nervous gasp. I glanced at the desk he'd abandoned: a laptop, and a workstation, plus a telephone and one file folder. Behind the desks and under a long window, a trio of bookcases lined the wall. Like Robbie's desk, it seemed neat, functional, unremarkable. That just amplified the sheer height of the chaos that sat on the desk opposite it.

It took my breath away.

That surface was completely buried in a hill of papers, no two of which seemed to point in quite the same direction. I blinked in surprise at what looked like a sock protruding from the top tier. Perhaps it went with the pair of slightly dirty sneakers, sticking out, on the side. Here and there the tails of candy bars were visible, as were copies of *People*, *Us*, and *Soap Opera Weekly*. If there was an in-basket or an out-basket, they were well and truly buried.

Surplus materials stacked on the floor, mostly manuals for software as far as I could tell, obscured the sides and front of the desk.

I tripped over one of the many cables trailing from the desk and onto the floor. As I picked myself up, I noticed the curling edge of an old sandwich. I figured that might have contributed to what looked distinctly like mouse droppings. Or the sardine can might have attracted furry visitors. Hard to say.

Somewhere underneath the haystack, a telephone was ringing.

A cast-off blue fleece jacket lay crumpled on the chair seat. I counted five cups: two beside the keyboard, two more on the floor, and another in between the ragged stacks of unfiled papers on the filing cabinet. I peered into it and recoiled at the crust of mold. The space under the desk was reserved for more sneakers. I tried not to inhale, as the sneakers and the moldy coffee cups made breathing a challenge. Of course, that could have been the empty take-out containers in the trash.

I could honestly say I'd never seen anything like it.

Fredelle bit her lip. She was in a tricky situation for sure if this was what she had to defend against critics.

I noticed a pack of cards sitting on top of that fleece jacket. *52 Tips To Get You Organized Fast.*

A sneering voice behind us said, "Disgusting, isn't it? I think we have to have it fumigated. That looks like rodent dirt to me. And who knows what's in the drawers. Dead rats? I could ask her, but big surprise, Barb's gone home for the day."

I turned to face Dyan. She stood with her arms folded in a way that emphasized her chest as well as her words. "I don't know how anyone could make that much disgusting mess so fast. She must have been working hard at it, that's all I can say."

I had a pretty good idea who had left the cards on the seat.

As the words left Dyan's mouth, Robbie Van Zandt scurried past her in the hallway, avoiding his own office area and shooting Dyan a look that should have blistered her tan skin. Ah, there's always so much undercurrent in every office, but Dyan was in a class of her own.

Dyan ignored Robbie, perhaps didn't even see him. She was glaring at Fredelle. "This is a disgrace. She should never have been hired. No one with a shred of competence would have let this oinker through the door."

Fredelle bristled, a fresh pink flush spreading over her round face.

I glanced at my watch, and turned to Fredelle. "What's left to see? Just the staff room?"

"Yes." She glanced at me with gratitude. "It's through here at the end of this corridor."

Dyan snorted as we slipped past her. "Although most of us lose our appetites before we get there. It's no way to run a business."

The staff room was unremarkable. I observed a couple of round tables, a half-dozen comfortable chairs, and a microwave, fridge, and sink. The dish towels with the pastel ducks in bonnets indicated that Fredelle kept things homey. It was tidier than most and better furnished, although perhaps it just seemed that way in contrast to Barb Douglas's desk. It smelled better, too. The bulletin board was tidy and well-ordered even if it was covered with photos and jokes and a thank-you card next to a photo of a smiling Missy Manderly and a pair of sleeping twins.

I noticed with approval that the large red fire extinguisher was in an easy-to-reach location. One of my tasks in a previous job had been volunteer fire warden in the office. I care about these matters. I'd noticed one in the IT area too, but it would have been hard to access it past all that debris. This was properly mounted, with instructions in large type posted over it. Number one being *CALL 911 FIRST.* And naturally there was a phone.

"Fredelle! Fredelle!" Autumn rushed down the hallway toward us, her hair streaming behind her. She mouthed the words, "It's Mr. Van Zee for you. He's on line one."

Fredelle gasped and her small pink mouth formed a perfect O. As Fredelle pivoted on one foot and skittered toward her office, Autumn turned back toward the so-called IT area and shook her head. "Oh wow," she said. "How is that possible?"

Dyan smirked. "Special talents."

Autumn's jaw dropped. "Really?"

Dyan rolled her eyes. "No, not really. Barb's a disaster and she's a disaster because the person who hired her doesn't know squat about how to run a business even if she thinks she does."

I made a point of looking at my watch and said, "Oops, better get going. Please tell Fredelle I'll call her tomorrow morning to discuss the next steps and the contract, Autumn. If you don't mind."

Autumn's smile lit up her vacant, pretty face. "Oh, I don't mind, Caroline. I am supposed to leave messages."

Right.

"Next steps," I repeated, "and contract."

Back across the office area, Fredelle's door slammed shut and blinds snapped down in the glass walls.

Dyan pointed a dangerously long fingernail at Barb's desk. "Miss Piggy shouldn't have been able to put one cloven hoof through the door. And someone else shouldn't be slamming doors and getting away with it."

Autumn's eyes widened. "Who?"

"Who do you think, Einstein?"

Autumn shook her head. "Fredelle? But she's so . . ."

"Useless?"

"No, Dinah, kind. She's so kind to everyone."

"Yeah well, this is a business and kindness has no place in it. If I were in charge, none of this bullshit would be going on."

Autumn glanced my way before staring at Dyan, a whisper of panic crossing her lovely young face. "But you're not in charge, Dinah."

"You think?"

Autumn raised her chin. "But you're not."

"Maybe, but it won't be long now. And it's good to know which side you are on, Little Miss Useless. And for the thousandth time, my name is Dyan. With a Y."

It seemed like a good time for me to make my escape before some of Dyan's animosity rubbed off on me and I offered a personal opinion beyond the scope of my project.

At least it had stopped raining. I was still pondering the evils of office politics as I tried to protect my suede wedges from the puddles and headed toward the Miata in the parking lot. I had never once regretted leaving the corporate world for small-town Woodbridge. It might be hard to get a good haircut in a town this size, but you didn't have to watch your colleagues routinely eviscerating each other. I didn't miss it, but at least I knew how to deal with it. And a glimpse at someone else's office miseries reminded me that I'd made the right decision in coming home to start my own business.

A heavy hand landed on my shoulder.

I jumped and spun.

I screamed for good measure.

Robbie Van Zandt jumped, too. I believe he also screamed in unison with me.

I slumped back against the Miata, gasping for breath.

He clutched his chest with both hands and bleated something that I didn't quite catch. Maybe I was still in scream mode.

"Sorry," I said finally realizing the source of the problem. "I have a tendency to overreact to sudden noises." *You're going to have to get a grip*, I told myself. *Can't go through life scaring timid men.*

He narrowed his eyes and said, "Well then, maybe you should just stay home."

I gawked at him. "What do you mean? What am I doing? Besides heading for my car."

"You know what you're doing." He'd dropped his hands from his chest. Of course, by now they were balled into fists.

"I really do not."

"Don't play that game with me. I heard you."

"Call me slow on the uptake," I said. "But what exactly did you hear?"

"I heard you talking about Barb's desk with that witch, Dyan. I was standing right by the door, even if no one noticed. Everyone here likes to pretend I don't exist."

He was right. I hadn't noticed him hanging around after he'd stormed out. Dyan and Autumn must have seen him but ignored him. And now that I did notice him, even with his fists raised, Robbie Van Zandt was probably the least scary man on the planet. For starters, his glasses were crooked and his socks didn't match. And he had tears in his pale rabbity eyes. For emphasis, he was shaking with emotion. I'm used to dealing with agitated people in my business. Even though he'd been aggressive, it was hard not to feel sorry for Robbie. The best thing to do was defuse the situation.

I said soothingly, "I can see that you are very upset. And honestly, I didn't say anything about the desk. From what I hear from Fredelle, Ms. Douglas is a valuable employee.

I am not here to make trouble for your friend. Trust me. And please don't worry."

"You can't fool me, with your nice little ways and your fancy little shoes and everything. You're a bitch like all the others. You came to Quovadicon to make trouble for Barb. To get her fired. Well, you won't get away with it on my watch. She's the best thing that ever happened to me. Just try to damage her and see what happens."

Keep a computerized master list of simple annual and seasonal business tasks. Do one whenever you need to fill a bit of time.

4

The message light was blinking when I opened the door, carrying a few groceries and the results of several errands. The message light is always waiting when I get home. Truffle and Sweet Marie woke up, stretched, yawned, and scampered over for a quick cuddle. I changed before getting back to routine office tasks. I hung up my pencil skirt and tossed the white shirt into the laundry. I carefully placed my shoes in the rack, where Truffle and Sweet Marie couldn't get them. I changed into a soothing Lululemon top and yoga pants. Bare feet felt good, too. Soon my second-floor apartment in the old Victorian home would be too cool for that.

As a rule, I'd catch the early evening news to bring myself up to speed on the world and Woodbridge. This evening, I couldn't bear the thought of watching Todd Tyrell salivating over some poor man's sad end in the trunk of a car. I'd had enough drama to last me for the day.

I did up a bill for the afternoon's visit and consultation. I drew up a contract outlining steps to sort out the wayward desk, including some time alone with Barb to help her organize her work space. I hoped she'd be willing. Most people were, if treated with respect. However, Quovadicon had already been full of surprises, and Barb had created a monster desk in a very short time. I dropped the bill and the contract into the Quovadicon file in my briefcase, ready to go.

I tidied up the day's business, opened my mail over the recycle can, and shredded envelopes with my name on them with my tiny, perfect shredder. I probably shouldn't love it as much as I do. I jotted down five messages from suppliers, clients, and would-be clients, ending up with Fredelle's.

"Charlotte, call me when you get in. Please don't wait until morning. Here's my home phone number." Fredelle's soft voice had a little quaver in it. Poor Fredelle. No wonder Dyan thought she was a pushover.

It was time to call it quits. I left the rest of the messages by the phone to be returned first thing in the morning during "office hours." If you work for yourself, you have to ensure that you have a life as well as make a living. I decided I'd make an exception for Fredelle. That quaver in her voice had found my soft spot.

But first things first: Truffle and Sweet Marie nudged my ankles to remind me that, as family, they had priority, and it was well past walk time, and anyway, where was their dinner? And what about treats, for that matter? They had a point. You can't bring two rescued dogs into your life and not spoil them.

I slipped on my flip-flops, picked up the pooches, and hurried down the stairs for a walk. As usual, Jack's apartment door stood not only unlocked, but open. The living room, furnished mostly in bicycle parts, philosophy books, and ancient *Mad* magazines, was unlit and empty. Was it just my imagination or did it look more forlorn than usual?

I'd been looking forward to sharing dinner with Jack. This charity race was eating his life. Never mind, the pooches were hungry and I was stuck making a stir-fry for one. Stir-fries are my signature dish. Actually, they're my only dish, which is a signature in itself. I'd picked up another tub of New York Super Fudge Chunk and tucked it in the freezer to serve when Jack drifted in. Not that it mattered. I could manage on my own. I may be a small person, but I'm a big girl.

Fredelle answered on the first ring when I returned her call.

She said, "Did Barb Douglas try to kill you today?"

"What?"

Her voice rose. "I know it sounds ridiculous, but that's what they're saying."

I said, "Who's saying?"

"Please, Charlotte. I have to know. Is it true she tried to run you off the road?"

I gawked at the receiver. "I don't even know what Barb Douglas looks like. But someone was definitely driving erratically when I was on my way to your office, and she would have hit me if I hadn't . . ."

I heard the gasp. "Then it is true. She tried to kill you."

"I didn't get the impression this woman was *trying* to kill me. So I didn't take it personally. It was a bit shocking, though."

"I can't really believe it. But did you see her?"

"I saw a woman in an SUV. I saw her face quite clearly. I've never seen Barb Douglas before, Fredelle, so it might have been her. She seemed panicky. I don't believe she even saw me. And it does seem highly unlikely that she'd try to run me off the road just because I'm being consulted on some office procedures."

"But our project is really a ploy to do something about her desk."

"Did she know that?"

"No. But she's very smart. She might have figured it out. Others in the office were making bitchy remarks."

"Even if she knew I was the person coming to look at her desk, what would she accomplish by running me off the road? The desk would still be there. Someone else would do something about it."

Fredelle's voice brightened. "Yes. That doesn't make sense, does it?"

"Not even a bit. And anyway, some of my colleagues might disagree with me, but people with messy desks can be valuable employees. I'm not sure yet what's going on with Barb's desk, and I'll have to have another look at it to analyze what's going on, but I do know it's not your biggest problem in that office."

Fredelle couldn't let go of the previous topic. "But this woman did come straight at you in a vehicle?"

"I'd just turned off Valley Drive and was heading toward your building. She shot down the wrong side of the driveway like the devil was on her tail, and I had to swerve to avoid her."

"You mean, you could have been . . . ?"

"She was just in a hurry and she wasn't expecting anyone. That's all. It was stupid and dangerous and whoever she was, she owes me an apology."

Fredelle said, "You are so right. I'll be speaking to her about it. In the meantime, you have my apology, Charlotte."

"Thank you, but not really necessary."

"So, you still will take this job? You won't just leave us in the lurch? Abandon us to . . ."

I said, "I plan to continue with this job. I'll have to have a word with Barb Douglas, of course."

"Of course."

"Since you're on the phone, I have something to ask you. Are you sure that Barb Douglas has no trouble getting her work done?"

"No. She's very prompt. And thorough."

"And except for Dyan, does anyone have any problems?"

She hesitated. "Not really. Everyone is quite pleased with her. She really knows her technology. Very up to date. And of course . . ."

"Yes?"

"Well, Robbie is quite smitten."

"I figured that out. So if no one is bothered, why is this a problem for you?"

"Dyan is doing her best to stir up some of the others. Even the guys on the other side and the salespeople. Now she says she's going to call the health department."

"And these other people are complaining to you?"

"That's not the problem. Someone is making sure that Mr. Van Zandt hears about it. That Dyan is so vile."

"And she wants your job."

"And she imagines she can use poor Barb to oust me. But she's not going to harm Barb, and she's not going to get her claws on my position. This office is everything to me. Everything. And she's not going to get to me. I have been with Quovadicon since Mr. Van Zandt came home and set it up. I would die before I let her rip this company apart. And Charlotte?"

"Yes?"

"We need you to help us. You can't leave us."

"I don't plan to. I'll see you tomorrow morning, Fredelle. How's ten o'clock?"

When you're single, you can find yourself alone when you don't want to be. This hadn't been such a problem for me recently, because Jack was always there, someone to talk to, someone to lean on, someone to eat New York Super Fudge Chunk with. Sometimes Jack was better than a girlfriend because you knew he would never borrow your clothes and forget to bring them back. And he was better than a boyfriend because he would never break your heart and cheat and lie and generally leave you no choice but to toss your engagement ring into the Hudson. Too bad Jack wasn't there this night. Pressures of organizing a bike race and fund-raiser and no need of my help whatsoever. Thank you very much, Miss Bossy.

Never mind, I have lots of good friends. I didn't need to be sniffling into my tub of ice cream just because he was hardly ever around anymore. I didn't have to wither on the vine. I picked up the phone and called my friend Margaret Tang.

"How about a movie?"

"I can't. Ow."

"Margaret?"

"Ow."

"What happened?"

"Ow. Ow."

"Are you all right?"

"I cut myself, if you must know."

"You cut yourself? Is it serious? Should I call 911?"

"Better not. I'm just shaving my legs. I have a date in twenty minutes."

"A date? You have a date? What date? Since when do you have a date?"

"Thanks for the vote of confidence, Charlotte. I am a reasonably presentable professional woman, not yet thirty-one. The kind of person who might even be able to get a date, in fact."

Oops. "I'm sorry, Margaret. I'm not suggesting that you couldn't get a date, it's just that . . ."

A chilly silence drifted over the line.

"Just what?" Margaret said.

"It's hard to know what to respond to first. The fact that you're shaving your legs while you are on the phone, a form of multitasking that can lead to permanent disfigurement, or the idea that you have your first date since moving back here and yet you didn't mention it to me, your friend for what? Nearly twenty years?"

"I didn't mention it to anyone because I didn't want to have this exact conversation. What exactly is wrong with me having a date, Charlotte? What am I, some kind of pariah?"

"Of course not, but didn't you tell me that *date* was a four-letter word?"

"That would be then. This would be now. Oh crap, it is bleeding. I don't have anything to stop it. I suppose I'll have to go on my date with scraps of tissue on my legs. Maybe I'll wear jeans. Maybe I will call 911. Mona Pringle probably knows what to do. Thanks a lot, Charlotte."

"But—" *Click.*

I didn't call her back merely because I wanted to know who the date was. I had advice. Good advice. That's my job. To help people.

"Try cornstarch," I said when she picked up the phone. I listened in disbelief as she swore. "I didn't know you had words like that in your vocabulary, Margaret. You've always been so . . . restrained."

"Shaving injuries change a person. Get used to it," she snapped.

I decided it wasn't the best time to ask who the date was with.

Margaret sniffed. "Did you say cornstarch? I have a box somewhere in my kitchen."

"Just pat it on and before you hang up again, I'm curious, who's the date with? Anyone I—" *Click.*

Oh well. Obviously, it was a tense moment and I had to

give her space. But who was she dating? Why wasn't I in on this? What was the good of being friends for all these years if we didn't share every little detail when we were lucky enough to have little details? What had Margaret done to get little details? That's all I wanted to know.

Next I tried Sally, just in case she was up to a second girls' night in a row. Sally's husband, Benjamin, informed me that Sally had had a rough day with the four children and was flaked out on the rug in the family room, snoring. I considered calling Margaret back to warn her that dating can lead to falling asleep on the rug after a rough day with the kids, but I didn't want to get another earful of new vocabulary.

So much for the misfits sticking together forever.

To top it off, my friends Lilith Carisse and Rose Skipowski were in L.A. on a belated visit to Rose's daughter.

It always pays to have a Plan B when you feel like company and find yourself alone. My Plan B usually involves decluttering. There's always something that needs to be done. I keep a list of tasks handy, especially the type of ten-minute chore that a person tends to forget about until it becomes a problem. I headed for my medicine cabinet and checked the expiration dates on my medications. Then I hit the fridge and checked the vitamins. I put the ones that had outlived their dates in a small basket and parked it in my cupboard out of reach of the dogs until I could take it to the local drugstore for disposal. I jotted that onto my master To Do list.

There's a great feeling that comes from getting rid of silly stuff that clogs up your life. Especially items you couldn't use because they were past their best-before date and still you couldn't quite bring yourself to throw them out because you paid good money for whatever it was.

Naturally you will feel so virtuous that you will reward

yourself. Enough work and worry. I knew exactly how to do that. I picked up my iPod and selected my James Blunt favorites. I curled up on the sofa with a cuddly throw and my pooches and a few purely medicinal chocolates. Luxury.

"You're beautifulllll," James warbled.

What a great way to make sure none of the toxicity of Fredelle's office and her office mates got under my skin. Wouldn't want that to contaminate my life.

My subconscious inquired exactly how Fredelle had learned that Barb Douglas had tried to run me off the road. My eyes popped open.

I hadn't told her.

I hadn't told anyone.

The truck drivers? Mel and Del? There had been no one else around. But could they be part of the great "get rid of Barb Douglas" conspiracy?

At five minutes to ten the next morning, I arrived at Quovadicon. There was a slight September nip in the air, and I wore a crisp fitted jacket to give myself that extra bit of authority I thought might be necessary, a flowered skirt, and my purple leather stiletto boots.

Fredelle was already hovering around the door spreading anxiety when I got there. Her cotton sweater today was a deep and beautiful periwinkle. The pin appeared to be a squirrel or possibly a chipmunk. I spotted a glimmer of lavender in her nail polish. Maybe it was the periwinkle that made Fredelle look pale as a breeze.

Autumn sat at the reception desk biting her lip and staring. The phone rang, but Autumn didn't appear to hear it. She watched, transfixed, as Robbie Van Zandt paced back and forth in front of the desk, clenching and unclenching his fists. Maybe that was why Autumn seemed on the verge of tears. Although possibly she was trying not to laugh. Robbie was definitely not the type to inspire fear.

I said, "Good morn—"

"She's not here," Fredelle whispered.

"Who?" I said, hoping the answer was *Dyan*.

"Barb. She didn't come in."

"Oh."

"Can you blame her?" Robbie blurted. "She's practically being persecuted by all of you she-witches, and you expect her to come in and take it day after day? What is the matter with you people?"

She-witches? Puh-lease.

At that moment Dyan slunk into the reception area and shot Robbie a look of pure tanned malice. Today she was even more dramatic in black with stud decorations than she had been in leopard pattern.

Robbie pointed at Dyan. "It's you. You're the one behind it. Don't worry, it will catch up with you. What goes around comes around. You will be sorry and I mean it."

Dyan upped the ante by laughing. Autumn emitted a tiny gasp.

Fredelle straightened and snapped, "That's enough, Dyan. Robbie has reason to be upset, even if he is misjudging *most* people in this office. You will treat him with respect. And you will treat Barb with dignity, too."

The tiny quaver in her voice hinted at how hard it must have been to stand up to Dyan.

Dyan sneered. At every encounter, she managed to act like someone who was auditioning for a B movie. A living stereotype of bad behavior, not to mention egregious style. "People should earn respect, if you ask me. I don't think too many people here can say they do." The sneer seemed to be split between Fredelle and Robbie, with plenty left over for the absent Barb, and spillover for Autumn and me.

What kind of workplace was this where an employee would openly disrespect the manager? Not to mention also laughing in the face of the owner's son? Dyan was special, that was for sure. I couldn't imagine why she'd been allowed to continue working there. She must have had something on someone. But what?

She slunk out of the room, swaying her black leather butt.

"Well," I said, "there might be a better time for me to talk about my observations, Fredelle."

"Please don't leave. I can use your support."

Robbie stormed past me and out the front door, his keys clutched in his hand. The heavy glass door closed with a *thunk* behind him.

"Perhaps in your office, Fredelle?" I said, with a reassuring smile at Autumn. "Everyone needs to chill out a bit."

—••—

Fredelle closed the blinds on her glass wall. "Perhaps it was a mistake to do this. Barb must feel humiliated."

"Fredelle, I didn't tell anyone that my visit was about Barb's messy desk. Did you?"

"Of course not, I would never do that. I couldn't single her out for that kind of bad attention. And I would never, ever, say anything about Barb to Dyan. I like Barb. She's kind and capable and cheerful. Dyan is . . ."

"A bitch," I said. "High-ranking, specialty type. So if you didn't tell Dyan, then who did?"

Fredelle stared at me. "I have no idea."

"Somebody wanted to make a bit of trouble for you and for Barb."

"I didn't tell anyone, because I felt that would be underhanded. I didn't want any of the staff to think that I would do things behind their backs. Although I suppose I did."

"What about when you spoke to me on the phone?"

"The door was closed, the blinds were pulled. No one could have heard, unless they were bugging my line, which is"—she paused to chuckle—"ridiculous."

I said, "I imagine we'll get to the bottom of it. So one more question: How did you find out that I had a near collision with Barb on the way in yesterday?"

Her mouth formed a perfect pink O.

"You're thinking about that, Fredelle. Is that because you believe there's a connection?"

She shook her head. "Couldn't be. I got a call from Mr. Van Zandt. He told me. He was upset that someone visiting our operation could have a close call as a result of an employee."

"Did you tell him why I was here? About the plan to have me come up with solutions to the desk problem."

"Oh no. He wouldn't have liked it. Might have been disappointed in Barb and anyway, I should have been able to handle it on my own. That's what I'm paid for. He has enough to worry about without having to run the office."

"Did he say it was Barb Douglas?"

"Yes."

"Did he mention who told him?"

"That wouldn't be like him. He just said to make sure you were all right and to find out—"

I waited.

She took a deep breath. "—to find out what the goddamn hell was going on over there. He meant here."

"And I'd like to," I said. "Do you think it could have been the two truck drivers who stopped to help?"

She stared at me blankly.

"Oh, I guess I didn't mention that. It didn't seem important. They were kind to me, that's all."

"I don't think . . . they wouldn't know how to reach Mr. Van Zandt at home. He's not listed. And why would they?

They could have told the foreman, but he was off sick yesterday and today. If they were really worried, they'd let me know. Who were they?"

"They said their names were Mel and Del."

"Mel and Del?"

"Yes."

"Are you sure?"

I laughed. "Well, who could forget that?"

Fredelle bit her lip. "But we don't have a Mel and Del."

Keep a recycle bin within tossing distance of your desk. Practice your aim and get rid of as much unnecessary paper as soon as possible.

5

"Most likely I'm mistaken about the names," I said. "I was so shocked at having avoided a head-on collision. But I really could have sworn that they said Mel and Del."

Fredelle shrugged. "I know everyone in this company, even the occasional drivers and the part-timers, and I'm one hundred percent certain there's no Mel and no Del, and I can't recall any names at all like either one of them. Did the truck have a Quovadicon logo?"

"I was kind of shaky. I didn't notice. It was black and silver."

She frowned. "Those are our colors. But I guess it's not important right now."

I reminded myself that Mel and Del were the only people who might have witnessed Barb Douglas running me off the road, so it was important and I didn't really plan to forget about it. I said, "I'm sure it will all become clear. In the meantime, here's an interim plan to help take the pressure off."

"You have an interim plan? That's so wonderful!" Fredelle actually clapped her hands.

I smiled and pointed to her chair. "Let's hope. It's fairly basic, but office politics can be worse than family dynamics. The big problem is often the most easily solved."

"It is?"

"Sure, it's the backbiting that will get you. Have a seat, Fredelle. I have some sketches and suggestions that might solve some problems. Most of them involve changing the placement of certain desks, including the IT area."

She nodded enthusiastically, the silver curls bobbing in agreement. I raised an eyebrow and she sat primly at the edge of her chair.

I took the chair next to her. I flipped open my notepad to show her the design. "I noticed a couple of problems here in the layout of the office."

The enthusiasm faded. "But the whole purpose of bringing you here is to have you fix Barb's desk."

"Actually it was to find a solution to the messy desk without causing Barb to get mad and quit."

"Oh. Right. Yes."

"So if we fix these other items, which really need to be fixed, then the solution to Barb's problem won't be as . . ."

"Insulting?"

"Among other things. I could help her get that desk under control, no problem. But you have to understand, that may not solve anything and you could end up looking for a new IT person."

Fredelle sighed tragically. "What do you propose?"

"Three things: First, reorient the reception desk so that Autumn can see people coming through the front door. It's a small change, but it will help her stay on top of her job and it will make clients and other visitors feel more welcome."

Fredelle's brow wrinkled. "You know, that desk used to be facing the door. I don't know when it migrated to its current position. Maybe when Missy was here?"

"Easy to bring it back?"

"Very easy. Not that Autumn Halliday would necessarily pay any attention to visitors as they arrived. She's a lovely girl, but I think you can see she may not be cut out for corporate life. But she loves it here and I don't think she was cut out for college, either. Although her father can't accept that."

I said, "She's still young."

Fredelle picked up on that. "Not even twenty. She'll find the right field." Fredelle was back in office-mom mode.

I moved on. "Next, since Dyan is always snooping from the photocopier, let's move that photocopier so that she doesn't have to stroll across the office and preen in front of the boardroom and your office to use it. I imagine that distracts anyone in a meeting and annoys you."

"You have no idea."

"I bet I do. Does anyone else do any amount of photocopying?"

"Hardly anyone. It's mostly her. And I'm pretty sure she uses it a lot more than she needs to. Most things are computerized now."

"Perhaps you should start comparing bills and usage month over month with last year. See if your photocopying costs are up."

Fredelle's face lit up with the possibility of giving Dyan a bit of well-deserved pushback.

I added, "And in the meantime, you have an outlet nearby; if you put the photocopier right outside her office, she won't get to use it as an excuse to swagger around. She may even use it less. That will save you money." I did ask myself why Fredelle wasn't on top of this fairly obvious situation. "I'd relocate any central printers there, too, in case she makes the switch to them."

Fredelle looked a bit worried. "Do you suppose she'll get the message?"

I couldn't help grinning. "Oh, she'll get it."

"Wonderful." Fredelle brightened at the thought.

"Be prepared for retaliation of some sort."

"I will. And what about Barb and the point of the whole exercise?"

"First off, reconfigure the IT area so that Robbie and Barb aren't visible on the path to the staff room or anywhere."

Fredelle blinked. "Will her desk still be messy?"

"Most likely, but Dyan won't have any business looking at it and therefore no legitimate reason to complain. It's a stopgap solution, and it may even seem silly, but until I meet with Barb, it's the best I can do."

Fredelle's round kind face fell. "What about the mouse droppings? The old food? Those are health issues."

"I have a feeling they might have been added to the scene to give someone else ammunition."

"Oh! So maybe this reconfiguration is all we need." Relief replaced worry on Fredelle's expressive features.

"Temporarily, for sure. It doesn't simply target Barb. It tells people that you are doing something and their own tasks should be their focus. But you will have to decide how you're going to deal with the desk if Barb doesn't respond to my advice. You only have two choices: It's okay or it's not okay." I thought about Jack's desk and those of other creative people I knew. "Lots of creative people function better that way. Other people can really work much better when they develop new habits to create more order. There's lots of debate about it. But as I keep saying, it's not the desk that's your big problem."

Fredelle nodded slowly. "I don't know how I let things get so out of hand. It used to be so easy in the old days."

The door to the office burst open and crashed against the glass. I half-expected to find the entire window wall in shards on the floor. Robbie Van Zandt loomed in the door, his normally ashen face red and blotchy.

"Now you've done it," he shrieked.

I dropped my notebook, and the design notes scattered on the floor. I'm not really used to men shrieking, I suppose. Although when you think about it, why should we women have all the best emotional outlets?

Robbie pounded on the desk. "I hope you're happy now!"

Fredelle reached over and touched his arm gently. "Goodness, Robbie. What is the matter with you? You have to calm down. Please."

He jerked away from her touch. "Calm down? Calm down? I'm not going to calm down. I'm mad as hell and I'm fed up. I've had it with this place. I've had it with these people and I've had it with you." He shook his finger under her nose. As a terror tactic, the gesture didn't do it for me. Sure, the crash of the door into the glass wall had been dramatic, but the finger pointing? Not so much.

Even so, Fredelle backed away and raised her hands in submission. "All right, okay. Please tell me what is wrong."

His voice hit a new register, and the red flushed face turned almost purple. Robbie leaned farther forward and tapped his finger on Fredelle's collarbone. "You know what's wrong. You had it in for her. You want to get rid of her."

I felt I had to intervene. I stepped between Fredelle and Robbie. "You're mistaken there. Fredelle has nothing but respect for Barb Douglas. She is making sure that Barb is treated fairly."

"Fairly? That's a laugh." He turned and banged on her desk. A pink china cat jumped. "Fredelle brought you in to put the nail in Barb's coffin. To humiliate her in front of this crowd of . . ." He turned back toward the door and stopped.

Dyan stood watching us. She was in full bitch mode, a scarlet smirk playing around the corner of her enhanced lips. Playing against the stereotype, she held a watering can, now suspended over the peace lilies. Autumn had been passing behind her and now stood rooted to the rug, her hazel eyes wide and one hand to her mouth.

"You see. Look at them. It's all for entertainment. And you—" This time he poked my collarbone with his index finger. "You made sure they got a great laugh out of the whole thing at her expense. She was the best thing to ever happen around this stinking hole and now you've got rid of her."

I decided against telling him that the poking of fingers on collarbones technically constituted assault. Sometimes you have to pick your battles. I took a step back and found my voice. "What do you mean, 'got rid of her'?"

"She's not here at work, is she? We had a significant software installation planned for today. Well, no one can do it without her, so you're all screwed."

Fredelle said, "Robbie, I will go and speak to Barb. I must assure you she was not the target of any unkindness from me or from Charlotte. I like and respect her, although I am aware that not everyone does." Fredelle and Robbie turned to glare at Dyan. I suppose I did, too. "But as office manager, I should have prevented this from happening. I will apologize to Barb."

Autumn had rushed over from her desk to see this scene and now gazed openmouthed. One hand was over her heart now, and her mouth stood open. Dyan rolled her eyes and gave Autumn a nudge. "Apologize? To Miss Piggy? As if."

I said, "You don't owe anyone an apology, Fredelle, although I believe other people do. You were kind and considerate. This whole situation has been misinterpreted and stirred up by others. I will be happy to speak to Barb and explain what really happened."

Robbie stared at both of us, his color still dangerously high. "What is the matter with you? Are you deaf?"

"Well, yes, a little bit, Robbie, you know that," Fredelle said. "But—"

I sputtered, "I don't think you should talk to—"

"She probably left town for good. And you know what, Fredelle Newhouse, you can apologize until the day they bury you, it won't change what you've done here. And I will see that you pay for it."

Autumn pressed herself against the exterior wall and Dyan deftly jumped aside as Robbie stormed out of the office. As he passed Dyan's cubicle, he swatted at her tiger lilies and sent vase and flowers flying onto the floor.

Sometimes the phrase *watched openmouthed* doesn't do justice to the reaction of onlookers.

Fredelle lowered herself onto the chair in her office and pulled out a tissue to dab at her eyes.

"Excuse me," I said as I closed the office door in poor little Autumn's stunned face. "Fredelle, are you all right?"

"Not really. But don't mind Robbie. He's upset. I thought he might have fallen in love with her. And he's right," she said. "This is all my fault. I mismanaged everything. I should have gotten rid of that tramp Dyan the first week she came in. We need to get Barb back here."

"He had no right to speak to anyone like that, Fredelle, especially not you. He was way out of line."

"I understand his feelings, though. Poor boy, he's never had anyone. Such a shy, lonely boy. Vulnerable. And I could see that he was growing fond of her. It was one of the reasons I wanted to do something about this situation, before she got fed up with the sneers and digs and quit. And left poor Robbie behind, too."

I stared at her.

"You're right," she said. "The absolute best thing would be if you went to see Barb and explain that we were just trying to improve the situation without embarrassing her. I don't want to lose a good employee over this. I think that perhaps we mishandled things and drove her away."

I said, "I'll be happy to."

"Once she meets you and sees what you're like, I'm one hundred percent convinced that she'll come around." She added, "I don't know what else to do. That system upgrade is being installed. I knew that. Why did I ask you to come here yesterday? Why didn't I wait until things were less stressful? Why didn't I speak to her about it? I feel like a total—"

"Okay, I will go and talk to Barb. I will explain and also say how distressed you are. And if I don't succeed in persuading her to come back, then you can still try. Can I have her address, please?"

Fredelle just stared straight ahead, imagining Barb's distress, I suppose.

"Fredelle?"

"Hmm?"

"Barb's address, please. I think I should do this quickly." I didn't add, *before I lose my nerve.* This was the woman who had almost wiped out me and my car just a day earlier.

Fredelle opened the left-hand drawer in her desk and fished out a file. She opened it, checked the address, and wrote it out for me without appearing to pay any attention to what she was doing.

"I am so grateful," she said, as she put the note with the address on it into my hand.

The phone trilled on the desk.

Fredelle glanced toward it and flinched. She picked up the receiver. "Hello, Reg."

Keep only one agenda,
whether it's paper or electronic, whatever suits.
Use it for all appointments, business and personal.

6

To tell the truth, I wasn't sure it *was* such a good idea to approach Barb Douglas. Whatever she imagined I was planning to do to her on my first visit to Quovadicon, she had certainly been extremely upset by it. Never mind. *You don't get anywhere in life by being a coward*, I reminded myself.

I found her building without any problem. Woodbridge is short of apartment buildings and condos, but if you're lucky you can find, as I did, an excellent unit in an older home that has been converted to multiple units. There are many throughout the city, and you just have to know someone to get one.

Barb Douglas had hit the jackpot with a place on Lilac Lane, a tree-lined cul-de-sac with just four houses. The white clapboard house looked well maintained, and the fresh green paint on the shutters and porch contributed to the cared-for look. A separate set of external stairs had been added on to the original building and ran up the side to the second floor. The mailbox indicated No. 4B. I recognized the dark-green RAV-4 parked in the driveway.

Whom had Barb known in town to rate this street and pretty house? I hurried up the stairs, smoothing my skirt. I was feeling anxious. Plus I wanted to get this situation over with, apologize to Barb, and assure her of Fredelle's innocence as well as my own. Soon after that, with any luck, I would never have to set foot in Quovadicon and see any of its employees again, especially the toxic and tarty Dyan.

The door to 4B stood wide open.

I braced myself for the conversation that would follow, knocked, and called out. "Ms. Douglas? Are you there?" I waited. I told myself the shiver down my spine was just because of a nasty memory of another open door and had nothing to do with this visit.

But if she wasn't answering, why was the door wide open? A mischievous wind lifted my flirty skirt and answered the question. The wind must have blown it open. After another two minutes, I whipped out my small notebook and wrote my name and phone number and a short message asking her to call me to discuss a misunderstanding. I was debating whether to drop it on the floor, where it might get blown away, or in the mailbox, where it might not be seen, when I heard feet thudding behind me on the stairs. As happened all too often lately, I jumped.

"Sorry," a cheerful male voice bellowed. "Guess I sound like a bull in a china shop." A white-haired man somewhere in his sixties puffed up the rest of the stairs, grinned, and held out his hand. "I'm Jim Poplawski, Barb's landlord, or as my wife calls me sometimes, the lardlord." He patted his substantial paunch, threw back his head, and shook with laughter.

I laughed, too, couldn't help myself.

"Don't mind me. I'm just jumpy lately. I was just about to leave Ms. Douglas a note. Would you be able to give it to her?"

"Barb must be home. Her car's here."

I shrugged. "But she doesn't answer."

"Gee, that door's wide open. I gotta get around to fixin' the latch. Sure, I'll give her the note. But why don't I just show you the thing?"

"What?"

"Seems a shame for you to have to come back again. You can save yourself a trip if it doesn't suit. Don't worry. I won't make you carry it down the stairs yourself." The staircase seemed to shake with each guffaw.

I knew the honest approach at that moment would be to say there'd been a misunderstanding. No one's perfect. I followed Jim "the lardlord" through the open door and into a bright and airy apartment.

"One minute. Just in case." He boomed, "Barb, honey, you better not be in the shower 'cause I'm here with a bunch of sailors droppin' by to say hello."

I blinked.

"Well, guess she must be out on the town." He chuckled. "Normally, that'd get a rise out of her."

"I'll bet," I muttered.

"So what do you think?" He stood watching me and obviously waiting for a response.

"It's beautiful," I answered truthfully.

"Not so bad." He smiled, apparently pleased with my response.

Of course, I just had to blunder on. "I love the windows."

It was his turn to blink. "It doesn't have windows."

Had everyone in Woodbridge lost their mind? I said, "Of course, it does. Are you kidding me . . . Jim?"

He frowned, puzzled. "No ma'am."

I said, "But . . ."

He cut me off. "Never saw a piano with windows. And I bet you never did, either."

"A piano?"

"Well, what did you think we were talking about?"

"The apartment. It's beautiful. So bright and open and all those lovely trees you see through all those windows that are definitely here."

He went back to booming. "That's pretty funny. The apartment. Yup, I think I made not too bad a job of it. Should have seen upstairs before we bought the place. Thirty-year-old wall-to-wall carpet with all the original dirt still in it."

I shuddered.

Jim just kept talking. "I resanded all this hardwood myself. And the wife picked the colors for the walls. This one's called Butter Pecan, although it looks like Taffy to me. The trim's called Vanilla White."

Butter Pecan? "It's lovely. The name makes me hungry actually, so I really should head out."

"Not so fast. Don't forget your piano."

"Oh, I don't . . ."

"That is really why you came, no?"

"Sure. Sure it is, but now that I see it . . ." I squinted at the apartment-sized piano tucked into a charming nook by the far wall. It looked as though it had been lovingly cared for.

"We can negotiate on the price. It's not like we're using it now that the family's gone. No shortage of hobbies to keep us busy. And we've got to keep it tuned and everything. Darn thing's nothing but trouble. The wife had to ride herd on those kids to keep 'em practicing. They don't want it and we don't have room for it now that we've downsized. Anyway, Barb needs the space for a desk. She's stuck working on the table."

I strolled toward the small dining table. It had two matching heart-shaped bright blue placemats placed across the table from each other, and two blue-and-white gingham napkins in white rings. A small vase with white garden lilies stood in between. Sweet.

"She keeps her computer here?"

"Just a laptop. She's getting desperate for a better work space. She's a real good tenant and I wouldn't want to lose her. So make me an offer."

Oh, what a tangled web we weave. "How about if I measure it and check to see if it will actually fit in my apartment?"

He raised an eyebrow. "You need to measure the piano?"

"My place is much smaller than this. I'll need to know if it will go into my tiny corner. In fact, this is such a beautiful big space." I turned to examine the living room. It was furnished simply in IKEA style: big comfy sofa in a bright blue denim slipcover, matching oversize chair, glossy white coffee table, cute little dining set for two, gingham cushions, and a couple of cheap and cheerful prints on the Butter Pecan walls. Pale yellow curtain panels fluttered at the open windows.

He glanced around. "Suppose so."

"Barb did a nice job of decorating." My eye was drawn to the open bedroom door. An inviting double bed was nicely done up in soft shades of taupe with crisp white touches. Lots of comfy cushions, soft puffy comforter, tailored bed skirt. Truffle and Sweet Marie would have loved that bed.

Jim said, "Barb rents it furnished. The wife did all this. She's got the knack for it. These days she'd have made a career in interior decorating." He beamed with obvious pride.

"Very nice. But I still need to measure. I'll let you know." I was twitching to get out of the place before Barb showed up and revealed that I was not a potential piano purchaser, but a nosy interloper with an inclination toward false pretenses and trespassing. That would be an awkward moment. Because. . . . I froze.

"Something wrong, ma'am?"

"Oh yes. I feel a bit faint. Could I have a glass of water,

please?" Okay, I realize that the feeling-faint thing went out long before I was born, but, hey, something was very wrong in this place.

"Sure thing." He rumbled toward the kitchen and whipped open a cupboard to get a glass.

I followed him, just to get a better look.

He glanced back at me nervously, perhaps imagining litigation of some sort. "Maybe you should sit down, ma'am."

"Don't worry."

The small kitchen was also cheerful and neat. No dishes in the sink. Clean appliances and floor. A cookbook open on the counter, an imported coffeemaker, and a matching grinder were the only objects on the spotless countertop.

"Ma'am?"

"Hmm?"

"Wouldn't want you to fall down."

"You're right. I'd better sit down." I made my way to the comfy blue sofa and plunked myself down. On the lower tier of the white coffee table, current issues of *Computerworld*, *InformationWeek*, and *Wired* were stacked neatly. On the top, a copy of *Wedding Bells* sat next to *Brides*.

Strange companions for *Wired*.

The white rug was clean and lint free. I turned my eye to the cat-scratching post in the corner, next to a kitty litter tray with fresh litter. I sniffed. No cat scent in this apartment. In fact, everything was clean, fresh, and orderly. There was no sign of whatever cat used that equipment.

Jim lumbered out of the kitchen, glass of water in hand, ice cubes clinking. I said, "Does Barb usually take her cat with her when she goes out?"

As Jim handed me the glass of water, I could only nod in thanks. He stared at me with worry written across his weathered red face. "No, Diablo's an inside cat. She never lets him out. And he never gets into the car without a fight. She has the scratches to prove it."

"Sounds like a real handful."

"For sure. Oh well, they probably just went off to the vet. Perhaps a friend gave them a lift."

"Right. And if she had to wrestle him into the car, that would explain the open door."

"You mean you didn't open it?"

That took me by surprise. "Of course not. That would be . . ." *Good point*, my good angel said, *how about 'nosy, intrusive, rude?'*

"Oh. I thought you had knocked and then just . . ."

"Tried the handle and opened it? I wouldn't do that. It's not even legal. At any rate, if she rushed the cat to the vet she might have forgotten to lock the door behind her; it probably just blew open. Pet owners can get pretty emotional when something is wrong. I once ended up at the vet's wearing mismatched shoes."

He chuckled.

"A small mystery solved," I said, before taking a sip.

"Sure, she would have had to wrestle Diablo into the cage, and her hands would have been full and that would be it. Got to admit, you had me worried for a minute, little lady. It's sure not like Barb to forget to lock her door, but like you said, a pet can make a person emotional. Hope Diablo's all right. Can't stand the critter, but our Barb sure loves him to bits."

I hesitated. "Um, did you say cage?"

"Well, sure. Not a cage, but you know those little carriers people use."

"She always took him out in the carrier?" I pointed across the room. "Is that it? Or did she have an extra?"

"Just the one. She's a restrained kind of person. Anyway, why would she need two? She's only got one cat, even if he is mean enough for two."

I got off the sofa and walked over to the carrier and peered in, hoping to see a mean cat.

"No luck. So not the vet, I guess."

He rubbed the back of his neck. "Darned if I know what's going on. She's crazy about that cat."

I took a gamble. "Maybe we can ask her husband?"

"She doesn't have a husband. Single gal. Works a lot."

"Boyfriend then? Maybe he picked her up?"

He shrugged. "The wife's convinced she might have a fella, but I've never laid eyes on him."

"I just asked because the dining table is set nicely for two."

"I didn't even notice that. For all I know it was set for that darn cat."

"Right. Well, I hope nothing happened to it."

"I guess we'll find out soon enough. So you're going to measure and let me know about the piano? If you want it, we can talk about the price, maybe do a deal."

"Thank you," I said.

"Paula, that's the wife, will be really happy to know if it's going to a good home. She's sentimental about stuff as well as people."

"Artistic temperament," I said. "I can tell by the nice job she did here."

"I'll tell her. And here, let me give you our telephone number so you can get back to us. Do you mind letting us know one way or the other? I'm going to have to put it in storage otherwise."

"Sure thing," I said.

Even as I walked down the outside stairs, my head was clambering with questions. The biggest one was obviously, how could this serene and well-organized spot possibly belong to the owner of the desk from hell?

"And the bedroom! You should have seen it. That bedroom was absolutely pristine," I said to Sally as we sat on her leather sofa watching the toddlers play and baby Shenandoah sleep. Truffle and Sweet Marie were snuggled in, as far as they could get from the rest of the children. One of the nice things about having a stay-at-home mom friend is that she will give you a grilled cheese sandwich for lunch with no prior notice required.

"Hard to believe how some people live. Do you think perhaps because there were no children?"

I nodded. "That could do it."

Sally shook her blond curls and stroked Shenandoah's tiny tummy. "Discarded socks, then. Must have been a few. Yesterday's underwear? Everyone drops those on the floor."

"Speak for yourself, Miss Messy. This bedroom was a regular oasis. It made me think it was time for me to redecorate mine. I like the taupe-and-white look."

"Listen, Charlotte. Don't make me smack you. You just decorated your bedroom when you moved back last year. Don't put me through another endless discussion of paint samples and fabric swatches. I couldn't bear it. Life's too short. Don't pull the doggie's tail, Savannah. Mommy told you that's a no-no."

"Friends are there for friends during redecoration. You can't just bail on me when I have the next one. But no matter; let's get back to the subject, which isn't paint or fabric, it's incongruity."

Sally said, "I suppose it is really weird for someone they called 'Miss Piggy' to have a spotless home."

"Yes it is. It's beyond weird."

"Although you also have to wonder about people who would call a co-worker 'Miss Piggy.' "

"Just one co-worker, really. Dyan the schemer. And I don't know, there was more to it than that. The whole scene just seemed wrong. And it makes me wonder what's really going on with that desk. I can tell you, Sally, my spider senses were tingling."

She shrugged and reached over to pick up a fallen toddler. "People can be very different at work."

"Maybe. And another strange thing, I can't believe anyone who loved her indoor cat would just leave the door open so it could run out. Awful things could happen. Her pet could have been hit by a car. Do you think she'd do that?"

"I'm not so in love with cats, so I couldn't say."

"Who are you kidding, Sally? You with four kids? You're a patsy for anything that needs to be looked after. Even me, sometimes."

"That's true enough. Even you frequently. By the way, that's why I really don't like to see you getting involved in something else that might be dangerous. I think we should have gotten that out of our systems by now."

"Dangerous? How could it be dangerous? It's broad daylight with people around. Everyone's always exaggerating."

"Call me nuts, but didn't you tell me that this Barb tried to run you over with her SUV?"

I shrugged and leaned back on the sofa. "Maybe she did. I'm not really sure. Maybe I just overreacted because I'm so jumpy. But I still wouldn't want to spot her coming toward me on the road again."

"Right, the too-much-murder thing. That is exactly my point. Dallas, don't put that in the socket." Sally heaved herself off the sofa and confiscated a fork. "What the hell happened to my plug guards?"

"Well, no one's been murdered. Fredelle wants me to speak to Barb because of this misunderstanding. We want to set the record straight. That's all. Maybe I'll talk to those two truck drivers again, in case I just misinterpreted what happened. I got their names wrong, so maybe I did."

"Listen, stay out of it. You've had too much bad stuff happen to you. Rest your brain. Do relaxing little organizer things. Sort my Christmas decorations by color and size and shape, for instance. Or maybe my spice drawer according to the color wheel. I have tons of ideas to keep your mind busy."

"Very funny."

"You get way too wrapped up with your clients. Let it go."

"Good advice, I guess."

"You betcha. Now let's catch the news."

"Noooo! Come on, Sal. Not Todd—"

Sunlight glinted off the most celebrated chompers in town. Of course, that could have been a trick of the camera. This time Todd Tyrell was on location in front of the Woodbridge police station. It was too late to cover my eyes. And I would have still been able to hear him.

In breaking news, Woodbridge police have confirmed that the man found in the trunk of a blue Impala had been shot to death execution style. They have still not issued any information regarding the victim's identity. The body was found in an isolated wooded area near Vineland Estates on the outskirts of Woodbridge. Anyone with any information is asked . . .

Todd's giant face was replaced by footage of the wooded area and the blue Impala. The scene surrounded by fluttering yellow police tape filled the screen. A white tent had been erected, over the site where the car must have been, I suppose. The red-haired detective was still there, still juggling his silver keys, still wearing what looked like the same suit, shirt, and tie as the day before. Perhaps he'd made the announcement about the execution-style killing. This time he was accompanied by Nick the Stick, who was wandering around looking goofy and probably trampling evidence. A small crowd of curious people hovered near the tape. I gasped and leaned forward to stare at one of them. An agitated woman with short dark hair paced back and forth behind the tape. She was wearing jeans and a hoodie and didn't seem to be aware of the rain. She held her hand over her mouth and appeared to be talking into a cell phone. She turned away from the camera, but not before I caught a glimpse of her face. Pleasant, thirtyish, and oddly familiar.

"Sally, you're always watching WINY."

"Not *always*."

"Okay, but you follow the news on that channel."

"Sure. You know how I feel about Todd."

I let the Todd part slide. "That wasn't the footage we saw the other night, was it? When he first talked about the body being found in the woods? Todd was in those shots and I'm sure that tent wasn't there."

But, of course, the news had moved on to another item by that time: Todd had put his "brain" to work talking about rising prices in our town.

Sally had turned her attention back to him.

I grabbed the remote and flicked off the television.

I said more to myself than to her, "In that case, they must be using voiceover with earlier footage of the crime scene."

"What are you talking about?"

"See? That red-haired guy hasn't changed his clothes."

"And that's important because?"

"It means it wasn't from today. We were able to see the car before, although I couldn't make out what make it was. Now it's under that tent."

"Have you lost your—"

"Plus, and this is really important. It was raining in this footage, but the sun's shining today and Sunday was a beautiful day, so the WINY camera must have been there during that rain shower yesterday afternoon."

Sally shook her curls. "What difference does it make?"

I sat up straight. "It started to rain just before two, although it could have been a bit earlier or later wherever that stretch of wood is."

"Todd said Vineland Estates. It's off the highway north of Woodbridge. You take the exit near the bridge."

"Not too far out of town. And the rain didn't last very long. Maybe an hour."

"Is that important?"

"I think it is, because she would have been there sometime between two and what, three?"

Sally said, "Who?"

"I just saw the woman who almost ran me off the road yesterday."

"You mean the owner of the weirdly messy desk and the flawlessly spotless apartment?"

"Exactly. Barb Douglas. Now what was she doing at the site of this murder?"

Assemble all the papers and documentation you need the day before a meeting.

7

Sally was right, of course. I did have my job to do, and I didn't mean to get overly involved in the Barb Douglas situation. By way of being normal, I dropped off a detailed work plan contract to my new closet client. It felt good having her squeeze my hands in gratitude when I hadn't even done anything yet. We agreed that I could start the next week with an inventory of her contents, much of which I knew would make my mouth water. I promised to drop off some closet designs and ideas on Thursday night, just to keep her in the mood for the purge the following week. Once that tough part was over, we'd work together to find just the right space for every object that remained. I loved my job.

Next, I headed back to Quovadicon. I hurried past Autumn without being noticed. I poked my head into Fredelle's office and said, "Barb wasn't home. I'll try again later. I'd like to have a quick look at that desk again. Will I run into Robbie?"

She shook her head. "He's gone. Do you need me with you?"

"Not at all," I said.

I thought she looked relieved, and I couldn't blame her.

In the office, I hurried, not just because of the nasty smell of old cups and sneakers, not to mention the sardine can. I didn't want Robbie to come back and threaten me again. Fredelle didn't think he was dangerous, but I had my doubts. I headed for his desk. The file folder was still there. I peeked back into the hallway and glanced around just in case. Then back to the desk, where I lifted the file folder. Sure enough, there were a number of photos of the woman I now knew as Barb: several shots of her at her desk, on her cell phone, smiling, tying her shoes, gazing at her computer screen. Did she know Robbie had taken these? My guess was no. I slid the photos back under the file, minus one with a clear image of her face. With one backward look at the unbelievable desk next to Robbie's and a shake of my head, I got the hell out of there.

The reasons why I hate the Woodbridge police station are too many and varied to go into here. Let's say I wasn't comfortable about dropping in and confiding my concerns about Barb Douglas to the red-haired detective with the icy eyes. Something about him made me nervous. Naturally, I wouldn't have considered discussing my observations with officer Nick Monahan, although I've known him since high school, as he could be counted on to do something inappropriate with the information.

That was why I was parked in the Miata on Old Pine Street getting up the nerve to knock on Pepper Monahan's door. Pepper is Sergeant Monahan, outranking her husband, when she's not on sick leave because of her difficult pregnancy. Old Pine Street is not my favorite place nor is Pepper my favorite person to visit. A shiny Chrysler Town and Country in deep crimson was parked in the driveway.

It didn't merit the garage, of course, because that's where Nick's vintage 'Stang was parked. It sat there along with his totally ridiculous giant truck when Nick wasn't speeding through Woodbridge pretending he was still a footloose chick magnet. I figured he was at work muddying the waters for the police force, and if my luck held, he'd stay at work until I was finished.

First I made a quick cell phone call to Quovadicon to see if Barb Douglas had shown up. If yes, my visit to Pepper could be purely social. I would have preferred that. But Barb hadn't shown up, nor had she called, according to Autumn. I had to believe her, as Fredelle and Robbie weren't available. And considering it was Autumn, she did seem quite certain of her facts.

Pepper's belly preceded her to the door. One of these days I am going to get used to having my friends be pregnant. That must be the curse of being in your thirties. People get baby crazy. In the last year or so, even Jack would get pretty excited about babies. But no one else was nearly as baby crazy as Pepper. No baby had ever mattered as much as this one.

"Don't laugh," she said.

"Who's laughing? That baby bump looks great." In fact, the bump did look cute. Pepper was another story. As she was the most elegant, put-together blonde I knew, it was a shock to see her with dark blue circles under her eyes, sallow skin, and—I could hardly believe it— a zit on her chin. The checkered flannelette pajamas and striped socks might have been comfortable, but they made Pepper look like a walking wall. Her normally perfect do was pulled back in a stubby ponytail.

"The bump, sure, but not the rest of me."

"Come on," I fibbed. "You look fine."

"Give it a rest," she said. "I own mirrors."

She had a point.

"Don't trust your mirrors. You look happy and pregnant, and that's really wonderful."

"Happy to be pregnant, yes. That is wonderful. Happy?" She shrugged her checked flannel shoulders. Of course, the Monahan household could easily be a minefield of buried marital explosives. Nick the Stick had a wandering eye at the best of times, as I knew the hard way. He'd be hard to keep on a leash by a pregnant wife who was on sick leave for a difficult pregnancy.

"I heard you haven't been well. Is it okay to drop by?"

"Sure. Come on in."

I followed Pepper into the house she and Nick had bought less than a year ago. So much had happened since then.

"Nice place," I said, glancing around.

"Right." She yawned. "This is the first time you've been here. Inside, I mean."

Resisting traps, I kept it straight. "Yes. I love what you've done."

That at least was true. The style of the older home had been respected, but updated, warmed, and brightened.

I said, "The yellow walls are really great."

"Thanks." She sank onto the sectional sofa and pointed to the matching chair. "Have a seat. You want something? Coffee? Soda?"

"I'm fine." I would have liked a coffee, but seeing Pepper with those deep circles under her eyes, radiating exhaustion and worry, I preferred to have her relax on the sofa. Obviously, that's what she'd been doing. A well-worn patchwork comforter was flung across the streamlined microfiber sectional. I remembered that comforter from our adolescent years. We'd always called it Pepper's security blanket.

She glanced at it and back at me.

"I hope everything's all right," I said.

"So do I."

She said, "Thanks for sending the flowers and everything. I appreciated it. I should have got in touch, but I was too . . ."

"It's okay. You didn't need to get in touch."

"But that was nice. Thoughtful."

I waited, watched, and prayed she'd be able to blink back the tears shining in her eyes. I knew she was desperate to have this baby, and I'd heard she was worried.

"It's nice to be sitting here together just like old times. In the middle of the day, too," she said finally.

"Couple of misfits, playing hooky."

"Brings back memories."

"Sure does."

"Can I get you something, Pepper? I'm happy to do that."

"The kitchen's a mess," she said.

"Misfits don't give a crap about messy kitchens."

She managed a weak smile.

I added, "Neither do friends."

"I'll have milk and cookies," she said. "And if I remember correctly, it's your turn to get them."

She had a good memory. After years of estrangement, that was not one of the things that stuck in my brain.

I returned with the milk and a plate of Oreos on a tray and settled it midway between us on the yellow leather ottoman.

"It's good to be back," I said.

"You know, Charlotte, I've come to realize that nothing really ever happened with you and Nick."

I felt a catch in my throat. I croaked out an answer. "You're right. Nothing ever did."

"It just looked . . ."

"You were my friend and I couldn't ever do that to you, even if the opportunity had really presented itself."

"I'm sure the opportunity did present itself. I know my boy. But I guess I didn't know him that well then. I was so angry," she said. "I thought you would take him from me. He had that thing for you in school. Every time I heard him call you Charlie, I'd just freak. I blamed you."

"He's just a flirt," I said. "He can't help it. We always knew that about him. Part of his charm, I guess."

She hiccuped. "Part of the challenge."

"What changed your mind?"

"I can't even talk about it. Let's say we had a conversation about a transgression and I threw it at him and he threw it back at me. This time I believed him."

"I'm glad. I've always known that you're the person he loves."

"I hope you're right," she said. "There's more at stake now."

"I am." I wasn't sure why I was offering this totally unmerited bit of support to Nick, but I was in friendship mode, and grateful to be there, and I thought that was what Pepper needed to hear.

"That's good. Because if we're lucky, we're finally going to have a baby."

I hesitated. There was a lot of subtext in that sentence. *If we're lucky?*

She blurted, "Tell me why Sally can pop out beautiful children as often as she wants and she doesn't even mess up a curl on her head. And I can't even . . ."

Oh boy. This didn't sound good. I had no idea what to say, or do. I reached over and squeezed her hand.

She said, "I've been having problems. Complications. There could bc a premature birth."

"Oh Pepper. I'm so sorry. I knew you were off work, but I didn't realize it was so serious. Is there anything . . . ?"

"Keep hoping with me, that's all."

"Charlotte?"

"Yes?"

"I'm glad we're friends again."

"Me, too."

"So stop hogging the Oreos."

"Me? Who are you to talk?"

Sometimes the best thing about reconnecting with a lost friend is what isn't said. Look forward, move ahead. Cookies and milk for the future. The plate was almost empty by the time Pepper lifted an eyebrow.

"What?" I said.

"So what can I do for you?" she said.

"What? Oh. Right."

"You came here for a reason. You didn't know I had forgiven you. So what do you want?"

"You're right. I did have a reason, but I almost forgot because this was—"

"A special moment. Yeah, yeah. Now cut to the chase."

"Ah, I see you haven't changed that much. Still the cop lady. Okay, I need some advice."

"As long as it's not about some case. I love my job, but right now I'm trying to concentrate on life. I don't want to hear about violence or crime. It's all Nick can talk about, although maybe it's a break from vehicles. Do you know he's a detective now? That event last year boosted his promotion possibilities. But for me, shop talk doesn't mesh well with staying positive and pregnant."

"I hear you. I just need to know what to do about someone who may or may not be missing, who may or may not be in a very fragile emotional state which may or may not be sort of my fault."

"As long as we're clear about everything." She popped the last cookie into her mouth and scowled at me.

I filled Pepper in on the events at Quovadicon, including my reaction to Barb Douglas trying to run me off the road.

She said, "Explain that to me again."

"Well, in retrospect I wonder if that's what really happened. I'm jumpier than I used to be, and maybe I just overreacted."

"Did she try to run you off the road or not?"

"Here's the thing. She was on the wrong side of the road. She had kind of a wild look on her face, like she was in a panic or something. So I don't really know if she was trying to get me, because why would she? She didn't even know who I was. Or was it something else, some terrible thing that led to her disappearance?"

"I don't see where you have any responsibility at all."

"I just think if we can make sure she's all right, then I can walk away from this really strange project and get on with things."

"Oh fine, what's the person's name again?"

"Barb Douglas."

"Humph. Never heard of her. And I'm on sick leave and not supposed to think about anything stressful, like you know, *missing women*. But since we're being all girlfriendy here, you might as well give me a description and I'll get in touch with the station and see if they can keep an eye out for her."

"I have a photo of her. What's the good of being an organizer if you don't have what you need with you?" I felt that if Pepper looked at the face of a real person who might be in some kind of real trouble, she might be more likely to make sure the police really did something about it.

Pepper didn't quite manage to ditch the bored expression on her face. "Oh fine, let's see then."

"And I was hoping you'd say that." I slid the photo across thc table. "I'm really grate—"

"Give it a rest," she said, reaching for her glass of milk. "I'm not saying they'll find her for you, but you never know."

I did notice that she ignored the photo on the table in

favor of the milk. I waited. After all, I was glad to be taking tentative steps toward repairing our ruptured relationship.

I tried not to twitch impatiently.

Eventually, she shot me a sneaky grin. "Okay. I couldn't help it. You look so serious. It just screams 'kick me.' I'll look at your dumb photo, not that it will do much good. Most people who go missing do so of their own free will and don't want to be found."

She leaned forward with an "Oof." We both laughed.

She said, "Beached whales are us."

I said, "But not all of us." And I dodged the mommy magazine she tossed in my direction.

"Don't get overconfident." She put the glass of milk down on the tray in front of her, which was good, because she's got a great aim and if she'd playfully tossed that at me, she wouldn't have missed.

This time, I picked up the photo and handed it to her. "Here, Mrs. Whale, no dodging the question."

She chuckled and glanced at it, obviously humoring me. So when she turned ashen, I panicked and jumped to my feet. "What is it? A pain? A contraction?"

Pepper glared at me. "If I didn't have high blood pressure before you showed up, I sure could get it while you were here. Calm down, Charlotte. It's just the baby kicking."

"Sorry, didn't mean to overreact. I don't know that much about these things. Let me wipe up that milk."

But I did know enough to detect a false note in her voice. After our years together as teenagers, I could always sense when Pepper was lying.

Pepper's eyes flicked back to the photo. She frowned. "As I said, there's not much the police can do when a functioning adult doesn't show up at work."

"Or at home. I know for a fact she's not there, either. As I said, her landlord is really worried. And there's the whole thing about the cat."

I left out the part where I'd actually gone into Barb's apartment looking for her.

"But I have to mention that I saw her on television near the spot where that murder took place. She must have gone there directly from work, because it had just started to rain. She must have found out about the murder, and I think she's connected in some way with that. And now she's missing. So that's why I'm here, really. In case there's some . . ."

If I'd expected a dramatic reaction from Pepper, I was disappointed. "I'm sure there's nothing to it, but I'll convey your concerns to the right people. You'll have to leave me the photo."

I managed not to say, *The one you're clutching with white knuckles?* I knew better than to grill her on that.

"Sure. That'll be good. By the way, who's the detective in charge of the case? I saw him on television, but I didn't recognize him."

"Nick's working on it."

"Yes, I saw him on the news, too." I chose not to mention that being Nick, he had been blundering around the scene looking even more useless than usual. "But there was this other guy who seemed to be in charge."

She made a face.

"Red hair," I said, playing to her reaction. At the same time, I hoped she didn't notice mine. I felt my heart rate rise at the mention of the new detective. "Pale skin, blue eyes. Looked sort of like a handsome goldfish."

Pepper snorted and then laughed. "That's Connor Tierney. I knew there was something fishy about him."

"Where did he come from?"

The laugh turned to a scowl. "He transferred in from the city. Thinks he can jump over people's heads just because he picked up a bit of experience in a large urban setting."

"Hm."

"Handsome goldfish says it all. Cold. Slippery."

It was my turn to laugh. "Don't hold back. How do you really feel about him, Pepper?"

"How do you think? I knew him from the police academy and out of the blue he shows up here and now he's supposed to be running an investigation? Get real. He doesn't even know where to get a cup of coffee in this town. I would have been in charge normally, with Frank D'Angelo. Nick's been here all his life and his father and grandfather were on the force."

There was something else behind her comments. If I'd had to guess, I'd have said that Pepper didn't entirely trust this guy.

"Oh right, Frank D'Angelo," I said, bypassing the distractions of Tierney and Nick. "Your partner. Looks like he should be on Mount Rushmore."

"What do you mean?"

"You know, chiseled face. Never smiles." I remembered the crazy crush that Margaret had developed on him. We'd called him Tall, Dark, and Granite. I decided not to mention this to Pepper in case partnership trumped friendship in the secret-spilling category.

"Frank's been on a task force dealing with a car theft ring. He's got a lot of years on the force, starting to coast a bit. This is good for him."

"Oh right. I forgot. He's a lot older than we are." *And older than Margaret is*, I thought.

"No kidding. Forty-five."

"Divorced?"

"What difference does that make? You want to hook up?"

I shrugged. "Just asking. I have some older friends who are always on the lookout for an available man without a lot of baggage."

For some reason, I thought it was better if Pepper didn't know that I suspected that Margaret had her date with that same Frank D'Angelo.

"Forget that. His wife died in a car accident three years ago. I think he likes being on his own."

"Point taken. So the new guy—"

"Is single. Interested?"

I was, but not for that reason. "Thanks, but I'm taking a break from men lately. Been burned a few too many times. I just wondered if he was the type to do a good job with this investigation, that's all. It seems like quite a high-profile crime and here's this guy we've never seen before."

Pepper peered at me through narrowed eyes.

I continued. "I wondered if I could approach him about the Barb Douglas situation. He might have noticed her at the scene. For all we know, maybe he spoke to her."

"Pay close attention. Do not approach him with your harebrained ideas."

"I was just going to—"

She pointed her finger at me. "I need you not to poke your pointed little nose into this situation, Charlotte. Do you hear me?"

"Loud and clear," I said, getting ready to leave. "Do they teach you to say 'I need you to whatever' in the police academy?"

She ignored that. "You must have heard that the victim in the trunk was a professional hit. He was shot execution style and dumped by people who knew how to cover their tracks and leave a message to others."

"I did hear that, but—"

"But nothing. Do not get involved. Don't discuss it with anyone. Go back to your closet makeovers and whatever else keeps you busy."

And as I slipped into the Miata minutes later, I had a

couple of questions to ponder. Why did Pepper have such hate on for the new cop? Was it merely because he would interfere with her ambitions for her dopey husband?

But more to the point, why had she lied when she said she didn't know Barb Douglas?

Shred documents with your name
and address before you discard them.
Identity theft is real.

8

I pulled up in front of the two-story house on Lilac Lane and stared at the green RAV-4 still parked in the same position in the driveway. I scampered up the stairs. If Barb had shown up, I could utter my little apology and get on with my life. The door was closed and locked this time.

Naturally.

I headed downstairs just as a tall, moonfaced woman in faded jeans and a paint-splattered green sweatshirt opened the door. Her cheeks were red, her feet were bare, and, even though that limp ponytail was about the least flattering style she could pick, there was something very attractive about her. Maybe the splashes of purple paint on her hands. For whatever reason, she was the kind of person you liked the moment you saw her.

"I'm here about the piano," I lied as I hit the bottom stair.

"You are? That's great. Come on in. I'll get the key to the apartment." She beamed.

I stepped inside. The entryway was cluttered with boxes

on their way in or out. A tantalizing smell of coffee drifted into the space. At the end of the long hallway, I caught sight of a conservatory. An easel with a canvas explained the paint splatters on her clothing

"I spoke to your husband earlier and took some measurements, and I think it might fit in my place if I move things around. But I realized that I didn't take the time to try it out. How silly was that? Anyway, I'd like to check that out. Is there any chance your tenant might be home soon so I could run my fingers over the keys?"

The pleasant moon face clouded briefly. "Barb hasn't been around these last couple of days, but I can certainly let you in. I'm Paula. I have the keys, and I'm sure she won't mind seeing as she's itchin' to get that piano out of there. Hang on a sec while I get my shoes on."

"I don't want to disturb you if you're in the middle of something."

"I'm always in the middle of something, and you're not disturbing me one little bit."

A minute later she'd slipped into her battered Birkenstocks and we were on our way up the exterior staircase.

"I loved this apartment when I saw it this morning. What a great choice of colors and furnishings. Your husband said you chose everything. Your tenant was lucky to get something like this in Woodbridge."

"We were lucky to get her. We were going to rent it unfurnished, but she made us a deal we couldn't refuse to furnish it for her. She thought it was perfect, and she was in a hurry to start this new job. She didn't want to find a hotel or anything while she set herself up, and she made it worth our while to furnish it for her. I enjoy decorating, so I whipped through that check and had a blast shopping. We'd already painted it and refinished the hardwood floors, so that speeded things up."

She unlocked the door and we stepped inside. From my

initial glance, nothing had changed inside the apartment. There was still no sign that Barb had come by and moved so much as a molecule.

"She's very neat, your tenant."

"Yes, she takes wonderful care of everything, and she's always friendly and pleasant."

"You were lucky. Well, I'll just try the piano now and be out of your hair in a minute." I crossed the floor to the piano, hoping I'd remember at least one of the scales from my childhood enforced practices. "Oh look, that's so adorable, those heart-shaped placemats. Where did you get those? I'd love to pick some up for Valentine's Day."

She looked puzzled. "What . . . ? Oh right. Barb must have found those somewhere. Nothing to do with me. But they are cute, aren't they?"

"Guess she had some romantic dinner planned for her boyfriend."

"I suppose so. Perhaps that's where she is now."

"Oh right, you mentioned she'd been away."

"Yes, and it's not my business of course, but I've been a bit worried about her. But I imagine he surprised her with a special trip or something and she didn't have time to call." A look of hope flooded her round face.

"He?"

"The man she was seeing. I guess you could call him her boyfriend. Silly. He wasn't a boy anymore."

"It is a ridiculous expression, isn't it?"

"For sure. They really hit it off. That must be it. Perhaps she took Diablo to a pet sitter and brought the crate back here."

"Oh right, Diablo the cat. Your husband was worried about that cat. Did Barb have a pet sitter?"

"She might have. I'm just the landlady. I mean we're friendly, but not exactly family, you know. I don't know that much about her."

"Of course."

"Even so, Jim and I would have been happy to look after Diablo. Well, I would have been. I love cats, even that one, but . . ."

"But?"

"She didn't ask, did she?" The anxious expression on her face deepened. "I think I should have told her that I'd be willing, I should have made it clear. But, look, I shouldn't be bothering you about this. I think I'm worried about nothing at all. Probably just a little fling. So, what do you think about the piano?"

"What? Oh right, the piano."

Something flickered across Paula's face, a bit of suspicion taking over from the anxiety. I decided, considerably behind schedule, that honesty might be the best policy.

I said, "I haven't been entirely truthful with you."

She stepped back, surprised.

"I actually came here to see Barb Douglas." I left out the part about the apology and the controversy at work.

"You mean you lied? But why?"

I could tell she was deeply disappointed in me. Frankly, I couldn't blame her. "Just about the piano. I didn't intend to. Your husband assumed that I was here to see it, and I didn't set him straight because I was worried about her."

"You were already worried about her? And you snooped in her apartment under false pretenses? I don't get it."

I nodded, feeling equal parts creepy and sleazy. "It just sort of happened naturally."

"Huh."

"Yes, I know. But she left work under really strange circumstances, practically ran someone off the road. And then she didn't show up today, even though it was important for her to be there. The woman she works for is very worried. And so are . . . some of her colleagues. And so, apparently, are you."

She crossed her arms over her chest and looked down her nose at me. "If you don't mind me saying so, wouldn't it make more sense to call the police, rather than waste time doing whatever you were doing?"

"Yes. It would have. That's the first thing I thought of. And I already spoke to a police contact about it."

"You did?"

I shrugged. "Sure, it's the first thing you think of, but I've been told she's an adult and she's free to do whatever she wants. She has no legal obligation to go to work. So I thought I'd check to see if she was sick. That's when the, um, misunderstanding happened. I didn't correct it because I was alarmed by the open door, and then your husband told me about Diablo."

All right, so I wasn't entirely forthcoming with her. I hadn't gone to see Pepper until after my first visit to Barb's place, and I hadn't told Pepper I'd gone in under false pretenses.

"The door was open?"

"Yes."

"And you didn't open it?"

"Of course not. That would be breaking and entering, or something illegal. I should have told him I wasn't who he thought I was, but . . . I made a mistake."

I guess at that point, she decided to trust me. "Did you tell the police about the cat?"

"No. I will. I'll talk to them again. But I started to think about the cute little placemats and I realized the table looked set for a romantic dinner. I wanted to check if you knew about a boyfriend. I thought if I had his name, I could call him and find out if he knows where she is."

She still had her arms crossed across her chest. And she hadn't let go of that wary look in her eye. "I don't know how to reach him. I'm not even sure of his last name. I keep telling you, she's new here and she doesn't really confide in me. As much as I like her, she's quite a private person."

"Quite a tidy person, too, wouldn't you say?"

She chuckled. "For sure, a lot neater than I am."

Another thing that didn't make sense.

"Randy?" she said.

"Randy?" I echoed.

"No, that's not it. That kind of a name, though. Boy, it must be menopause, but I can't remember anything lately. I'm sure she mentioned his name in passing, but . . . pfft, it's gone."

"Did you ever meet him?"

She shook her head. "No. He took her home a couple of times. Parked outside and chatted for a while. Jim couldn't resist spying from the window. He feels kind of paternal. A bit ridiculous when you think that Barb's in her late thirties."

"Mmm." Margaret's parents came to mind.

"She's not much older than our own girls. He misses meddling in their lives. No wonder they moved so far away."

"Did you see this man?"

"Jim might have, but I didn't. I told him to get away from the window and give the woman some privacy. Had to make a fuss to get him away from there."

"Do you think Jim saw him when he got out of the car?"

"He didn't actually get out. Or anyway, Jim didn't mention it. I think they talked in the car and then she went upstairs by herself."

"But you think it was a romantic interest?"

"I didn't ask, but she mentioned a guy a couple of times, and you know you can tell by someone's tone that they're taken with that person. Oh, why can't I remember his name? I heard it enough."

"Of course, you wouldn't think you'd need to remember it," I said. "But if it's in your head, it will pop out sooner or later." I reached into my bag and brought out my card. She stared at it and then at me.

"Oh boy," she said, "to think I let an organizer into my chaotic house. I must be nuts."

"Your house isn't chaotic."

"Oh, sure it is. Don't know how you could miss that." She shot me a suspicious look, as though she thought I was lying again.

I said, "Are you an artist?"

"Yes. A messy one." She laughed.

"Are you happy and comfortable in your home?"

"Well, sure."

"Are you productive?"

"Most times."

"Can you find what you need when you need it?"

"Of course."

"Then you don't have anything to worry about."

She smiled, and then the smile slipped from her face. "Except Barb."

"Right. And let's hope I'm wrong about her."

"Robert, I think," she said.

I stared.

"Yes, that's it. I'm sure she mentioned that." She tapped the side of her head. "You were right, it was in there."

"Do you have a last name?" Of course, even as I asked the question, I was pretty sure of the answer.

"It will come to me."

I suggested *Van Zandt*.

She shook her head. "Not sure. Not even one hundred percent sure about the *Robert* part."

"I think I know how to find out."

I turned to leave, hoping that Paula didn't see the worry on my face.

She touched my arm. "Let me know, please. As soon as you have any news about her."

—

I pushed open the glass door of Quovadicon and waved to Autumn.

"May I help you, miss? Oh hi, Caroline," she said, as I walked past her and through the offices. Fredelle was in her office, looking paler than usual. Her periwinkle cardigan had lost its crisp clean look.

I closed the door behind me and Fredelle gasped.

"She's still not at home," I said.

Fredelle's hand shot to her mouth.

"The landlord doesn't know where she is. The door was wide open and the cat was gone."

"Oh, goodness! Do you think she left town?"

"If so, she left everything behind her. She didn't seem to have packed." I continued, "I thought I saw her on television."

"What?"

"At the scene of that murder. One of the bystanders gawking at the site looked like the woman at the wheel of the SUV."

"I don't understand. Why would she be there?"

"No idea. I thought perhaps you might know something."

"I heard about the murder." She stopped talking and shuddered. "But how could Barb be connected with that? Perhaps she saw the site and stopped out of curiosity. It doesn't make any sense to me."

"Me neither. Maybe you're right."

A connection was beginning to flicker in my mind. "By the way, Fredelle, were you aware that Barb was going out with Robbie Van Zandt?"

She stared, her hand hovering at her throat. "No. I mean,

she never let on and neither did he. I knew he had a huge crush, but who would ever imagine that they . . ."

I understood Fredelle's reaction. That sardine can would have been a powerful deterrent for me if I'd been Robbie. On the other hand, Robbie's personality would have been an equally daunting prospect if I'd been in Barb's sneakers. Still, wedding magazines can make people unpredictable.

"I think it's true, and I want to ask him if he has any idea of where she might have gone."

"Oh, dear. Do you think you should? He's so angry about everything."

"I have to ask, and I prefer to do it here."

She stood up and clutched the edge of her desk. "But you don't think that Robbie would have anything to do with the fact she's missing?"

"He probably doesn't."

"What if he . . . ?" Her hand was back in front of her rosebud mouth again.

"Not too likely, but just in case, I wanted to talk to him here where there are lots of—"

"Witnesses?" she blurted.

"Is he back?"

She stared at me and then at her phone, which had started to ring. Mr. Van Zee, I imagined.

I left while she took the call and practically knocked over Dyan, who once again was pretending to water the peace lilies outside the door. At this rate, both plants would be washed away before the end of the week. I said hello and headed toward the IT office from hell.

Robbie whirled in his chair as I walked into the space. "What the hell do you want?" he said.

"I want to talk to you about Barb Douglas."

"Haven't you done enough harm?"

"I don't believe I've done any harm."

"That's your story. Of course, you'd say that. You drove her away. They put you up to it. They're horrible, always cackling and whispering. They put things on her desk to make it worse. It's like a coven in here. Witches as far as the eye can see."

"You're dating Barb," I said.

He snapped his mouth closed, practically cracking a molar. He stared at me through thick lenses. Up close I could see that the left arm of the frame was held together with duct tape. Not a good look for him, but also probably the least of Robbie Van Zandt's problems.

"Yes?"

He shook his head.

"You've been seen."

A flush crawled up his neck and began a slow ascent up his cheeks. "So what? There's no law against dating."

"True. And no problem with it, either. So why didn't you just tell the truth?"

"Haven't you ever heard about that rule you can't date your co-workers? Where else are you going to meet people you have something in common with? Why is everyone so determined to make people miserable? Barb is such a nice person. So calm and smart and levelheaded. She's got a sense of humor, even about the desk situation. She's the nicest person I've ever worked with."

I couldn't imagine that Robbie Van Zandt was too hung up on the rules. I had no idea why he'd wanted to keep their dating a secret, but decided to let that go. For one thing, it wasn't my business, although I felt her whereabouts was. "Do you have any idea where Barb could be?"

"Why should I tell you? Do you feel guilty?"

This time I told the truth. "I do, in a way. I don't want to be responsible. If she's upset, I want to talk to her and explain that I was not part of a conspiracy to diminish her. Fredelle regards her as an excellent employee."

He glanced past me. "I don't see what the fuss is about the stupid desk. She gets her job done."

"That's what I think, too. I was going to offer a few approaches and suggest that in the end, maybe a screen might be the best solution."

"But you singled her out. No wonder she's not here."

"I didn't single her out. I have advice for everyone in the office. And anyway, Barb took off before I even got here. We both know that's true."

He nodded and frowned absently.

"I know it's true because she almost ran me off the road."

He jumped to his feet. "I don't believe that. She wouldn't do that. She's a really nice, kind person and . . ."

"She did. Trust me. She may not have meant to, but she did. Right outside Quovadicon."

He slumped back in the chair and unbuttoned his collar. His color still hadn't returned to normal and was now somewhere between putty and cold oatmeal. I watched him squirm and resisted the urge to tap my foot. I also fought off the equally strong urge to straighten the files on his desk and empty the trash.

He said, "There must be some kind of explanation, but I don't know what it is yet."

"Did something happen to upset her? Do you think someone talked about my visit?"

"No, Dyan and Autumn were just outside whispering and giggling as usual. Barb and I knew you were coming in, and we knew that you'd be looking at her desk and then something would happen. Dyan used to plant things there. Like old food and things like that. The sardine can, this time." He picked it up and tossed it in the wastebasket. "Barb didn't even eat at her desk. Anyway, she was prepared for a bit of ritual humiliation. We planned to have a laugh about it afterward."

"She tore out of here. Something must have triggered that. Something they said?"

"She got a phone call."

"You mean, just before she left?"

He bit his lip so hard it must have hurt. I waited until he unleashed a torrent of words. "I should have stopped her. I should have asked her what was going on. I should have told her I'd take care of it. Anything, anything at all, but instead I just sat here like a dumb, useless, stupid—"

I actually felt sorry for him. "It's not your fault."

"Of course it is."

"I doubt that very much."

"Yeah, well, you don't know much about me. I've never been able to get anything right."

"I'm sure that's not true."

When I arrived, I'd been convinced he was involved in Barb's disappearance, and now I was practically patting his hand and saying, *There, there, don't cry.*

"Let's pull ourselves together and try to find her," I said. "What was the phone call about?"

He looked down at his feet as if the answer might be written there. "She didn't say."

"Did she say anything?"

He shook his head. Sad puppy.

"Was there anything in the conversation that might give us a clue about what upset her?"

"Do you think I haven't asked myself that a thousand times?"

"Maybe some small thing that could help. A word. A phrase?"

"She gave a little cry, and then she jumped up and raced out the door. I ran after her trying to find out what was wrong, but she just pushed me away like she didn't even know it was me. Didn't see me. Then she kept going."

That fit in with the woman who drove as if she didn't see me or my car.

"And you have not a single clue who or what?"

"None. It was like she was too upset to talk. I didn't take it personally when she pushed me away. I knew she had to get out of here. You could tell she was hurting." He looked up miserably.

"So the prospect of me didn't send her over the deep end. It was the call."

"Yes."

"We need to find out who called her."

"I love her," he said. "Go ahead, and laugh."

"I'm not laughing. You may have some horrible co-workers here, but not everybody in the world is a total jerk."

Robbie had obviously met more than his share of total jerks. He looked suspicious.

I added, "Why shouldn't you love her?"

"She accepted me for what I am. Now she's gone. I don't know what to do."

"Well, first of all, she hasn't been gone long. So let's work together to find out what happened. Perhaps she got a message about a family member. Maybe it has nothing to do with you or me."

"I'm sorry; I kind of lashed out at you. I feel helpless."

"Well, let's start by checking her phone to see who called."

"Won't help. The call came on her cell phone."

"And, of course, that went with her?"

"She had it in her hand when she left."

And I hadn't seen it at her apartment, although I chose not to mention that.

I said, "Wherever she's gone."

"Yes."

"Okay. Let's think. She must have said something when she answered the phone. *Hello? Hi?* Can you recall the moments before?"

"She was in a good mood. We were talking about new movies that were coming to town. Stuff we might like to see. We'd been to a couple together. Just like friends, you know. And there's a new Coen brothers picture in town. She's a big, big fan."

"Go on."

"She said we should go to see it and then she'd make dinner for me at her place. Just simple, she said, but we'd have fun. That was great. I was looking forward to seeing where she lived."

"You'd never been inside her place?"

He shook his head.

"You just drove her home and said good-bye?"

He stared at me. "I didn't drive her home. She had her own car. We used to meet at the movies."

"Oh. Did you pick her up?"

Sad puppy eyes again. "I don't even know where she lives. I could have found out easily I guess if I wanted, but it seemed wrong, like a stalker. Creepy. Anyway, now I had an invitation."

I felt a lump in my throat. "Were you nervous?"

"I was pretty revved about the dinner offer, but yeah, I was nervous. She was relaxed. She probably didn't know how much . . . I can't believe I'm telling you these things. I feel like such a loser."

"You're not a loser, Robbie, and you're the best chance we have of finding out what happened to Barb. So after the dinner offer . . ."

"We were laughing about popcorn or caviar. Menu choices. Beans or boeuf bourguignon. And her cell phone rang."

"Well, did she say anything at all?"

He closed his eyes, thinking back. "No. She just stood there listening and then that little cry of distress."

"She didn't mention anyone's name?"

He shook his head.

"But she recognized the voice?"

He blinked behind the thick glasses. "Yes. She must have."

"Have you tried calling her cell phone?"

He actually hung his head.

"What's wrong?" I asked.

"I don't have her number."

Now that was unusual, no question about it. I kept my mouth shut. From the look on Robbie's face, he knew it was weird, too.

"Well," I said, at last. "You did work side by side, so you probably never needed to call her."

He managed a weak smile. "I suggested it a couple of times. I gave her my number. She just forgot, I thought. When I'd remind her, she'd say, 'Oh right, gotta do that.' "

For some reason, I felt the need to comfort him. "Well, you could just wave at each other. Probably didn't seem pressing to her at the time."

"I think she didn't want people calling her. She was very private. But I thought we had something special."

"Right."

Someone had called her, though. Figuring out who that had been through Robbie wasn't going to be easy. I tried anyway. "Did she have any other friends or colleagues in Woodbridge?"

"Not that I knew of."

"Family? Maybe someone—"

He paused, thought a moment. "No. She never mentioned anyone. She never got calls. You know what? In four months, that was the first time I ever heard her cell phone ring."

"Really? The first time?"

He shot me a reproachful look. "Mine never rings, either."

"Hmm. We don't have much to go on."

"No."

"What did you do after she left?"

"I didn't know what to do. I just paced around here and then you arrived, and I figured that you were the cause of the problem."

"If you didn't have her cell phone number, then I can't imagine any of the Quovadicon staff would. It seems unlikely that someone outside this office would call her and say that I was coming in to check out her desk." I looked him straight in the eye. "Admit it, Robbie. That's not what happened."

"I realize that now. I guess I was trying to find a reason for it. I wanted someone to blame."

"How would you describe her reaction? That cry. What emotion do you think caused it?"

He stared back at me without speaking. He no longer saw me as the enemy, but I thought I saw panic lurking behind the thick glasses.

He said at last, "I don't know how to explain it. I would have to say it was a cry of anguish."

Keep the office items and supplies that you use every day within easy reach of your desk.

9

I had squeezed no more useful information out of Robbie by the time I left, even though I felt he was holding back something. Of course, I was hardly in the position to browbeat him any more than I already had.

On the way out, I ran into Fredelle, still looking peaked. I followed her into her office, glancing back at Dyan, who was keeping a heavily made-up eye on the two of us.

"Hi, Fredelle." I had the contract in my briefcase, but clearly this wasn't the time to talk about it. "I just had a long talk with Robbie."

"He didn't do anything to her. He wouldn't. Not Robbie. He just wouldn't." She twisted her hands as she spoke. I figured she was on the verge of tears. It struck me—and not for the first time—that for a practical business like shipping and logistics, everyone in Quovadicon seemed overwrought all the time.

"I didn't suggest that Robbie did anything to harm Barb, Fredelle," I said. "Why would you even mention that?"

She pulled a tissue from her periwinkle pocket and honked. I waited.

Eventually she said, "Some people are talking."

" 'Some people.' You mean Dyan?" I turned back and closed the door. "Don't give her the satisfaction of getting under your skin. The situation will only get worse if you do."

"It's just that I'm so worried about Barb and now about Robbie and you've been dragged into it."

"For sure, this is an upsetting day, but . . ."

"And then she called me a stereotypical interfering mother hen. Said I'm the cause of everything wrong in this office."

"What?"

"She—"

I held up my hand. "Sorry, I actually heard you, but I couldn't quite believe it. That's ridiculous. How could *she* call anyone a stereotype?"

"What do you mean?"

"She does dress almost like a cartoon character."

I found it hard to imagine that Fredelle wouldn't have noticed this. Of course, she might almost have been a cartoon character herself. If only she'd worn a long skirt and a blouse with a cameo and kept a canary.

Fredelle's jaw dropped. "Overly glamorous, you mean. Do you really see her as a cartoon character?"

"Never mind, Fredelle. I shouldn't have said that. But you are certainly not a stereotype. You are warm and caring and kind and obviously committed to your job."

She went back to twisting her hands. "We're all types, I suppose. Robbie's the sad little boy who could never get out from under his father's thumb to have a relationship with a woman. Dyan George, well. And even little Autumn Halliday: pretty face, empty head—oh, I shouldn't say that. You know what? Barb Douglas is the only one who's unusual."

"In what way?"

"She's tough but warm, effective but messy. Friendly, but private. She's a whole lot of contradictions." She grimaced. "Maybe that's why I like her. She's the only one of us who seems real."

"I suppose I'm a bit of a stereotype myself." I grinned.

"I suppose you are," she said.

That wasn't the answer I was expecting.

Fredelle said, "I know what you mean: a bit bossy, a bit uptight, kind of vain about your appearance. Maybe shallow."

Ouch.

"Back to Robbie. Is there something to worry about?" If she'd been pale before, she was bleached white by my comment.

"I said there wasn't."

Now I was worried. I'd had the feeling there was something wrong in Robbie's behavior and Fredelle was confirming it.

I looked her straight in the eye. "I know what you said, but you're acting as though there is, so please tell me what it is."

She straightened up. "I think that this arrangement is not working out. I'm going to terminate it. Right now."

"What?"

"I'll pay you for your time, and extra, of course."

"Fredelle. What's going on here? I rearranged my schedule to make room for your project."

This had been no big deal, a small switch here and there, but never mind.

She raised her small round chins. "And as I have not signed a contract, that's even easier. I want you to leave the premises."

"No problem. I don't know what you're trying to hide, but I'm going to head straight for the police and tell them that you threw me out of the building because you didn't want me to ask questions about Robbie Van Zandt and the missing employee that you claim to care so much about."

I whirled and whipped open the office door.

"Wait!"

"Too late," I said. "I don't know what you're trying to hide, and I don't like being treated like this."

Autumn was standing by the filing cabinet, wide eyes even wider. "Awesome," she said.

Dyan smirked from the photocopier. Had I been shouting? I sure hoped I hadn't been. I held my head up and nodded to them. "Thank you, ladies, you've been very helpful."

Of course, that didn't make any sense, but I couldn't let Dyan think she'd gotten to me, even if it was clear that Fredelle had.

"Charlotte!"

Fredelle stood in the doorway, gripping the frame. I turned back toward her. She looked like she'd had a shock, lost a loved one or a pet. "Please, come back in. I don't know what got into me."

I glanced at Dyan, who mouthed, *Losing it*. Autumn mouthed *Awesome* again and then *Wow* for emphasis. She didn't have the range that Dyan did, but I guessed she was working on it.

"I think we're done here."

"I'm sorry. Very sorry. But I have no choice. You must stop nosing around Barb and Robbie's private life."

"Nosing around? First you insisted that I come here to do something about the desk, which is the least of your problems. Then you begged me to go to Barb's place. I think there might be something funny about Robbie's behavior and you call that nosing around? Fine. You want me to leave? Now I'm out of here."

Fredelle caught up to me in the parking lot. I could hear her huffing. Now she was pink with exertion, I suppose, or anxiety.

"I'm so ashamed. Please forgive me." She leaned against the shiny red Ford Focus coupe. She was breathing heavily and her face was flushed, no doubt with embarrassment.

"I don't know what you want from me, Fredelle. Our deal, which was really a verbal contract, is over. I don't work for people who yell at me. I have more business than I can handle. And if you're firing me to protect Robbie, you can forget that idea. I have to tell my contact at the police that you were worried about Robbie. I have no choice. If something has happened to Barb Douglas, and I know damn well something has, this is no time to keep secrets."

"He didn't do anything. I didn't mean that. He's so vulnerable, that boy. He's always had such a hard time making friends, meeting women. I was just afraid . . ."

"What? That things didn't go well and he lost it? Or worse?"

"No!"

"And you want me to keep quiet about that so his feelings don't get injured?"

She narrowed her eyes and crossed her arms. The sweet and gentle Fredelle was displaced by a much tougher version. "Maybe he'll hurt himself. I'm trying to tell you, he's sweet and fragile and I think he's in love for the first time in his life. I intend to protect him and so now I'm making it clear that you're not welcome here anymore. You are not involved in anything to do with Quovadicon or Barb Douglas or Robbie Van Zandt. I think the police will believe me and Reg Van Zandt before they believe you. After all, neither of *us* has ever been hauled into the police station for questioning. And I think they'll agree that you have no business making trouble."

I resisted the urge to stamp my feet. I felt furious at Fredelle for creating the situation, angry at Robbie for holding back on whatever, but most of all, royally ticked off at myself for getting overly involved in yet another bizarre and emotionally laden situation and failing to mind my own business.

As I drove away, Fredelle was still leaning against the Ford Focus, her arms crossed over her chest. She was partly blocking the vanity plates, but I did catch a glimpse of *FRED* as I left. I picked up speed. Quovadicon was a toxic volcano. Everyone in it seemed ready to blow at any minute.

There are times when nothing does the trick like the public library. I got the last parking spot and strode through the doors, hoping to catch Ramona. She waved to me across the reference desk, where she was helping out a gangly teenager. I waited and paced until she finished her job. Ramona is not one to hurry. She gives new meaning to the word *thorough*.

"Sorry to keep you waiting, Charlotte," she said.

"No problem. I can see that you're up to your—"

"I have bad news."

"What?"

"Those file materials on Quovadicon never showed up. I've searched everywhere, and I've had the rest of the staff on alert. They're gone. Pilfered. Pinched. Purloined. Ripped off," she added. "Because not everything in life is alliterative."

"Who would pilfer something like that?"

She shrugged her indigo shoulders. Her silver earrings danced. "Who knows? Files go walkabout from time to time. Kids doing projects, practical jokers, distracted staff. I'll let you know if they do turn up, and I'll see if I can pull together some new info in the meantime."

"Thanks. And I have something else I want to know."

"Go for it, Charlotte. We aim to please. Even when we are up to our patooties in whatever."

"Reg Van Zandt's son Robbie. Do you have any information about him?"

"Like what? Business information? That would probably be in the missing files, but I'll check anyway."

"I was thinking more along the lines of personal information. I'm asking you as a friend. Controversies, that kind of thing. Any problems with women?"

Oops. I should have known better than to ask Ramona for gossip when she was in her full professional mode.

She snorted. "You must be kidding. I can't imagine what kind of controversy Robbie would get into."

"What?"

"It's Robbie, for heaven's sake. Maybe jaywalking. Feeding the pigeons against city regulations. On a really bad day, wearing mismatched socks."

Aha. Mismatched socks. "You know him?"

"Well, sure."

"But you didn't mention anything about him when I asked about Quovadicon and Reg Van Zandt."

"I said I knew the family. Robbie's Robbie. He's nothing like his father. And to tell the truth, I didn't even think about him when you mentioned Quovadicon. I suppose he must work there, but he sure wouldn't be running the place."

"But how do you know him?"

"Charlotte, this is Woodbridge, population less than twenty-five thousand. Not New York City."

I bit my tongue so as not to say that Robbie must have been nearly ten years younger than Ramona. She must have read the expression on my face. "I remember him as a kid. He used to come to the pool when I was lifeguarding. Worked my way through school doing that."

"And you remember him after all these years?"

"Absolutely. He was one of my favorite kids."

"Really?"

"Sure. He was so nervous. Scared of everything. Shy. Awkward. It was painful to watch. And he was terrified of the water. His father insisted he learn how to swim. No choice in the matter. Poor little guy."

"And what happened?"

"It took until the end of August to get him used to the water and then another summer until he really caught on, but in the end, he was one of my successes. Got his medals and even swam a bit in college, I think. I learned a lot from working with him."

"Like what?"

"Like how not to raise your kid. I still can't stand the sight of that father. Everyone thinks he's such a hero, but with Robbie, I thought it was all about control."

"Where was the mother?"

"Died young. One of the father's staff used to bring him, take him home. Busybody mother hen type. Sad, really. Oops, got a line forming back at the desk. I'll let you know when I get anything worthwhile on Quovadicon, but I'm not going to dig around for Robbie. Not personally and not professionally. It's not my business to do that, and it's not yours, either."

After a quick trip to Hannaford's for replacement vegetables and ice cream, I headed to Old Pine Street, where I caught Pepper getting out of the car. No sign of Nick the Stick's big honking truck, I noted quite happily.

Pepper waved. That was good.

"Hey," she said. "Want to see my latest ultrasound printout?"

My mouth opened, but no sound came out. Pepper interpreted that as an enthusiastic yes. "Come on in," she called over her shoulder as she lumbered up the walkway to the front door.

I followed.

Pepper pointed to the sofa and I plunked myself down. She sat beside me, rested her hand on the bump, and said, "I'll get you a coffee or something in a second, but I want to show you this first."

I stared at a black-and-white wavy image on grayish paper. Words failed me, which doesn't happen that often. "That is *so* interesting," I finally managed. "And so you can tell—"

"Yup. It's a boy," she said. "But we already knew that from the previous one. His name's going to be Garrett."

"Nice."

"He's really developing."

She stood up and reached for another sheet of paper, much like the first, and passed that to me, too. Again, I groped for the right thing to say. *He's pretty wavy* didn't seem right. *How bloblike* also struck out. I could have said either to Sally at any time during her four pregnancies. She would have just laughed. But I knew there'd be no joking with Pepper about this baby.

"Gonna be a big boy," I said, hoping that would do the trick.

"I think so. Like his daddy."

Crap. I reminded myself not to blunder onto the daddy topic. That was a minefield for Pepper and me.

"And your brothers," I said. "Big guys."

"It's in the genes, I guess. I just love looking at him. But never mind, you want a coffee? Or a glass of wine or something? I can't have one, but it's no trouble."

I shook my head. "Just one thing, and please don't get mad at me. I'm really worried about this. I know you said you didn't know anything about Barb Douglas, but I've also been your friend for a thousand years, give or take a few. I'm familiar with your reactions."

Pepper scowled. "I don't know anything about her."

I said, "Save it. I can tell when you're lying. We used to practice telling whoppers together to get out of school. Remember?"

She glared at me, our lovely if weird little ultrasound moment ruined. "Leave it, Charlotte."

"I'd be happy to leave it, but there are a couple of bits of information to share. Remember I told you I saw a brief clip of Barb Douglas at the crime scene? You know, the one with the guy in the trunk, in case you get coy. I now know that she got a call on her cell just before she tore out of Quovadicon. Robbie Van Zandt described her reaction as anguished. He doesn't know who she was talking to and claims he doesn't have her number. But most likely, she was in a panic over some personal disaster when she ran me off the road. Nothing to do with me at all, which would make sense."

"Oh, I don't know," Pepper said. "Sometimes I feel like running you off the road. Like now, for instance."

"Very funny."

"The truth hurts."

"Hey, I'm almost finished. So, the other thing is that she was seeing Robbie Van Zandt. By the way, do you know him?"

"I am aware of who he is. Everybody knows the Van Zandts. They're big Kahunas around here."

"The father may be, but Robbie is very socially awkward and he is way over the top over Barb Douglas—the missing woman, in case you've forgotten her name. I think Fredelle Newhouse, the office manager at Quovadicon, is afraid he may have flipped out and done her some harm. Maybe Barb had another boyfriend and he found out and he . . . couldn't deal with it. I don't know if I'm right about this, and I realize I'm not in a position to find out, but the police should be aware. Did I mention her apartment was left unlocked and her car's in the driveway, but her cat's gone?"

"Her cat's gone? That is a disaster! More a matter for the National Guard than the Woodbridge police, though."

"Who do you think I should talk to? Or will you let the right person know?"

"Charlotte?"

"Yes?"

"Drop it."

Sometimes the best antidote for a tough day at the office is a long soak in the tub. Keep a supply of soothing bath products handy, grab a big fluffy towel, select some relaxing music, and let the toxic experiences just float away.
Do not attempt this at work.

10

I was annoyed that Pepper showed me the door without giving me any information about Barb, but at least Truffle and Sweet Marie were glad to see me. As we hoofed it down the stairs for their constitutional, Jack popped out of his apartment and waved both hands in greeting. He hopped on his bike and skidded out onto the street.

"Jack! I need to talk to you."

He called over his shoulder, "Can't talk, Charlotte, late for an organizational meeting. Catch you later."

Not so fast, mister.

"At least you could introduce me to your friend," I called back, pointing to the woman hurtling down our street at warp speed.

"Oh," Jack said, stopping. "Sure."

As the cyclist whipped up beside us and stopped by some miracle, she flashed Jack a grin that could rival Todd Tyrell's for whiteness, brightness, and bigness. That cycling outfit had been designed with her long, graceful frame in mind. Comfortable yet clingy. How lucky is that?

"Hello," I said, politely.

Jack shot me a look.

"Charlotte, I'd like you to meet Blair. Blair's the chair of our organizing committee for the fund-raising race."

Blair took off her helmet and shook out an amazing mane of blond hair. Even damp from her helmet, it managed to look very sexy. Without a break in the grin, she shook my hand. Bone-crushing grip, I noted.

"Hi, Charlotte. I've heard all about you," she said.

"Nice to meet you, Blair," I said. I did not say that I'd heard nothing whatsoever about her, even if that was true. "I hope the planning for the race is going well."

She gave Jack a nudge. "How could it not be? Jack here is just an amazing inspiration."

"Is he?" I said. Jack shot me another look. Oh well, maybe he shouldn't have called me bossy.

"Later, Charlotte," he said as they took off down the road.

"Nice seeing you, too," I remarked as his Hawaiian shirt and her clingy sports gear vanished around the corner. Inspiration, my backside. Jack was one dropped sock short of complete chaos. Who was she kidding? Well, with all these so-called organizational meetings, I sure hoped he got everything right. Or she did. Or WAG'D might end up with its tail between its legs.

Never mind. I still had an evening to fill.

Switch to Plan B. As the doggies sniffed every tree and bush along our street, I tried Margaret on my cell phone. "Feel like a spontaneous dinner out? I can tell you about Pepper's ultrasound," I said. "And maybe—"

"Ultrasound? Ew. I mean, love to. Really. But, um, I have to work tonight. Urgent matter. Gotta go. See you soon."

Right. I know when Margaret's lying, too. She's not as good at it as Pepper. Less practice back in the formative years, maybe. What was going on there? I had my suspicions. I tried Sally next, a bit reluctantly, because it was getting close to dinnertime, and that's a pretty intense time of day at the Januscek residence.

"Rescue me," she said.

"I'd love to. How about dinner out?"

"Can't. I'm stuck here, with three howling kids. And the last holdout looks like she's on the verge of joining the choir."

"Is Benjamin there?"

"Long, tedious board meeting. The lucky devil."

"Well, you've been in the house for too long. What about getting a sitter? What was that horrible noise?"

"That was me snorting in derision, Charlotte. There's no way I can get a sitter for four small children on short notice at mealtime. How happily unmarried of you to even suggest such a thing."

"No need to get personal," I said. "I can come over and help you with dinner. Then maybe we could play with them for a bit and then put them to bed and—"

"Charlotte?"

"Yes."

"Remember how that doesn't always work?"

"Are you referring to the spaghetti-on-the-ceiling incident? Because, if so, it's time to put that behind us."

"It's all coming back now. And no, it wasn't just that."

"The incident with the glue in the hair?"

"Mmm."

"Not my fault. How was I to know they'd use craft scissors on each other?"

"Mmm."

"It grew back, didn't it? Anyway, I'm just trying to help."

"Tell you what. I'll get a sitter lined up for one night later in the week and we'll go into the wide world as adults. But tonight, as soon as the last little head hits the crib, I am going to bed myself. With a box of chocolates and a mystery."

Motherhood. I like kids, and I love Sally's in particular, but I'm not very effective with them. I certainly don't long for my own, and I consider a night at a trendy restaurant more rejuvenating than scrubbing finger paint off the walls. What can I say? Sally loves being a mom most times, and Pepper had been miserable until she knew she was pregnant. Maybe I was missing that gene. Margaret was, too.

My revised Plan B was to settle the pooches in, feed them, and actually for once make myself a stir-fry. I eyed the New York Super Fudge Chunk, but decided to save it for some time when Jack was available. I ate my stir-fry. It was all right, I suppose. I polished it off in front of the television. I didn't care how many nutritionists I offended. Of course, I regretted it when Todd Tyrell loomed onto the screen again. Detective Connor Tierney scowled into the camera. Perhaps he'd already heard Todd's words. Whatever the reason, even scowling, he looked a lot better than Todd.

Woodbridge police continue to be tight-lipped about the man found shot to death in the trunk of a blue Impala on the outskirts of town. So far there seem to be no leads in this bizarre case. Stay tuned to WINY for hourly updates.

Flash back to Todd's magic teeth, flash back to blue car in wooded area. The crime scene tape was still fluttering gaily. I saw no sign of Barb Douglas's anguished pacing in the background or of Nick trampling evidence. What kind of an update was that? A special information-free spot? Useless as always.

I clicked off the television and headed back to the kitchen, still caught up in the situation that everyone said was not my business. Why did I feel involved? Definitely not because of the unpredictable Fredelle or the socially inept Robbie. I washed up the one pan, one plate, knife, fork, and glass and put them away.

The expression on Barb's face, that was what had hooked me. I'd seen how she looked as she raced away. I wanted to know what had happened to her. I wanted to know she was safe. I wanted to know her connection to the man in the Impala. Did it mean that she was truly in danger? Because there didn't seem to be anything I could do about that.

When the kitchen was done, I kept busy preparing invoices for the previous month's projects and put the copies in my tickler file for thirty days later to track them for payment. I took care of a couple of items from my master list, and I checked over the files of the projects I had going to see if I was on target.

I did not let my mind drift to Barb Douglas. I did not dwell on Quovadicon. I did not give a moment's thought to Robbie and whether he'd been lying about not knowing where Barb lived. I definitely did not think about Jack.

When I finished my tasks, I decided to reward myself with a nice bath. That wasn't so bad. I made myself a cup of pomegranate tea, ran the bath, and dropped in a mango-scented fizzy bath ball. One of the nice things about having an apartment in a converted Victorian house is that you can end up with a big bathroom, and I mean *big*. Mine was probably a nursery originally. So my kitchen may be the size of a phone booth, but the bathroom more than makes up for that. I placed my giant fluffy bath towel and my terrycloth dressing gown on the chair near the claw-foot tub and lowered myself into the warm welcoming water. I lay back and closed my eyes to let the tension of the day slip away. I wanted all the talk of bodies in trunks and missing IT people and suspicious boyfriends to float away. As Fredelle and Pepper and even Ramona insisted, it was none of my business.

I inhaled the scent of mango, sipped the pomegranate tea, and sighed happily. The dogs watched me from the bath mat, intrigued but cautious and close enough to the open door to bolt if they decided I was trying to trick them into a bath.

The tense muscles in my shoulders and neck began to relax. My eyes closed. My breathing slowed. Bliss. And I'd even had a decent dinner, making my quick trip to Hanaford's pay off, too.

My eyes popped open. Hannaford's. Of course. That's where I'd seen Missy, the perfect admin assistant who was on maternity leave. She'd been noticeable wheeling a basket through the produce section, smiling happily while two infants slept in a double carrier. I sat up, splashing scented water over the floor. Truffle and Sweet Marie leaped from the room and vanished.

When had I seen her? She was supposed to be terrifically organized, so most likely she had a shopping schedule. Once a week. My regular time was around four in the afternoon. A low-productivity time of day for my work and yet good for getting groceries ahead of the after-work rush. But it hadn't been then. It had been a quick dash through to pick up diapers for Sally, who'd been marooned because Savannah had an ear infection. Last Tuesday? No, Wednesday. Hmm. That would be tomorrow.

I don't work for free. I let people know that up front, and they sign a contract. If they choose not to proceed, they pay me for my initial time. This business has a lot of emotion in it, and people often change their minds. That's code for chickening out. Easy to do, but I have to make a living.

I had an invoice for Fredelle, and first thing Wednesday morning, I headed out to Quovadicon with it. Oh sure, I could have put it in the mail. The odd thing about an invoice, particularly delivered face to face, is that the client often has a change of heart—in part to avoid paying for something they won't receive, and in part because a little time lets the fear and anger dissipate. I have to admit that sometimes it's an effort to face the person, but it's important to be resolute. In spite of the lure of the messy desk, I wasn't keen to continue my Quovadicon contract, but I had a small piece of information I wanted and I had been booted off the property. This seemed like the best way.

Autumn was on duty when I opened the door, the invoice already out of my briefcase and in my hand.

"Hey, Caroline," she said, without any great interest.

Hey? Never mind business etiquette, had she totally forgotten that I'd been unceremoniously ushered off the premises just the day before?

"Can I help you?" Naturally, there was no great enthusiasm to match the interest level.

"I'd like to see Fredelle, please."

Autumn looked puzzled. "Fredelle?"

I kept my sharp little tongue in check. *Never alienate the receptionist* is a first rule of business. "Yes. Fredelle, your office manager. I have something for her."

"Oh." She nodded sagely, as though that explained everything.

I smiled, patiently.

"Is she expecting you?"

"I'm pretty sure she isn't."

"Oh that explains it."

"Explains what?" Having a conversation with Autumn was like fighting your way through an invisible verbal jungle; you felt caught in the tangle of irrelevant responses and general vagueness.

"Fredelle is tied up right now. I don't think she's available for the next few minutes, so while you're waiting, I was wondering," she said, "if you would mind filling out a little survey for me."

I stared at her.

She said, "You are Caroline, aren't you?"

"Close enough," I said.

She gazed at me anxiously. "So can you do it? You can't believe how hard it is to get people to fill these out. I am trying to do well at this job so my dad doesn't force me to go back to some college. I hate school, and I really like it here. Sometimes it's interesting, especially lately."

No kidding, I thought.

She handed me the printed questionnaire before I could think of a good excuse.

"All right," I said, hoping it wasn't a client satisfaction survey or one that sought to determine Autumn Halliday's suitability for employment. I put the questionnaire on the small counter by the side of the reception desk. Still clutching the invoice, I fished out my pen. I placed my handbag and briefcase on the floor as there wasn't enough room for them plus the questionnaire and the invoice on the counter. It was hard to feel satisfied with Autumn's services, but I didn't mean her any harm. I could always say *not applicable*, as I was a supplier and not a client.

She said, "It has to do with impressions."

I said, "Huh."

Autumn smiled in her hazy way and went back to playing with her hair.

I stared at the questionnaire, hoping I could deal with it.

Autumn jerked her attractive yet seemingly empty head and glanced behind her, leaning to see around the corner.

"Oh, there goes Fredelle now. She's heading to the staff room. If you hurry you can catch her." She smiled the way you smile when you've done someone an immense favor.

I grabbed the envelope with the invoice and dashed down the hallway after Fredelle.

"Hello," I said when I caught up to her.

She lifted her chin.

"I don't have an appointment with you, but I needed to drop off this invoice for my consultation and time worked. I wanted to make sure you got it personally."

I handed her the envelope.

She took it without a word.

I held out my hand to shake hers. "Too bad it didn't work out with us. I hope things . . . improve."

She didn't shake my hand. "I'll send the check tomorrow. But you'd better leave now. And I don't want you dropping in here anytime it suits you."

"Trust me. I have no intention of coming back."

Dyan must have followed me down the hall, hoping for some drama. I ignored her curious stare as I passed her, my head high, naturally. For some reason the office seemed full this day. I assumed the extra people were sales staff, and one or two might have been clients or even suppliers. No way to know. I thought I saw Robbie scurry by, but that may have been my imagination. I snatched up my hastily abandoned handbag and briefcase as I passed Autumn's desk.

"Will you finish the survey?" she breathed.

"I'll mail it in," I fibbed, picking that up, too. "Oh, by the way, I thought I saw Robbie, but I didn't notice his car outside. Is he in today?"

"Robbie?"

"Yes," I said patiently, "Robbie Van Zandt. The owner's son?"

"Oh right. Yeah, yeah, weird Robbie. Everyone knows him. I didn't notice him come in."

"I was almost certain I saw him in the parking lot. What kind of car does he drive?"

She shrugged. "I have, like, no idea, Caroline."

I gave her a tight little smile. "You know, if you reoriented this reception desk, you could actually see people come by. They'd see you, too. That would probably be a good thing."

"Awesome, Caroline."

"Yes, and you could probably get them to fill out that questionnaire, too. There are quite a few people here today."

"Thank you!" Her lovely face lit up. "That's a great idea."

On that note, I headed for sanity.

Next stop Hannaford's, and not a second too soon. I slowed my pace as I headed through the automatic doors. Ten o'clock seemed like a good starting point. I'd taken a little extra time styling my hair and doing a restrained but effective job on the makeup. I wore a crisp cropped jacket and a Pucci-inspired patterned skirt in yellow and charcoal. My pewter heels finished off the look. I'd chosen a contrasting handbag. No point in looking like the neighborhood lunatic if you were planning to ask a total stranger some very peculiar questions in front of the baby powder section. I grabbed a grocery cart and began to prowl through the store, seeking my prey. The baby products aisle seemed like a good place to start, but it was empty.

I returned to fruit and vegetables to pick up a few boring but necessary nutrients. Maybe someday I'll get excited about food that doesn't have chocolate as a first ingredient, but I wasn't there yet. So lettuce, red peppers, broccoli, and some ripe and fragrant pears. Couldn't hurt. I glanced around as I selected each one, but no petite blond smiling mommy caught my eye.

I hurtled around the perimeter of the store, glancing down each aisle as I passed by. No sign of her. By this point, I had no choice but to wander down the candy aisle, where a package of Mars bars jumped into my basket.

Back again, this time on the lower end of the aisles.

No luck.

I returned to the produce section to start all over again. This time I picked up and examined every orange in the store. I kept an eye out, but no Missy appeared. I selected two oranges that had looked pretty much like all the others and decided to keep hunting for Missy.

By the fourth trip around the store, I'd collected a box of ice cream sandwiches, some microwave popcorn, and three containers of B & J's. Jack, if he ever showed up again, could make short work of those. I'd make sure he knew I had them.

Forty-five minutes later, I still hadn't spotted Missy and I had admitted defeat, but had stocked enough ice cream and candy to take me through Halloween. I was headed toward the cash registers when I caught a flash of blond hair. I made a U-turn, abandoned my cart, and whipped down the baby aisle.

Missy was stopped in front of the disposable diapers. "Thank heavens," I said. "You look like you know what you're doing." I pointed toward two sleeping infants.

Missy smiled. "That might not last long, but so far so good."

"They're such beautiful babies," I said, although to tell the truth I can't tell one baby from another one, something I never ever mention to my friends. "What are their names?"

"Riley and Ryan."

"Beautiful names. They seem like such good babies, too. Look, I don't want to hold you up, but could you help me out, please?"

"Sure, if I can."

"Thanks," I said, radiating gratitude. "I promised to get some baby powder for my friend. She's stuck in the house with a couple of sick children, and I said I'd swing by and pick it up. Her baby is six months old. Shenandoah. Another beautiful child. But I don't remember what brand my friend told me to get. What do you use?"

"I've always been happy with this." She picked a familiar container from the shelf and handed it to me.

"That's it. That's the one she prefers. I wasn't sure and I didn't want to add to her troubles, or make a return trip." I was about to drop the baby powder into the cart with my purchases when I realized I'd left the cart behind in my dash to catch Missy. Sally would be bemused to learn she'd been part of my info-gathering conspiracy, and she'd think the cart thing was hilarious.

"I don't blame you. Once a week in the grocery store is enough," she said, confirming my opinion of the type of organized person she was. "Your friend's a lucky girl, though."

I did a little fake double take. "I hope you don't mind me saying so, but you seem quite familiar."

She looked at me, seeking signs of familiarity, I suppose. I tried not to feel guilty over the subterfuge. I reminded myself that Barb Douglas was missing under strange circumstances, that the police had no intention of getting involved, and that someone at Quovadicon could well be at the heart of her disappearance.

I said, "Oh, I know what it is. I have a contract at a business on the edge of town. Quovadicon? I saw you in a photo yesterday. Unless it was someone who looked a lot like you."

She laughed and pointed to the twins. "It would have been me. I was as big as a house with these two bruisers."

"I didn't like to say that. It was your smile that I recognized."

"Wow. Say hi to everyone for me. I have to get in again

to show them how the twins are growing, but the days are so busy. You can't imagine."

"I'll pass on your greetings."

"Thanks!"

"Fredelle says they miss you a lot."

"She would say that. She's such an office mom. I miss her, too. It must be hard on her. A lot of new people."

"Right. Dyan, who replaced you . . ."

"Hmmm. Actually, we overlapped."

I figured Missy was too kind and probably too smart to trash-talk Dyan to a stranger.

I said, "And I guess the receptionist hadn't been there long, either. Did you have to train her, too?"

"Autumn. She's young. I guess she's still managed to avoid going back to school."

I didn't want to change the subject. "So Robbie's been there for a long time."

She smiled. "Oh, Robbie, so shy. Tell him I said hi."

Here was my chance to find out about Robbie's car. "Sure. In fact, I have to talk to him later today. I'm embarrassed to say that I think I drove right by him this morning and didn't acknowledge him." I paused to consider the most unlikely vehicle for Robbie to drive. "He was in an SUV, a big red one. A Jeep, I think."

She frowned. "I can't imagine Robbie driving an SUV. Or anything red. He's too self-effacing."

"Really, I was sure it was him. So what does he drive?"

"An old silver Camry. He's had it nearly ten years. He's not a person to spend money on luxuries. He's probably got plenty tucked away for emergencies. He's always expecting one."

"And what about what's-her-name, right, um, Barb, who works next to him? I have to talk to her tomorrow. Or did she join Quovadicon after you left?"

One of the twins opened a tiny rosebud mouth and emitted a squawk.

Missy leaned forward and rubbed the little tummy. "Shh, shhh, shhh. No, she was there before I left."

The other twin's eyes opened, followed by his identical rosebud mouth. I knew that Missy wouldn't stand around chatting with a stranger if both babies started crying. I spoke quickly, because I wanted to hear if Missy had anything to say about Barb Douglas. "Really, I didn't know that. Did you have to train her, too?"

"Shhh, shhh, Ryan. No, no, she was technical. I wouldn't have known where to start. She knew her stuff, though."

"Did she? I haven't talked to her yet, but I'd heard she was really smart. Must have been why Fredelle recruited her."

"Oh, Fredelle didn't recruit her."

"She didn't? I thought she did all the hiring."

"There's not that much hiring, outside the warehouse, and Fredelle doesn't do that. We've always been a stable group until this year, when everything changed for a number of reasons." She cooed at the fidgeting babies. A serious bleat came from the baby on the left, echoed by a matching one from his twin on the right. Missy said absently, "I'd better get moving. I want to finish before they hit high C."

Not just yet, I thought. "Didn't people like Barb?"

Missy had already started to move down the aisle. "Most people did, but that's the thing. It didn't matter two cents whether people liked her or not, because Mr. Van Zandt handpicked her."

When you make an appointment,
note the contact number of the person in your agenda.
If you have to cancel in an emergency,
you'll have the number handy.

11

I grabbed my missing cart, checked my watch, and high-tailed it to the cash register. I had a consultation soon, but I had another important item to check out first. Luckily for me, it was on the way. I popped the groceries in the car and raced off to Lilac Lane.

Fortune was with me, and Jim Poplawski was just about to wedge himself into an ancient station wagon. He was carrying a small animal crate. Worry clouded his broad, cheerful face.

"He turned up," he said. "Not sure whether that's bad or good."

"Who?"

"Diablo. Barb's cat, remember?"

I'd been worried it might have been Robbie.

Jim said, "Someone turned him in to the shelter. Said they found him a few blocks away from here. Now I'm worried."

I felt that sinking sensation. "Because she hasn't been calling looking for him?"

"You got it. So did you decide on the piano? I'll have to help you out with it after I get back with the cat."

"Sorry. Not the piano. Something else." I figured Paula hadn't filled him in on my duplicity. "I need to talk to you."

"Sure."

"Thanks. I think the man Barb was seeing might have been a friend of mine. I don't want to stick my foot in it because I'm not sure and he's very private. Paula thought you might have seen his car."

"I did see Barb with a guy a couple of times. They were just chatting. No harm in saying that. You think he had something to do with her taking off?"

"Most likely not. Was it a silver-gray Toyota?"

He scratched his head. "Toyota? Nah, it was a big sedan. Didn't see the make, but I remember it was blue, not silver."

"Oh!"

"Hey, I guess I got the wrong answer. You all right? You look awful pale."

I said, "Could it have been a metallic blue Impala?"

He nodded. "Sure. Big American sedan. Not too old. Wasn't a Toyota, for sure."

I wasn't sure whether that was good news or bad. On the one hand, it meant Robbie might not have been lying about knowing where Barb lived. On the other, it might have meant that he'd spotted Barb with the still-unknown man in the Impala. This was yet another connection between Barb and the murder victim.

"Did you hear about the man who was shot in the woods at the edge of town?"

Jim shook his head.

I said, "It's been all over the news."

He chuckled. "Can't be bothered with the news. Hardly ever get that TV turned on for it. Got my hobbies and the wife has hers, and one of hers is keeping me busy. Anyway, we don't like the news much. Gets depressing."

"No argument," I said. "This victim was found in a blue car. You can see why that would be important."

"Sure can. Heck, how 'bout you tell the wife this story? She'll never believe me. She's upstairs washing the cat dish and putting out fresh food for Diablo. Just head on up."

Paula Poplawski had just finished setting out Diablo's dinner when I knocked. I followed her into the apartment. Her round moon face paled when I explained about the man in the Impala and the car that Barb had been in. She sank onto the blue sofa.

"I can't believe Barb would be involved in something like that. It's so . . ."

"Not involved. But afraid, maybe. It might explain why she would make herself scarce."

"I'll watch the news, and Jim will, too, whether he likes it or not. We can't stand that Todd Tyrell. So full of himself."

"I hear you." I slid my card over to Paula and said, "Please call me and let me know what Jim says. Or he can, if he wants."

"Whatever we can do. But aren't the police . . . ?"

I shrugged. "You'd think."

As I got into the Miata, I felt that someone was watching me. Was I getting more paranoid by the minute? I looked up the stairs and saw Paula's kindly face staring down at me. She waved as I pulled away.

I was home by lunchtime and did a quick sprint around the block with the pooches before panting up the stairs. It was a good time to practice for the Therapy Dog evaluation. We worked on STAY. It needed work. Apparently to floppy-eared creatures, it sounded just like CHASE EACH

OTHER AROUND THE ROOM. Never mind; through the magic of liver strips, we made a bit of progress. Follow your dreams, as the motivational poster in Fredelle's office said.

The dogs lost interest before I did and called it quits. No problem. I hit my desk and looked through my contracts schedule to see which projects I might be able to reallocate to Thursday and Friday, so the week wouldn't be a total loss.

I decided on the couple who wanted to clear up their crowded finished basement to make room for a combined exercise room, TV room, and spare bedroom. Easy and fun for me. I called and left a message to book time the next day.

I headed out to the exercise gear shop to see what kind of equipment people were using and what storage solutions might be required. I checked out rowing machines and Nautilus machines and elliptical trainers. Stationary bikes had quite a big footprint, I noticed. There seemed to be compact versions of most of the equipment.

Next stop was the linen shop, where I looked over the latest in coordinated bedding and checked out the sales. I could make suggestions to make the guest room space look larger and brighter. Naturally, I made a couple of quick stops at my favorite storage and container shops to see what fun new possibilities existed. My clients would thank me.

By midafternoon, I had to admit to myself that I was killing time with pleasant tasks that could be done at another time, rather than face up to whatever I should be doing about the situation with Barb Douglas.

But what was I supposed to be doing?

Pepper had warned me against going to the police. Fredelle wouldn't give me the time of day. But the fact remained that Barb Douglas was missing. She'd left her door open and let her beloved cat escape in her hurry to get away. She must have been running from something or someone.

I didn't know why she'd fled, but it was down to me to make sure the right person knew about it.

I'm never comfortable in the police station, but I stiffened my spine and marched up to the desk. It didn't matter that there was something about the red-haired detective that I found disturbing. He was a police officer and he was involved with the case, which was more than I should have been. All I wanted to do was fill in the appropriate person on the odd connections of Barb Douglas and this strange and horrible case.

"I'm looking for the detective in charge of the case of the man in the trunk of—"

The desk sergeant cut me off. "You just missed him."

"Oh."

"Didn't you see him drive away?"

I shook my head. "Thanks. I'll try later."

"Leave him a message if you want. I'll get you his voice mail."

I spotted the cocky walk of Nick the Stick. "No problem. I'll pop in again. It's probably nothing anyway."

"Suit yourself."

I made it as far as the door but didn't have time to get back to the car before Nick spotted me. "Hey, Charlie. What are you doing here?"

Visions of Nick mishandling the information about Barb Douglas and Robbie Van Zandt and the dead man danced in my head: Nick tramping over the crime scene, Nick manhandling Robbie Van Zandt and tossing Barb's apartment. Nick releasing the cat, Nick finding new ways to be inappropriate.

"Nothing," I said. "Just came in to . . . see how Pepper was doing."

"Pepper's not here. She's on sick leave because of her pregnancy. Thought you knew that."

"I do. But I wanted to ask you how she was really doing."

He shrugged. "Fine, I guess. You know Pepper. Tough as nails."

"I think I'll drop in and see her, then. I just wanted to make sure that would be okay."

"Sure. Don't tell her I told you she was tough as nails, okay? She might not like that. She's kind of touchy lately."

"I wonder why," I said.

"Oh wait, I think she's at her doctor's now. She has to go a lot. Something about the baby."

"I wouldn't be surprised. Maybe I'll pop by tomorrow."

"Great. But remember . . ."

"Not a word out of me."

Poor Pepper. You would think her husband, useless as he was, could stir himself to attend some of these appointments with her. Other husbands sat in on ultrasounds. Who did Nick think he was?

I sat in the Miata and decided to call Pepper and leave a message to ask when I could drop in. But my cell phone was not in my handbag. Truffle and Sweet Marie, as much as I love them, were the most likely suspects. Usually they liked to hide keys, which would eventually turn up behind the hamper, or buried under a sofa cushion, or in a shoe. I've installed a high shelf in my entranceway to put an end to that. Until they find a ladder, the keys are safe.

For a while, my shoes and boots went AWOL at the worst possible times. Usually just one of a pair. I installed a set of shoe racks on the second tier of my closet to solve that little problem. Luckily, being an organizer means you have to know how to use a drill and install shelves. I can do that in my sleep.

I'd left my handbag by the front door that morning while I double-checked the ice cream situation in the fridge before the trip to Quovadicon and Hannaford's. It was out of my sight for only a minute. How had they managed that?

I squealed out of the lot and raced home to chastise the little beasts. In my business, you need a cell phone and you really must have it with you if you want your clients to take you seriously.

By four o'clock, searches, threats, and cajoling still hadn't worked. I'd searched my entire apartment, under the bed, under the sofa, behind cushions, and in the dog blankets. Not a sign.

"You'll pay for this," I said for the tenth time. They ignored me but tilted their heads with interest as my home phone rang.

I said, "Hello?"

"What kind of business are you running where you don't even answer your cell?"

The grating tones could only belong to Dyan. I winced, as I knew it was the same question I'd just asked myself. No need for her to know that.

"I've answered now. What can I do for you, Dyan?" I said, keeping my voice even.

Her sneer hit my ear. "Maybe you should ask what I can do for you."

I took a breath. "Okay, what can you do for me?"

"Why don't you drop into the office and I'll show you."

She didn't bother to keep the gloating out of her voice. This woman was a walking, talking manifestation of every bad emotion I could think of. I couldn't imagine anyone I'd rather not see. Or anywhere I'd rather not be.

"Sorry," I said. "I have a very tight schedule. I'll just have to pass on your kind offer."

"Your loss, Miss Smart-Ass. This was your last chance to find out what Pigpen Douglas was really up to."

I hesitated. I really hated to give this woman any satisfaction at Barb's or anyone's expense. On the other hand, if she knew anything that would help find Barb, that would be worth a bit of irritation. Could she? Dyan was the one who hung around the office after people left. I'd seen firsthand how nosy and interfering she was. Fredelle was too innocent, Robbie too ineffective, and Autumn too vacant. If anyone could have found something about Barb, it was Dyan. No question about that.

"Okay, bye," she said. "Other people will want to know. It's probably worth something to somebody."

"Wait. I might be interested."

"Thought so."

"Well, what is it?"

Distinctive laugh. "That's dumb. If I could tell you on the phone, I would have told you on the phone."

"Fredelle has asked me not to come back."

"Like anyone cares what Fredelle says."

"Okay, you said you had information about—"

"Forget it. You know what? You really piss me off."

"I'm sorry. I'm not trying to," I bleated into the now-silent phone.

Too late.

I glanced at the time. Quovadicon was a good drive away, and this would be the start of what we call rush hour in Woodbridge. Still, I decided I wouldn't be able to relax without knowing what she was talking about. Maybe it would clear up the mystery of Barb.

Make sure you have at least one number programmed into your cell phone. If someone finds it, they can call someone close to you.

12

As I pulled into Quovadicon, I noticed only one car left in the lot, and it wasn't a silver Camry. That was weird. There must have been a separate lot for staff parking that I wasn't aware of. I hopped out and checked the time. Four thirty. A few minutes dealing with Dyan and I could get home and get back to the search for the cell phone.

The large glass doors were open. The lights in the reception area were out. I hesitated before going in, considering I was persona non grata with Fredelle.

"Hello," I said, walking past the empty reception desk into the office area. "Autumn? Are you here?"

The lights were out in the boardroom and the main office area, but still on in Fredelle's office. There was no sign of Fredelle, though, which was just as well considering the conversation we'd had the last time we spoke.

Where was everyone? It didn't seem like Fredelle to depart early without making sure the place was settled.

Never mind; since Fredelle and I were both going to be involved with Therapy Dogs, we'd have to have a civilized discussion soon about what had happened and put it behind us. People say things when they are shocked and upset. Sometimes you just have to forgive and with luck forget. But anyway, I hadn't come to deal with Fredelle or to talk to Autumn. I wanted to talk to Dyan as quickly as I could and then just get out of there.

I looked around. No sign of Dyan. And she was so nosy that she would normally be checking to see who had come in the front door.

"Dyan? It's Charlotte. You win." *Keep it light*, I told myself. *Don't let on she's getting to you.*

It would be just like Dyan to sit smirking in her cubicle, like a nasty spider waiting for me to fly in. I stiffened my shoulders and stuck my head around the corner. But her work space was empty, too. The leopard-patterned trench coat was still hanging on the hanger, and her oversize orange patent leather handbag was sitting on her ergonomic chair. She couldn't be far, that was for sure. She wouldn't leave her money and ID for anyone to plunder. She didn't strike me as the trusting type.

Maybe she was just playing games with me. Or in the heat of the moment, she'd marched off to fling the so-called information about Barb Douglas in someone else's face.

Either action would be just like her. On the other hand, perhaps she was in the staff room having retyped a nasty note about the state of the fridge. That would be like her, too. I hurried down the hallway to get it over with, although by now I'd decided that the whole trip to Quovadicon was a waste of time and bad judgment on my part. Most likely Dyan had cooked up some nasty tidbit of gossip or indulged her talent for speculation.

I kept going even though I concluded it had been less than wise for me to engage in whatever nasty little game she was playing. After all, she didn't represent the management except in her fevered brain and I decided to tell her that. As I passed the IT section, I noticed that Fredelle had arranged a pair of baffles blocking it from view. I peered in and noticed that the towering pile on Barb Douglas's desk was lower than it had been the day before, partly because half of it was now lying on the floor.

Not your problem, I told myself. *Keep going, speak to the mean lady and get the hell out. And next time, use your brain.* I peered around the staff room, expecting to see Dyan preening or scheming or whatever she did after office hours. But she wasn't there, either.

I conceded defeat. I was about to head back toward the front door, mentally kicking myself. As I turned, I heard a strange scraping sound. I glanced around. Nothing. No one. There it was again. And a low moan.

Help?

Yes, I was sure I'd heard a soft gasp for help.

The hair on my arms stood up. My heart began to pound. Was Dyan likely to play a practical joke on me? What did I know about her anyway? Did she know how many terrifying situations I'd found myself in since I'd come back to Woodbridge? Did she think that would be funny? Maybe she was . . .

Stop hyperventilating, I told myself. *This is just your imagination. There's nothing to worry about. Run!* Okay, that was a bit of a mixed message.

Do you want to spend the rest of your life in a panic over things that may not ever happen? Do you want to be a victim forever? Shape up! And while you're at it, get out now.

Even if I did want to get out, I was in the back end of the office, with a moaning, scraping *something* between me and the front door.

I told myself it must have been something scraping on the roof, a branch perhaps. Or perhaps something in the warehouse. There'd be a foreman there, and maybe a lift operator, someone to help me check and see that the moaning was just my imagination. They might be parked in a different area. I pushed open the door between the staff room and the warehouse. I stared wildly around. No one. Not a driver, not a forklift operator, certainly not a foreman. Just a vast empty space. Worse, the doors were all closed and I had no idea how to open them.

Behind me, I heard the moaning again. Fainter. *Welcome to my horror movie*, I thought, with me playing the dumb one who rips off her clothes and runs into the basement at midnight.

Imagination or whatever, I picked up the phone in the staff room, selected line one, and pressed 911.

"I am calling from Quovadicon at 120 Valley Drive in Patterson Business Park. Something bad is going on. The building's empty and there's a strange moaning noise. I think someone's injured or . . ."

"Charlotte?"

Why does it always have to be Mona Pringle? Didn't anybody else ever take 911 calls?

"Can you send someone?" I said, making sure I got my message out before Mona got me sidelined.

"We haven't heard from you in a while," she said cheerfully. "Months. Must be the off-season. Ha ha."

"It's not a joke, Mona. Someone could be in here injured or . . ."

"Or what?"

"I don't know," I said. "I just know that it feels all wrong."

"I'll need something better than that."

"All right. I was supposed to meet someone here."

"Oh yeah? Like who?"

"Well, not like that, Mona. I was supposed to meet Dyan . . ." I paused. I couldn't remember Dyan's last name.

"Uh-huh. And what makes you think there's something wrong? Maybe she got delayed."

"I didn't expect the building to be empty. There's no sign of her and now there's this moaning and I can't figure out where it's coming from."

"Hmm."

"And then there's the fact that her handbag is on her chair in this apparently empty building. And her jacket's here, too. I can't believe she'd go home without either of those things or that she'd leave them in the open in an unlocked building. Anyway, no one else is here, but there's still one car in the parking lot. It must be hers."

"You should . . ."

"Please don't argue with me. Just send somebody. If it turns out to be nothing, I'll apologize to everyone."

"Sure thing, Charlotte. We've had a lot of demand tonight, but a unit is on its way."

"She could be hurt. Send them as soon as you can."

"I'm already convinced. Now in case something is wrong, you'd better go stand outside. Get in your own vehicle. You've found one too many bodies, Charlotte. You're developing a reputation."

"What if . . . ?"

"Unit's on its way. Leave the building, Charlotte. Charlotte?"

I am not going to spend the rest of my life hiding under the bed as soon as I hear a noise, I said to myself. Out loud, too. If Dyan was still there and injured for some reason, I had to help her. I didn't have to like her, but I couldn't just leave her for ten or fifteen minutes while the next available unit arrived. She was so nosy. I could imagine her standing on a chair to reach a tall shelf or snoop behind someone's poster and tumbling in slo-mo. Maybe she was lying somewhere with a broken neck.

"Charlotte? Are you listening to me?"

"Sure thing, Mona. Stay on the line. Just in case. This phone isn't portable. I'll be right back."

I thought hard. I'd heard the moaning after I'd passed the IT area. I pushed myself to move along the corridor. It was hard to believe a new building could be so creepy when you could still see the sun shining through the windows. It was only late afternoon, but the place had a midnight-in-the-graveyard feel to it. *Don't be stupid*, I said. *This is not midnight in the graveyard. It's just an office in an ordinary business. That sound is probably somebody's radio and you'll have to apologize to Mona and everyone else connected with emergency services in Woodbridge. Just check it out and put your mind to rest.* I paused at the entrance of the IT area and peered behind the baffle before stepping in. I resisted the urge to pick up the papers that had toppled from Barb Douglas's desk. I stopped and listened. Not a moaning sound, more like a soft gurgle, but it was definitely coming from behind the desk.

I checked behind the desk, my heart thundering like a locomotive. Dyan lay in a crumpled heap, her head under the desk, her legs at a strange angle. Had she tumbled from the chair? I glanced up at the bookshelves. Nothing seemed out of place. I dropped to my knees and leaned forward. I touched Dyan's back. She was warm and breathing. She moaned again, softly, not like Dyan at all. Alive, but not conscious. I stroked her head and said, "Don't worry. Help is on the way."

I got to my feet, somewhat shakily. That's when I saw the blood on my hands. It seemed to be on my knees, too. I forced myself to wobble back to the staff room and yell into the phone. "Mona!"

Mona yelled back down the line, "What?"

"It's her! It's Dyan. She's badly hurt. Get that unit here as fast as you can. She's alive, but she's bleeding. I'm—"

Unconscious as it turned out.

If you are interrupted reading a document, use a sticky note to mark where you left off. You won't lose time finding your place.

13

It's bad enough to wake up covered with blood, but even worse if someone is slapping your face. Much worse if that someone is Nick Monahan.

"Pepper is going to be so pissed," he said, scratching his handsome blond head. "What were you thinking, Charlie?"

I sat up a bit too quickly, and my head spun. "Why should Pepper be upset? I'm the one who got bashed in the head."

"With a stapler, looks like," Nick said.

Have I mentioned that Nick is not the brightest bulb in the chandelier? "You're right, Nick. It is a stapler. You really are a detective."

"Aw, Charlie, I get lots of mean at home. Don't say stuff like that."

"Forget it. Where's Dyan?"

"Who's Dyan?"

I took a deep breath. After all, this crisis wasn't really about me. "She's the injured woman. That's why I called 911 and spoke to Mona."

"Someone must have whacked her with the same stapler they hit you with." Nick picked up the stapler, which had a bit of blood and dark hair on it. Mine, I thought.

I said, "That's evidence. Aren't you supposed to leave it for the crime scene techs to bag?"

A sharp intake of breath from Nick. At least he had the sense to look embarrassed as he dropped the stapler.

It's hard to believe anyone wouldn't know this, let alone a third-generation Woodbridge cop, currently pretending to be a detective. But then again, it was Nick. Chances were that he'd zoned out during the relevant training sessions.

"You better tell them you moved it," I said. "They'll find your prints on it."

"They'll find yours, too," he shot back.

"They will not. I didn't knock myself out with it."

He frowned, pondering that. "I'll think of something."

A man and a woman in white paper suits, blue booties, and what looked like latex gloves waddled into the office. Someone at the police station was on the ball. The woman had a camera, which she raised to take a picture. Nick the Stick leaped to his feet and jumped back out of the room. "Don't want to get in your way."

Right. More likely didn't want Pepper to come across a shot of him face to face with me, even if I could feel a trickle of blood running down the side of my face. Probably not a good look for me.

I said, "Please tell me, where is Dyan?"

The technicians exchanged glances.

"Dyan?" I repeated.

"They took her away."

"And was she . . . ?"

"Didn't look good."

Nick stuck his head back in and said, "I think there are paramedics here to see you, too."

"I'm all right," I said, struggling to my feet. It's just

a—" I stumbled and hit the floor, jarring my spine. It would have been worse if that pile of paper hadn't absorbed the shock of my fall.

Nick said, "Aw, come on, Charlie. Stop fooling around. They'll take you to Emergency and get you fixed up before we haul you into the station for questioning."

As I was hustled by paramedics into a waiting ambulance, I glanced around the parking lot. Even though my head was swimming and the flashing lights of the emergency vehicles made things worse, I could still recognize some of the Quovadicon employees huddling in anxious groups in the parking lot. Why had they come back? Most looked like warehouse workers and drivers. I caught a glimpse of Fredelle, pale, stressed, and wringing her hands. Autumn's pretty face was streaked with tears. She was shaking and clinging to a tall, handsome man in a white shirt and dark business suit. He must be her father, I decided. And he's as mad as all hell.

Mr. Halliday held Autumn in a protective hug, then turned to Fredelle and said in a voice that commanded attention, "I trusted you people to provide a safe place for my baby to work. And now I find out someone's been attacked in your office. What the hell is going on? Reg Van Zandt has a lot to answer for."

I agreed.

Autumn wailed, "But I'm not a baby, Daddy. And Mr. Van Zee has been your friend for years. It's not his fault. Anyway, what happened to poor Dinah?"

Before I conked out again, I thought, *You mean Dyan, you silly girl.*

Never mind the police station, if you get hauled into the hospital there's questioning, too. It starts the second you open your eyes.

"How many fingers?"

"Does this hurt?"

"And does this?"

"How about this?"

"I need you to close one eye, so I can look in the other. Can you do that?"

"Now can you close the other one?"

"Okay, miss, let's take off your shoes. We need to test your . . . Is something wrong?"

If you're lucky, the hospital gods will let you make a phone call. And if you're really lucky, your friend Sally will answer the phone. Being married to Dr. Benjamin Januscek gave Sally an awesome amount of influence at Woodbridge General. And you never know when you're going to need a bit of influence. Say, when you're having a neurological examination just before you're about to be questioned by the police, and, may I add, not for the first time this year.

Sally arrived fast enough to suggest a wormhole between her house and the hospital. She turned her gaze from the doctor who was tapping my knee.

"Cute," she mouthed to me.

But not blind, I thought, giving her a *shut up* look.

The emergency room physician was about my age, tallish, fairly easy on the eyes in a pale exhausted way. As far as I could tell, he was completely devoid of humor. A smile or a bit of eye contact can be very reassuring during a neurological exam.

She said, "I talked to Nick, before I came in."

"Don't make my head hurt more."

"They seem to think you had something to do with what happened to that woman."

I said, "For the record, that woman is called Dyan. And do they have a theory that I hit myself in the back of the head with a stapler after calling 911? Because it doesn't make sense."

"It's Nick, doesn't have to make sense. Anyway, they are convinced you were involved. I told him to get off his butt and start detecting, because you couldn't have been. You're a victim, not a villain. They should leave you alone."

"Thanks." I hoped that Nick wouldn't mess up the investigation any more than he had already.

She shrugged and smiled winningly at the stone-faced doctor. "Didn't do any good. They've got a police guard on you."

"Oh great," I bleated.

"I took the liberty of calling Margaret. She didn't answer and I had to text her. Can you believe she was on a dinner date? Did you know Margaret was dating?"

A look of guilt must have flashed across my face because Sally pursed her lips. "You kept that from me? And to think I dropped everything to rush over and take care of you."

"Sorry. I've had a lot on my mind."

"Sure, like a stapler. And don't change the subject. I shouldn't be the last one to know about Margaret's date. Nobody tells me anything. But I am glad you're all right. Margaret better get here soon and she'd better dish."

Margaret folded her arms and shot me a look that clearly said I'd ruined her evening. Not what you want to see when your lawyer shows up at the hospital. Never mind, when dealing with the police, you can always count on Margaret to know what to do.

I pleaded my case. "I didn't know you had a date. How could I know? You hardly talk to me anymore. And that's twice in one week. It's not like I planned any of this. I found this poor woman—well, she wasn't a poor woman, she was the office bitch—but anyway, she wasn't so bitchy that she deserved to be lying in a pool of blood on the floor in an empty building."

"We'll come back to that," Margaret said. "I'd like to know what you were doing there."

"Well, she called me. She told me she had some information about Barb Douglas. You'd know more about Barb Douglas, who is missing, except you've been . . . Is your lipstick smeared?"

Margaret's hand shot to her mouth.

"It is! And since when do you wear lipstick anyway? Are you telling me that you've been smooching that detective right here in the hospital? In broad daylight!"

"It's dark out," Margaret said. "After eight. And it wasn't here, not that it's any of your business. You were in that examination room a long time. And that bop on your head looks like the least of your problems."

I held up my hand. "Never mind about me. Please tell me what happened to Dyan. Is she going to be all right?"

Margaret shook her head.

I said, "Oh no. That's horrible."

Margaret avoided my eyes. "DOA, my sources tell me."

"Your sources? Oh right." The tall, dark, and way-too-old detective.

Dead on arrival? The full impact of Dyan's death began to sink in. Even if I hadn't liked her much, I still felt sick to my stomach that she'd died in such a horrible way. And even worse I knew that I'd been so close, but hadn't called for help in time to save her.

Margaret looked up and said, "It is horrible. So you can see why the police are determined to talk to you."

"Well, I want to talk to them, too."

Her eyebrow rose. "No, you do not. You want to keep your mouth closed. Let me stall them until we think of something."

"We don't need to think of anything. I didn't do anything."

"Charlotte, Charlotte, Charlotte."

"What?"

"They're going to tell you they think you killed her, and they're going to want to know how, and to a lesser extent why. So if you talk to them when you've obviously been injured, you won't be in the best position to tell a coherent, credible story."

"So why wouldn't it be credible? It's exactly what happened."

"My source tells me you were instructed not to return to Quovadicon."

"Well, I suppose that's sort of true—"

"Sort of?"

"Fine. It's totally true, but it wasn't because I did anything wrong. Fredelle, who is the office manager—you would know all this if you hadn't been so remarkably unavailable lately—Fredelle was a bit upset because I asked some pointed questions about Robbie Van Zandt. And how would your source know this?"

"Word came down the pipe from someone who is important to the brass, I gather. So let's see if I understand. You grilled the office manager—"

"Who was my client—"

"—about the son of the owner?"

"Since you put it that way, I suppose it was a bit shortsighted. But he's connected to—"

"To a very important man in this community."

"To a missing woman, Barb Douglas. Robbie might be involved in the death of that guy in the trunk of the blue Impala. Barb Douglas knew him. I would have told you all about this, but you've been tied up shaving your legs and going on dates and pretending you have to work late. Anyway, Dyan called me this afternoon and said she had information about Barb and to meet her at the office. Dyan hated Barb and had to be the snoopiest—"

"So you met her at the office that you were specifically instructed to stay away from?"

"Well, if you want to put it that way, yes. Don't roll your eyes, Margaret. You never used to do that."

"And you never used to get involved in murder."

"Anyway, when Dyan asked me to go back, I assumed she'd cleared it with Fredelle. She worked for her." I caught Margaret's eyebrow lift again and said sheepishly, "You're right. I shouldn't have gone. But don't you see—"

"The optics are bad, Charlotte."

"But Dyan claimed to have information about Barb Douglas and now she's dead, right behind Barb's desk, which incidentally is right next to Robbie Van Zandt's. So if I have to be questioned, he should be, too."

"Words fail me."

"They don't seem to be failing you." In fact, Margaret had become a lot more forthright than she used to be. She'd been easier to take in the good old days, for sure. Of course, I hadn't needed legal help quite so often back then. "I didn't know the building was empty. I'd planned to see Fredelle on my way in. But she wasn't there. Robbie wasn't there, either. Autumn, the receptionist, was gone, too. Even the warehouse was empty."

Margaret said, "You checked the warehouse? Unbelievable."

"Do you know why the staff came back? They all seemed to be in the parking lot when the paramedics took me."

"The manager got a call. Everyone was summoned to Mr. Reg Van Zandt's home on an urgent matter. They all showed up, expecting to hear some dire news. The rumor was that the company was being shut down. The receptionist had a meltdown, and some of the drivers were pretty vocal. And before you ask, the police have interviewed everybody, and everyone seems to check out. People were in view of the security cameras at Van Zandt's place, too. Looks like none of the staff did it."

"Well, Dyan wasn't at Van Zandt's. Did anyone notice that?"

"Apparently, she volunteered to stay and lock up."

"Of course. She would have loved being in charge, too. Probably moved everyone's stuff around." I caught myself with a frisson of guilt. After all, Dyan was dead. I changed the subject. "At least that call explains a lot, and it definitely vindicates me."

"I wish. There are two other problems."

"And they are?"

"Mr. Van Zandt didn't plan to make an announcement. He was quite surprised when all those vehicles pulled up at his home."

"Oh. So was it some kind of a prank call?"

"Hard to say. It seemed real to Miss Newhouse."

"Okay, what's the second problem?"

"Well, it's the really big one."

"Spit it out then."

Margaret said, "Apparently, that phone call came from you."

Five minutes of filing at the end of every workday can save hours searching through piles of paper for documents later on.

14

"What? I thought you said—"

Margaret repeated, "The police claim the phone call came from you."

"But I didn't make that call."

"No need to yell, Charlotte. I believe you, because I know you. But the police say they have proof."

I raised my voice. "It's perfectly ridiculous. Why would I do that?"

Margaret shrugged. "Don't shoot the messenger, who is also in this case the lawyer. The police seem to think you wanted to get Dyan alone."

"This is crazy-making. And by the way, even if I had made such a call, which I didn't, why would anybody follow such a ridiculous instruction from me?"

"Keep in mind I'm just telling you what the police are saying. They think you didn't say you were you."

"Well, I wasn't me."

"They confirmed the source of the call as your cell phone."

"That's not . . . wait a minute. My cell phone was lost. I reported it." I felt a tingle as odd events fell into place. My voice rose. "Obviously someone took it to frame me. You know what's weird? This time last week, I hadn't met any of these people and now one of them is missing, another one is dead, and I'm the fall guy."

"Stick to your story. Don't deviate. Don't talk about this other missing woman. Don't volunteer anything. Don't badger them for information. Just answer the questions truthfully and don't allow yourself to be questioned without me present. They're stirred up enough already."

"I'd be stirred up too if the first cop on the scene was Nick the Stick. I mean really, he had his hands all over everything—"

Margaret said, "Ew! How could you stand that?"

"Not me," I yelped, "but the evidence. The stapler and who knows what else he contaminated. He has the brains of an acorn, you know that."

Margaret narrowed her eyes. "I've told them you're not in any shape to be questioned yet. Maybe it's making them cranky."

"I don't blame them for being cranky. But why should I suffer for it?" For some reason, when Margaret left the examining room, no doubt to wring some more information out of Detective Tall, Dark, and Granite, the doctor seemed just a little bit, oh, I don't know, on edge?

I lay there with my head still throbbing and wondered about what I might have forgotten in the shock of Dyan's murder. Did I have appointments? I sat up, causing my head to spin. Therapy Dogs orientation. No, that was Friday. At least someone had retrieved my handbag. I was glad it wasn't Exhibit B. I had promised to drop off brochures and design ideas to my latest closet client that evening. I didn't like to let her down and I wanted her to keep her enthusiasm for the project. After all, I only had a headache and a bit of dizzyness. I've worked through worse. And I'd been really looking forward to this project. But the shadow of the police guard on the white curtain surrounding my emergency room bed brought me back to reality. I staggered out of bed and tapped the officer on the shoulder. She was a stocky young woman of the keener type.

"I have a meeting tonight at seven. It's very important. I feel well enough to go home and get over there. I might take a taxi. So I wonder if you could just keep an eye on me there, instead of here." I smiled brightly to defuse any suggestion that I was an unreliable character.

"You're kidding, right?" the officer said.

"No."

She rubbed her nose.

I chirped. "What harm can it do? I have to make a living and—"

She held up her hand. "Let me explain this. The only reason you're not at the station is that you are in the hospital, which usually means you're not well enough to go to the station without some risk. I am not here to protect you. I'm here to make sure you don't disappear to avoid being questioned in a murder."

At least she didn't roll her eyes.

"I'm not planning to disappear."

"And I'm not planning to argue. For one thing, it's already nine o'clock, so you've missed your meeting. Anyway, if you're well enough to go, and they check you out, it's the station for you."

"Fine. Let's get it over with. Where's that doctor?"

Apparently wanting to be cleared to depart and actually being cleared to depart are two different things. Our original doctor had gone off shift. The new one was round, fresh, and cheerful.

"No way, José," she said when I tugged on her sleeve. "Not until I see those X-rays. And even without seeing them, I'd say you're not going anywhere for the next forty-eight hours. You won't be able to stay alone."

"Will I be able to drive?"

"In your dreams." She chuckled.

Even at the best of times, I find it hard to make a telephone call to cancel an appointment. With a police officer looking over my shoulder, it was even worse. Eventually, I persuaded a nurse to transport me in a wheelchair to the pay phone in the nearest hallway. The officer came along. Luckily I had my client's name written in my agenda next to the date, time, and address. I asked the officer to make the call as I seemed to have a bit of trouble focusing. When my client answered, I apologized for not being able to drop off the brochures as promised. I explained that I had run into an unexpected problem and had been unable to contact her earlier.

She said, "Well, I've been concerned about you. I saw them lift you into an ambulance on the news. I hope *you're* all right."

"I will be. And I'll get in touch as soon as I know when I can get back to work." I paused to give her time to wiggle out of the contract.

"Don't worry about me. Anyway, you must be really shaken up. You weren't even supposed to drop off the brochures until tomorrow night. Never mind that. The weekend would actually work better for me. You just take care of yourself."

That was nice, if a bit embarrassing. Lots of clients drop you at the first sign of trouble with the police. I had a lump in my throat when I called to leave a message with the Therapy Dogs coordinator.

To my surprise a familiar human answered, although she did say "Woof! Woof! Woof!"

"Woof," I answered automatically. "This is Charlotte Adams speaking and . . ."

"Oh Charlotte! We met at the booth on Sunday. Everyone's looking forward to seeing you at the orientation session and we're dying to meet Truffle and Sweet Marie, too, when the time comes. Of course, we've all seen you on television. I am sure those little cuties will make wonderful additions to the team."

"The problem is that I'm in the hospital."

"Oh no! Not surgery, I hope."

"No no, just a small injury." I was glad she hadn't been watching the news that evening. "But I don't know when I'll be released, and I don't know if I will be able to make the orientation session. I am wondering if there are any other options."

I decided not to mention that the police might still be grilling me by then. That's a seemingly endless process, a fact I've learned the hard way.

"Well, I sure hope you're feeling better soon, otherwise we'll have to send a therapy dog team to cheer you up."

I chuckled. "I hope I'm not here that long, as much as I'd enjoy that visit."

"The session is full. It's probably too late to fill your place, so if you get a chance to come by, that would be great. Otherwise, we'll fit you in the next time. Might not be until spring, though."

"Thanks." Such lovely people. So kindhearted. That reminded me. "Oh, by the way, there's been a death at Fredelle's workplace. She's very upset. I don't imagine she'll make the event, either. I am sure she'll contact you, but just in case . . ."

"Who?"

"Fredelle."

"Fredelle?"

"Fredelle Newhouse. I met her at your booth the other day."

What is known as an awkward silence drifted over the line.

"Hello?" I said, after a while.

"Um, was it a head injury?"

"What?"

"Did you have a head injury? Is that why you're in the hospital?"

"Um . . . yes, sort of a head injury. But why are you asking?"

"Well, because we don't have anyone named Fredelle who is part of the Woodbridge League of Therapy Dogs."

"What?"

"I know every volunteer, and there's no Fredelle."

"But I saw her there, by your booth."

"Sorry, but that doesn't make her part of our organization."

"Oh." I searched for something to make sense of this. "Maybe . . ."

She filled the awkward pause. "In fact, I know Fredelle Newhouse very slightly, and we'd be glad to have her. She could help with lots of tasks, but she hasn't volunteered to date. Maybe she was thinking about it and mentioned that to you." She didn't bother to mention the head injury again, but I could tell she figured it accounted for my mistake.

"Sorry, I must have misunderstood."

"No harm done."

"You're kinda pale," the stocky officer said after I hung up.

No damn wonder I was pale. Innocent round-faced silver-haired fairy godmother type Fredelle Newhouse had deliberately misled me about her involvement in Therapy Dogs.

The only reason, I imagined, was to entice me into Quovadicon and the rat's nest it had turned out to be. Looked like Fredelle was just one more person who couldn't be trusted.

—⁂—

Of course, it was just a matter of time until the defective detective showed up again.

"Hey, Charlie," he said.

"Nick." I sat up. A bad idea, as it turned out.

He said, "Okay, you want to start by telling me why you hit that lady? Was it an accident?"

I lay back again, causing a bit of havoc in my head. "I think you're supposed to take my statement before you pull out the rubber hoses. Where's Detective Tierney, by the way?"

"Didn't anyone take your statement?"

I bit my tongue so I wouldn't blurt out that the detective shouldn't rely on the suspect to do his job for him.

I said, "No one did."

"That's weird."

The keen officer stared at Nick with astonishment. Or at least that was my assumption.

I would have rolled my eyes, except I thought that would hurt. "I have been here in Emergency under police guard since the ambulance picked me up at Quovadicon."

"Oh, so no statement. Hmmm."

How long, I wondered, before the Woodbridge police department found itself under the media microscope for some essentially stupid miscarriage of justice due to the sheer incompetence of Nick Monahan? How would Pepper ever hold her head up in town?

Oh well. Not my problem. I'd warned her not to marry the jerk.

"You could take the statement," I suggested. "Then I could get out of here and . . ."

"Unless we arrest you."

"Bad idea."

"It's my job, Charlie. Sometimes I got to do the hard stuff."

"Margaret just went back to her office to get some work material. We'll wait until she gets back."

"Margaret? Why do you need a lawyer?"

My head throbbed. Nick can have that effect. And I hadn't done anything. "Fine. Just take the stupid statement and you'll see why that won't be necessary."

"Okay, then. Want to tell me what happened?"

"Sure. But you have to write it down."

"Course I'm going to write it down, Charlie. I'm the detective, remember?"

I did my best to describe my trip to Quovadicon without making my behavior look suspicious or, worse, lunatic. A challenge. As writing was never Nick's best thing, the statement took longer than it should have.

Nick frowned and said, "Why did you go again?"

"I've explained that. Dyan called me and said she had something to tell me."

"What was it?"

"Well, I don't know, Nick. I never found out. We didn't talk. She was badly injured when I got there."

"And no one noticed this? Only you?"

"Do you recall the phone call that requested all staff to go to Mr. Van Zandt's home? And Dyan didn't go."

"So she stayed behind?"

I massaged my temple. "Yes."

"To meet with you."

"Yes."

"And that was because . . . ?"

"She claimed she had information for me. Perhaps Dyan made the call, a bit of subterfuge to clear the office of witnesses."

"What?"

"She claimed—"

"No, that word."

"Subterfuge? Means a trick."

"I knew that. How do you spell it?"

"S-u-b—"

Nick stopped to scratch his head again. "I'll just put *trick*."

"Good thinking."

Nick glanced over at me, looking sneaky. "The only thing is that Dyan didn't make that call: You did."

"I did not."

"The call came from your cell phone."

"That cell phone was stolen."

His look morphed from sneaky to smug. Possibly he planned to run through all known facial expressions starting with S. Say *strange*, *stunned*, *stupefied*. Any of them would have worked. Or maybe he was just tired of writing and had decided it was more fun to tease me.

He said snidely, "Oh, yeah. Did you report that?"

"I didn't because I thought my dogs had hidden it. We are still working our way through . . . issues about possessions. But it is patently untrue that I made the call."

"Patently. Big word for a little lady."

"Untrue. Bad word for a cop."

"But maybe Fredelle Newhouse made that call herself. She misrepresented herself to me."

"Your cell phone number showed up on the call display record when that call was made. Fredelle Newhouse didn't make it. The call was transferred to her from reception. The number's right there on the screen. Now, don't go saying your dogs made the call."

"Now I see that it must have been stolen by someone who . . ."

"Tough one, Charlie. Not sure if a jury will buy that."

"What jury? I didn't make that call, and I wish you'd get that through your—"

He raised his hand. "Okay, don't panic. You don't need to take everything so personally."

"Don't take it personally? Don't take a jury personally? Don't take insinuations that I may have killed someone personally? Are you . . . ?"

Before I could choose between *demented* and *dimwitted* in reference to Nick, the sturdy cop stepped forward. As if he needed protection from me. Nick the Stick had obviously found another emotional patsy. Better her than me, although I wanted to warn her not to let Pepper ever get a look at that lovesick cow expression or this officer would be looking for another police force. In Montana maybe.

At that moment the curtain was flung back with more than a little drama. Nick gasped, the officer gasped, and I gasped, too.

Pepper raised an eyebrow. She was in full makeup, nicely dressed, and with her hair fixed. This was the Pepper I was used to.

"I'm so glad you're here," I blurted. "Nick wants to arrest me for murdering Dyan. He's hoping I'll get discharged soon."

"Is that a fact?" Pepper said.

The female officer stared at Pepper's bump with barely disguised something. Envy maybe. Nick stared at Pepper with fear and confusion. I just stared. I would need to know what was going on before I could conjure up the right kind of emotion.

I said, "It goes without saying that I didn't do it."

Nick said, "All the evidence points to her, no question about it. You never really know about people, do you, babe?"

The officer said, "She's been stalling to stay in the hospital, but she won't be able to get away with that much longer."

Pepper said, "Do I have to do everything around here?"

"What do you mean?" Nick squeaked.

"Am I or am I not on sick leave because of this pregnancy?"

"You are, babe."

"Did we not both create this baby? And do we not both want this baby to go full-term?"

Nick scratched his head. That kind of complicated negative sentence was bound to throw him off. After thirty seconds he said, "Yeah, yeah. We did. We do. And you look beautiful. More beautiful than ever. You ask me, you're the most—"

"Blow it out your ear, Nick."

Nick's mouth shut with a click of his teeth.

I took a chance. "But you do look good, Pepper, even if you're not feeling well. Motherhood agrees with you."

"Yeah well, getting hit on the head doesn't agree with you. You look like crap and you have blood oozing through that bandage. Someone has to see to that. Where's the doctor?"

"There's blood oozing out of my head?" I said woozily. "Really? Are you sure, because—"

"Lie down and shut up, Charlotte. You." She pointed to the officer. "Get a doctor in here, right now. Unless you want to be part of some kind of lawsuit."

"Lawsuit?" Nick said.

"You know, harassment, mistreating witnesses."

"But, babe, I didn't . . ."

"Just take a hike, Nick."

He gawked at her. His mouth was open again, slack-jawed, in fact.

"Now!"

I lay there not knowing whether to be more concerned that my head was oozing blood and apparently people died of that sort of thing, or that Pepper and Nick didn't appear to be getting along. I was pretty sure that wasn't my fault, but I could never really tell what was going on with them.

Nick slunk out through the curtain. The officer had already scurried off in search of a doctor.

Pepper narrowed her eyes in my direction. "Look at you," she said. "Didn't I tell you not to stick your pointed little nose into this business?"

"And I didn't!"

"Oh, not so much, Charlotte."

"This woman, Dyan, called me to tell me that she had to talk to me about Barb Douglas. It was the middle of the afternoon, during a workday in a respectable business. How could I know it wasn't safe?"

"That's not what I said. I told you not to get involved. So when the woman called you, you needed to tell her that it had nothing to do with you. You could have referred her to the police. And now look."

I felt tears sting my eyes. "Pepper, they told me she's dead."

She was pale under her makeup. Up close I could see that she wasn't feeling as well as she looked. "I am aware of that."

"I tried to get you to listen to me. Do you think she'd still be alive if I'd sent her to the police?"

Pepper slumped into the hard plastic chair next to the chrome bed. "Maybe, maybe not."

"And I suppose I could sue the police for harassment."

"Don't be ridiculous. I just said that so that Nick would learn a lesson. He's putting his feet in everything lately."

Pepper stroked her baby bump and glowered. Something told me that Nick had been foolish enough to make some remark to send Pepper through the roof. His life would be hell until he groveled enough to make that remark go away. I almost felt sorry for him.

"So you don't really think that I killed that woman?"

"Of course not. But you could have been killed. And this was a clumsy attempt to frame you. What will it take to keep you from meddling in police business? Just go home, do your little closet fix ups and your color-coded rituals and leave the investigations to people who know what they're doing."

Behind her, the curtain was whipped open again. I saw the pasty face of the young cop. She was hovering behind the fresh new doctor.

"What's going on here?" the doctor said.

Pepper barked, "She's bleeding. Someone has to take a look at that wound."

"Actually," she said, "it's just a scrape. I've just been able to get a look at her X-rays, and she was very lucky."

I sat up. "As it's *my* X-ray of *my* head, Doctor, I think you should talk to me. Directly."

"Very lucky and very crabby, too," Pepper said.

"Another inch to the left and a blow like that might have been fatal." She did turn to me, but her gaze drifted back to Pepper.

"Told you," Pepper said, shooting me the kind of look your mother used to give you when you got hurt falling out of a tree you'd been told not to climb.

"So I was lucky?"

The doctor said, "Yup. Are the police still waiting to question you? Because we want to monitor you for another two hours. And I don't think you should be under any more stress. I'll keep you overnight if they're talking about taking you in."

"They have her statement," Pepper said. "She should just go home and go to bed."

"Is there someone who can keep an eye on you?"

"Oh sure," I said. "Maybe a few too many people."

"You don't fool around with head wounds, even superficial ones. Any dizziness, nausea, and you get someone to bring you back in right away. Are you paying attention to this?"

"She is," Pepper interjected. "And she will. There are half a dozen people waiting to take on the job."

"Good."

"Thank you," I said, but the doctor's white coat had already disappeared behind the curtain. "Thank you, too, Pepper, for intervening with Nick and this officer."

The officer sniffed.

Pepper said, "Now you listen up. Your luck can run out, you know. This better be the end of it."

I nodded, although it hurt.

Pepper said, "Margaret called me. She's on her way back. Sally had to go home for a bit to give Benjamin a hand, but she'll be back, too. They'll take you home."

"Sure thing. Is Jack coming, too?"

Pepper looked uncomfortable, although I told myself that could have been the bump. "No."

"Oh. Didn't they call him?"

I noticed that she wouldn't meet my eyes. "I guess they couldn't reach him."

"Right," I said brightly. "He's been involved in this bicycle race, hard to connect with him lately."

"Exactly," Pepper said, sounding relieved for some reason. "When you do get home, you'll rest and recover from your head injury, and then you'll just go about your own business. No more nosing around. You see where it leads. Right?"

"For sure," I said.

I meant it, too. There was no way I'd have anything else to do with anyone at Quovadicon. But it bothered me that I still had no idea what Sergeant Pepper Monahan really knew about the brutal killing of one woman and the disappearance of another.

Having trouble making a decision at work?
Write down the pros and cons for your top choices
and give a numerical weight to each.
Add up the numbers and the best option will be much clearer.

15

I jerked awake in a foggy state and gasped as a pair of icy blue eyes sent a chill down my spine.

"Don't get up," a voice said from the chair next to the hospital bed. The voice had a cool edge to it, too. Nothing warm and fuzzy about this visitor.

"Gaak," I said, struggling to sit up.

"Sorry?"

"My head is spinning again," I said, speaking more cogently this time.

"I'm Detective Connor Tierney with the Woodbridge police." He was sitting, fiddling with his silver keys, but Margaret was watching quietly from the sidelines.

"I've seen you on television," I said, trying not to be hypnotized as the keys spun in his hand. Up close, I could see that the keychain was a silver lion's head.

"Hmm. I've seen you on the news, too."

"None of that was my fault," I said.

"It's never my fault, either," he countered. "I'd like to

ask you a few questions about what happened today. Are you up for that?"

"I guess so. Nick Monahan already interviewed me. Am I still a suspect? Are you going to haul me in for questioning? You'd better check with the doctor first. And my lawyer . . ."

"You won't be hauled anywhere. Nick Monahan is—"

"Special, I know."

"I've read your statement. You said you misplaced your cell phone."

"I did not make that phone call in order to clear the building so I could bludgeon Dyan with a stapler."

"Glad to hear it. We do know that the call came from your cell, so work with me here and let's try to figure out where it could have been taken from you."

"Taken from me? Oh. I thought my dogs hid it. They do things like that. They're very cute, though. I love them a lot and—"

"I know you've had a blow to the head, but let's assume your dogs didn't make this call. I'm guessing they don't talk. So who had access to your cell phone?"

I stared back at him. He was better looking in person than on television. But he still made me nervous. Pepper didn't seem to like him, and I'd had the impression that she didn't trust him, either. That sure didn't make it easier for me to open up. At any rate, I still couldn't remember. I shook my head.

"Try."

"I have an incredible headache," I said, trying to ignore the pounding in my skull.

Fifteen minutes later, I still hadn't remembered. Connor Tierney reached into his well-tailored pocket. A different suit, I noticed despite the headache, from the ones I'd seen on television. Classy, well-cut. Not at all Woodbridge. He handed me a business card.

"Think about it," he said. "Give me a call if you remember."

"I'm trying. Whoever did that wanted me to look guilty."

He raised a pale orange eyebrow but didn't say anything.

He made me very nervous. I found myself talking way too much. "Why did they bother to hit me on the head? Who ever heard of a self-clobbering suspect?"

He stood up to leave and tucked the keys into his pocket. "Think about that cell phone. And if I were you, I'd make sure I wasn't alone."

"Don't worry about that," Margaret said.

Even though I felt better when I got home, Margaret insisted she'd sleep on the sofa bed in the living room. There was no sign of Jack, and anyway, I might need a lawyer, she added.

The next morning I began the day by sitting up in bed and cuddling with my dogs. Sally arrived to take over. She made me breakfast in bed. Hot buttered wheat toast with homemade strawberry jam and a giant mug of hot chocolate all arrived on a tray. That distracted me as she moved the television set into the bedroom. Margaret spent her time on the phone doing business, but she must have cleared her parents' convenience store out of Mars bars. I found that endearing. Our friends Rose and Lilith phoned from L.A. I gathered that Sally had texted Lilith with the news. It all helped, including knowing that the Mars bars would be there for snacks. I needed to keep up my strength.

Still no sign of Jack. I pretended that I wasn't pouting about that.

As the headache faded, I distracted myself by checking through my agenda and trying to assess whether my weekend appointments would need to be rescheduled. While my nose was in the agenda, I worked through my schedule and tried to figure out when I had last seen the phone.

I'd had it to try to call towing before Mel and Del showed up. That reminded me about them. Were they really employees of Quovadicon, or had Fredelle lied about that, too? I made a note to myself to mention it to Connor Tierney when I called him about the phone.

I'd used the cell to call Margaret about a spontaneous dinner the night she had the date. I'd first noticed the phone missing when I was outside the police station, and I'd searched my apartment afterward. Where had I been in between? A lot of my activities hadn't been in my agenda, as they fitted under the "spontaneous snooping" category. I'd been to Barb's apartment, but I hadn't used the phone. Nor had it been out of my possession. I'd been to Sally's place. Though one of the children might have played with it, they couldn't have made a phone call to clear Quovadicon.

I'd been to Pepper's. I'd left her alone with the phone when I got the Oreos. I wouldn't put it past her to sneak my phone to see if I'd called her sleazy husband, but again, why would she make the Quovadicon call?

Then I'd returned to Barb's apartment, but again, no way to lose the phone there.

I'd spent time with Robbie, but he hadn't been alone with my handbag. I'd been to the library to see Ramona. Ditto.

After that, I'd gone back to Quovadicon. I left my handbag and briefcase in the public area for a couple of minutes while I rushed after Fredelle. Anyone could have swiped my cell phone then. There'd been a lot of extra people milling about the office that day. Could one of the clients or suppliers have taken it?

Dyan could have taken the cell and faked the call herself. She was nosy and bold and didn't seem to understand the notion of boundaries.

Autumn was such an airhead that she wouldn't have noticed any or all of them rummaging through my possessions. If Autumn had seen Dyan, she might have been too intimidated to question her.

Just in case, I made a note to myself to ask her.

At one point I'd chased after Missy in Hannaford's and left my cart behind, complete with handbag where anyone could have rifled through it. That meant the entire population of Woodbridge and neighboring communities could have swiped it, although logically, I knew it had to be someone involved in this case, especially as the thief had left my wallet with cash, ID, and credit cards.

I bit my lip at this. People were right. Leaving my handbag where anyone could get it? How dumb was that? Obviously, I was losing it over this whole business with Barb Douglas.

I picked up my phone and called Connor Tierney's number. It went straight to voice mail. I left a message saying where the handbag had been out of my sight, although I hesitated before including Hannaford's. What kind of flake leaves her handbag alone in a supermarket? Of course, I was pretty sure he already thought I was a flake. And I prefer to be a flake than a suspect, any time.

After that, I took out my frustrations by building a case against the people who seemed to be involved with most aspects of this troubling case. I jotted my points down on separate pages in my spiral notebook. I discounted Paula and Jim as well as Missy early on. The only thing against either of them was that they knew Barb and had been near my purse. That left Fredelle and Robbie. It helped that I was really ticked off at both of them.

The case against Fredelle

- *Lied about Therapy Dogs. To get on my good side? Create sympathy? Trust?*
- *Used intro to bring me in on very short notice to see Barb's desk. Why urgency?*
- *Set up whole situation. Was I a ploy? For what?*
- *Had personnel files with addresses and contact numbers*
- *Could have seen the man in the blue car, heard news, and made connection with Barb*
- *Did she call Barb with bad news?*
- *Fredelle got frequent calls from Reg Van Zandt. Why wouldn't she recognize his voice?*
- *Banned me from the building after questions about Barb and Robbie*
- *Did I touch on something threatening? What?*
- *Said Mel and Del didn't work there—lying?*
- *Threatened by Dyan, who wanted her job. Was Dyan about to reveal something?*
- *Overprotective of Robbie. How far would she go?*
- *Would she kill Dyan and try to frame me? Two birds with one stone?*

The case against Robbie Van Zandt

- *Unpredictable and emotional, poor social skills*
- *Infatuated with Barb*
- *Could have spied and seen man in blue car with Barb*
- *Did he kill him? Overcome with jealousy?*
- *Overreaction about Barb's desk. Why? Did he know she was missing?*
- *Angry with me*

- *Hated Dyan and threatened her*
- *Had access to my cell phone in office*
- *Could he have made the phone call? Faked his father's voice?*

I obsessed over both lists. Robbie seemed more likely than Fredelle, but there was no question they were both behaving erratically. But really, Fredelle seemed so kind and gentle and Robbie so inept it was hard to take them seriously. Deep down, ticked off or not, I hoped that neither one had shot the man in the Impala or caused Barb to disappear. Not to mention killing Dyan and injuring me.

I turned to Sally. "I wonder if I should just give these lists to Pepper."

"Why bother? She's being a total bitch," she said.

"She's not," I said, "although a reasonable person could be forgiven for thinking that. When Pepper's being a real bitch, it's much worse than this. Remember? She's just trying to keep me out of it."

"You're such a pushover, Charlotte." Sally sniffed. "Although maybe she's on to something. That head wound was pretty serious."

"The serious part is Dyan's death and the guy in the Impala, plus Barb Douglas's disappearance. Pepper knows something about this case and about Barb, too, and she's known right from the beginning. That's why she warned me off."

"What do you think she knows?"

"I could tell she recognized Barb Douglas from the way she reacted to the photo. At that point, I thought maybe they'd been friends, neighbors, who knows. Now, I'm not so sure that she actually knew Barb or whether she knew something about the case. Nick could have blabbed at home about something. I can't figure it out. She also told me to mind my own business, but what else is new?"

Sally perked up. "What if the cops know that Barb's dead, and they also know she has a relationship with the victim, but they don't want the killers to know that they know? Face it, Charlotte. This guy had to be a criminal. The average citizen doesn't get killed and stuffed into a car trunk."

"Are you suggesting that Barb might be a criminal, too?"

Sally shrugged. "Makes sense."

I said, "That might explain it."

"What?"

"Everything. Barb wasn't running to this man."

Sally said, "Just say it, Charlotte. Don't drag it out."

"Okay, Barb heard about the murder at work. She was shocked, horrified. Robbie said she sounded anguished. I saw her face. She had one hell of an emotional reaction. But maybe she wasn't just running to him. She was also running away."

Sally blinked.

"Think about it. She rushed to the crime site. Then she must have raced home. She was in such a panic that she left the door open even though her beloved cat might escape. She grabbed whatever she would have needed to survive. If she knew things could get dangerous, maybe she kept a little suitcase packed. Anyway, she took off. No one has seen her since."

"But her SUV was still there," Sally said reasonably.

I said, "Maybe she couldn't take the chance of being seen in that car. Maybe she took a cab. Or walked. Although the crime scene was miles from Lilac Lane."

"What if she rented a car?" Sally said.

"That's possible. Or maybe she had access to another one somewhere. Or maybe someone she trusted picked her up and drove her. However she traveled, she was scared, and I am sure that she had good reason to be."

Sally frowned. "But she'd be exposed. Woodbridge isn't that large. Someone would be bound to see her. She'd need a place to stay, food—"

I thought about our friend Lilith, who had told me stories from her life on the streets. "You can disappear easily. You can sleep in the woods, change your appearance. You can steal a car if you want."

"That's right," Sally said. "Todd Tyrell mentioned that there's an epidemic of car thefts in Woodbridge."

I sniffed. "With Todd's love of exaggeration, that probably means one."

"But that's good news. If Barb is alive and hiding out because she got mixed up with dangerous people, then you don't need to get involved. Right?"

"Wrong. Someone killed her boyfriend and also killed Dyan." I stopped talking and touched my head. "And they tried to kill me, too, for whatever reason. I guess that means I'm still very involved whether I want to be or not."

"And that's why I'm not leaving you alone."

"I'm fine today, really. My head doesn't hurt. I'm thinking clearly." I protested. "I have the dogs. And you have your kids. I appreciate everything you've done for me. Now get out of here."

Five minutes later, Sally headed out, yawning. I followed her downstairs and glanced at the open door of Jack's apartment. Jack was fiddling with his bike in what passes for his living room. He rarely opens CYCotics before eleven in the morning, as he's not the quickest person out the door at dawn. This morning he was still in his pajama bottoms, and he had a bad case of bed head. He blinked as he noticed my bandage.

"You okay?"

"Sure thing. You should see the other guy." Of course, then I thought of Dyan and it didn't seem funny.

He turned his attention back to the bike. "Good. Call me if you need me."

Sally shot him a poisonous look, but he'd already vanished deeper into his apartment. "Can't count on some people."

"Relax." I grinned. "I'm much better and I have the best locks in town."

True enough. I put in extras for very good reasons. I have an alarm system. I even have locks on my windows. I am not taking any chances. But if someone really wants you dead, they can find a way to make that happen. Not necessarily when you're sleeping with one eye open in your bed, but sooner or later you have to go out. You have a living to make, friends to see, places to go, dogs to walk.

I wasn't looking forward to nonstop worrying about it. That kind of fear is made even worse if you have no idea who you are supposed to be afraid of. I knew I had to face it sooner rather than later, because the minute I climbed the stairs again, the dogs decided it was time to go.

Just to be on the safe side, I called into Jack's apartment on the way out. "Pooch parade!"

He stuck his head out of the bathroom and waved his toothbrush at me encouragingly.

Thanks a lot, Jack, I thought.

Never mind, I told myself. It's like a vote of confidence. You don't want to be a prisoner in your apartment for the rest of your life. Pull yourself together. I squared my shoulders and marched out to the curb in my froggie pajamas and pink fluffy slippers. It was a nippy morning. The dogs hate the cold, and they broke their current speed records. "That just earned you a treat," I said.

A shadow loomed behind me just as we hit the front

steps on our way back. I squeaked in alarm. I paused mid-squeak because it wasn't my worst fear. No armed thugs, no Barb Douglas ready to bash my head with a stapler, just the khaki-clad Robbie Van Zandt.

"Oh, you frightened me for a second," I said. But only a second, because, despite his outbursts, Robbie was one of the least intimidating people on the planet. Even Truffle and Sweet Marie didn't bother to bark. They sniffed his shoes.

"Why shouldn't you be frightened? Look what you've done."

"What are you talking about?"

"Duh. Barb Douglas. Things were fine until you showed up, and now everything in my life has fallen apart."

"It wasn't my doing, Robbie. Not Barb and not Dyan."

He scowled at me. "Who cares about Dyan? She got what she deserved."

My mind was working fast. I had made, after all, a case against Robbie. I glanced at the window, but, big surprise, Jack wasn't watching. Probably waxing his bike or something. I noticed a retired neighbor across the street pottering around the garden. A bit too far away to attract attention, but close enough to get to.

"Let's go for a walk and talk about this," I said, smiling brightly.

"How stupid do you think I am?"

Crap.

"Actually, I don't think you're stupid at all."

"I *was* stupid, though, so that's something else you don't know."

"Not sure what you mean," I said, wondering if there was anything I could use as a weapon to bean him if I had to defend myself. Somehow pallid, shy Robbie seemed very threatening.

"We're going inside," he said.

"It's such a nice day. Why don't we talk out here?"

"Because there are witnesses."

"Oh. Well, I hope we're not going to need witnesses."

"I don't care what you hope. I have a gun. It's pointed straight at you. Get in that door and keep moving. You are going to do what I want."

I'd heard that if someone threatens you with a firearm, the best thing to do is run in a zigzag uneven pattern because the chances that you'll be hit are slight. The odds seemed somewhat higher with a weapon aimed at me, one foot away. No one was close enough to hear me, and even the neighbor across the street had gone inside.

I could make enough noise to attract Jack's attention, but then what? Would Robbie shoot Jack, too?

"I'll make you a coffee," I said. "We can talk over that. You can tell me why you're so angry."

"Well, now *I* think *you're* stupid," he said.

"Maybe, but I could really use another cup of coffee this morning. You can have one or not, suit yourself."

The hardest part is to keep the fear out of your voice. Inside the apartment, Truffle and Sweet Marie launched themselves at Robbie's legs, wanting to be picked up.

"Shhh," I said. "Try to be good. Go lie down."

As if.

"I don't mind them," Robbie said, to my surprise. "I like dogs, especially little ones."

For a heart-stopping moment, I thought he was mocking me and threatening the tiny naughty creatures I loved so much. Then I realized he meant it.

He bent down and scratched their necks, then rubbed their bellies. They fell for him hook, line, and sinker. The little rats. I should add that they are no judge of character.

Lucky for me, I can practically make coffee in my sleep. I carried in two oversize Woodbridge Library mugs that

Ramona had given me for an organizing talk I'd given. I loved the huge blue mugs. Could I heave one at the head of the man who was threatening me for whatever unfathomable reason? That might give me time to . . . no, not a good idea.

Turned out he didn't drink coffee. "Makes me jittery," he said. His hands were definitely shaky already. For the first time, I understood that Robbie was as nervous as I was. Maybe more.

"Have a seat. Here's a nice selection of Mars bars," I said. "They won't make you too jittery, and we may as well be civilized."

I perched on the end of the sofa. He took the only chair. The dogs lay down at his feet. Little traitors. I took a sip of my coffee.

"She's dead," he said.

I blurted out, "Who?"

He jumped to his feet. "Who do you think? What is the matter with you?"

I gasped. "Barb? She's dead? That's horrible."

He nodded.

"I am so sorry. I hadn't heard. I tried to get the police to—"

"They're useless. They won't listen. That's why I'm here. You are partly responsible and you are going to help me find her."

My jaw dropped. I managed to speak. "But you just said she's dead. You mean you don't know where her . . . body is?" That sounded insensitive even to my own ears.

I watched his pale anxious face. I could almost feel his misery. He said, "She must be. Why would she do this to me otherwise? But if she's not, we have to find her. But I don't know what to do anymore. I'm not even making sense."

"Robbie, I really want to find her, too. Believe me. And

I need to know that you won't freak out over anything I say. I won't put up with any more accusations or blame or threats."

His chin wobbled.

I said, "So whatever we do from now on will be on my terms. Or we don't work together. Your choice."

"All right. I don't know where to start."

"Do you really have a gun, Robbie?"

He shook his head. "I was just bluffing. I didn't want you to run away. I needed to—" He pulled a Baby Ruth candy bar from his pocket.

I felt like a doofus for being spooked into thinking a candy bar was the muzzle of a gun. But I wasn't frightened anymore. "Okay, listen and don't get upset. The problem is that Barb Douglas knew the man who was found dead in the blue Impala on the edge of town on Sunday. Did you hear about that in the news?"

"She knew him?"

"Yes. I don't know in what capacity, but he had driven her home a few times. The people who own her building saw them. I think that news is what sent her running from the office."

"But what does this mean?"

"I don't know. They could have been colleagues. Could have been friends. I haven't been able to find out anything more. Except that they saw each other a lot."

To my horror, tears welled up in Robbie's eyes. "Maybe they were related."

"I hadn't thought of that. The police haven't given out his name. They're playing their cards close to their chests on this one. Maybe if we knew where she was from—"

"I thought she loved me. I think she did. Does. I believe it. I believe in her. I won't let this change that." He stopped and glared at me. "If we can find her, I know she'll have a good reason for having disappeared."

"You're right. She doesn't want the people who killed this man to kill her. She has panicked and gone into hiding. Let's hope she can keep a step ahead of them."

"Maybe she's gone home to her family."

I almost spilled my coffee. Of course. Her family. "Excellent idea. Do you know anything about them?"

"She never talked about them." He looked at me sheepishly and glanced away. "I tried to Google her, but there were so many people with that name. None of them her."

"Listen, Robbie. I have some ideas to follow up on. I'll check car rental agencies, for instance, but I'll need a photo of her, because I'm sure she wouldn't use her real name. Do you have one?" I knew he did, but I didn't want him to know that I knew that. I didn't figure I'd get my stolen copy back from Pepper without a hair-pulling session.

"I have one, on my phone. We were clowning around in the office and I snapped a picture of her. I can send it to you. Do you have a printer here?" Robbie did his best to look casual, but his deep flush gave him away.

"I have a mini-printer for photos," I said, pointing toward my office. "E-mail me the photo, and I'll print it for you."

"I'll just use my memory stick," he said.

Minutes later, as the photo of Barb slid from the printer, Robbie said, "I can come with you to the rental companies."

The last thing I needed was Robbie threatening a car rental employee and having the strategic response team show up.

"I have a better idea. You can get her personnel file from Quovadicon."

"That won't take any time. We can just ask Fredelle."

I shook my head. "I don't want Fredelle to know that I'm involved in any way."

"Why not?"

"Because she lied to me, Robbie, when she asked me to come to try to help about Barb's desk. I find that suspicious. And later she told me I wasn't welcome at Quovadicon."

He flushed and looked away. "I think all that was my fault, because I was upset about Barb. I told my father you were making trouble."

"Even so. I don't want to deal with Fredelle. I don't know what she's really up to. And anyway, I can't go back to Quovadicon because some people believe I tricked the staff into leaving and then killed Dyan."

"So we're stuck again."

"Not really, Robbie. You have the run of the place. Nobody finds you suspicious."

"What can I do?"

He sure wasn't one to pick up on an idea quickly. "You can get your mitts on Barb's personnel file without anyone knowing, not even Fredelle. It's underhanded, but we need to find out where she comes from. She might be hiding with a relative or former co-worker. Remember, we don't want anyone to know that we're doing it. Or that you have any connection with me. And don't get caught. Remember what happened to Dyan."

He nodded. "I'll do it. The office staff is all in by nine. Fredelle will be at her desk. But maybe I should wait until tonight. I like it better when no one's around, just a few guys in the warehouse and the truckers."

"Did you say the warehouse guys and truckers are there in the night?"

"Depends on what's coming in and going out, but I don't usually see them."

"That reminds me. Two guys in a truck helped me after . . . the situation with Barb. I thought their names were Mel and Del, but Fredelle said no one with those names works for your company. Do they sound familiar?"

He shook his head. "I don't mix with those guys. I might recognize their faces."

"Oh well. Try to get the file in the daytime without attracting attention."

"I know where the keys are kept. You really think this file might help?"

"Let's hope."

Robbie looked bleak. "We have to hope that things don't get any worse."

Reserve one outfit for disaster mornings:
no hot water, slept in, sick pet—you know the scenario.
Make sure it's professional and comfortable
and looks good on you.
It will help you stay confident as your day wears on.

16

By eleven, my head felt much clearer and I decided to make the rounds of the car rental companies. It was time to shower, shampoo, ditch the pajamas, and dress like big people. I reached for my disaster-morning outfit. I slipped on the raspberry sleeveless turtleneck and matching cardigan, enjoying the feel of soft cotton cashmere. September days can freeze or fry, so I could always slip off the cardigan if the temperature soared. I kept this favorite, two-year-old outfit ready for rough days: the chunky dark necklace would keep it on the right side of snazzy. The plain chocolate lightweight wool trousers had a comfortable stretch, and my glossy short boots were butter soft and easy on the feet. I was ready to go.

As I was leaving home, I got a call from a woman who was desperate to deal with her teenage daughter's disastrous bedroom. "Emergency," she said. "Can you come tonight?" I explained that I'd had a head injury and there was a small chance I might have to cancel, but I would do my best. I wrote down her phone number and address. I felt good doing something so normal.

Luckily, there were only three car rental offices in Woodbridge, and by noon I'd been through them all. No one had recognized Barb from her photo, although one customer had noticed Barb on television.

So the car rental was a dead end. That left stolen cars. Maybe even harder to get information on those. Unless . . . I got into the Miata and cruised by the police station. I kept going and pulled in front of Doug's Donuts, a favorite spot of the Woodbridge constabulary. Sure enough, parked at the counter, leering at a glazed chocolate number with white chocolate filling, was Nick Monahan.

"Hey, Charlie. You look good enough to—"

"Don't go there," I snapped. I then moderated my tone quickly. "So, Nick. I need to know something, and you're the one person who probably knows the answer."

His chest puffed up. Predictably. "Yeah, what is it?"

"Stolen cars."

He frowned. "Your car get stolen?"

"No."

"But—"

"Long story. It's a bit of research I'm doing."

He nodded knowingly. "You taking a course?"

"In a way. I was wondering if the type of cars that are stolen on a typical afternoon would be different from the type of cars stolen in the morning."

"Boy, it would take a while to go back over the year and figure that out."

"Sorry," I said, "my research just focuses on this week."

"Just this week?" Nick was losing interest in me and eyeing the doughnut lustfully.

"Yes."

He nodded, eyes still on the doughnut case.

"Let me get you another couple of those, Nick."

"Thanks, Charlie, but it's not much work. We only had one car stolen here this week and it was, hey—"

"Hey!" I echoed. "I bet that means Monday? Late afternoon?"

"Yeah, how did you know?"

"I'm a good guesser. Was it near Lilac Lane by any chance?" I gestured to the man behind the counter. "Half dozen chocolate glazed for my friend here." I slapped Nick on the back.

He frowned in concentration. "You know, it was maybe two blocks from there. Iris Street. You're good."

"No one knows cars like you do, Nick. What make of car, by the way?" I said.

"Well, that's true. I do know cars." He chuckled a bit at his own cleverness. "It was a black Civic, '99, new paint job, though. Mint condition."

"A black Civic."

"But you could have guessed that."

"Why?"

"Thieves love the older Honda Civics. Pop the locks like that." He snapped his fingers. "And if they don't have an alarm system or keyless entry, they're gone, looking like half the other cars on the road. Ten minutes later, they're in a chop shop. Thought you'd have picked that up in your research."

"Thank you," I said. "That's impressive, Nick."

I had a feeling this was one Civic that wouldn't end up in the chop shop. Black would be good for Barb. Why rent and be identified when you could pop the lock and off you go? Black would be pretty well invisible at night. I had a feeling the plates would have been switched with some other vehicle's, something with a bit of dust on it. I was smiling as I said good-bye to Nick.

"Let me know how your research turns out, Charlie."

"Sure thing," I said.

I had a few other errands while I was in the uptown area. I swung by Kristee's Kandees and picked up three boxes of black-and-white fudge, gift wrapped. A box for Sally, a box for Margaret, and a spare one in case I needed a quick gift. I got a plain box for me, too. If a head injury doesn't entitle you to black-and-white fudge, I don't know what would.

On my way out, I headed over to check out Dream Stories, the linen boutique that had opened recently. I like the boutiques uptown and downtown, and in my business I have to know what's cutting-edge on all fronts. I hoped to see some innovative storage as well as gorgeous bed and window coverings. I knew that would be great ammunition for the consultation about my new client's daughter's disastrous bedroom. I knew from previous experience that youthful décor plus the right storage options had been known to win over most adolescents.

I picked up a cheap cell phone and bought enough minutes to keep me going until I settled with my provider. I'd already canceled the other one, although not in time to save me grief.

On the way to meet Robbie, I stopped for gas just off the interstate. As I left the service station, I noticed a nondescript white van at one of the pumps. More to the point, the driver noticed me. So did Del, who was filling the tank. Something told me that stopping to ask them about Barb was not an option. Del dropped the nozzle and raced to the passenger side. Before he jumped in, I gunned the Miata, which has a lot more pep than any old van. I shot out of the service station and sped back onto the interstate. I'd always thought that feeling someone's eyes on your back was a cliché. This time, it felt like a threat. I got off at the next exit and took the secondary roads to my destination.

I hadn't been worried about Mel and Del before this. Now I was.

I used my new cell phone to call Robbie. We arranged to meet at Betty's, my favorite diner. Well, everyone's favorite diner. Sooner or later, you'll run into everyone in Woodbridge and surrounding communities there. Despite the fact that Robbie and I were now in cahoots, I wasn't crazy about spending time alone with him. Betty's was perfect. It wasn't far from Quovadicon, and I'd never seen a police officer in the place. Not that there was anything illegal about having a bite to eat with Robbie Van Zandt. The rest of what we'd be doing, well, it was necessary.

Robbie burst through the door just as I was polishing off one of Betty's famous club sandwiches with hand-cut fries.

"Sorry," I said, "I couldn't wait. The sight of all this food reminded me I'm behind a few meals."

"Bad news," he said.

Patsy Magliaro, our aging hippie waitress, sashayed up to the table at that exact minute. "Oh, hi, Robbie. I didn't know you and Charlotte knew each other. That's nice."

The deer-in-the-headlights look didn't really suit Robbie. For a moment, I thought he'd been stunned by her tie-dyed skirt or maybe the long gray braid.

"Colleagues," I said, hoping to nip Patsy's conversation in the bud. Of course, I had no such luck.

"That was a terrible thing about the murder at your warehouse," she prattled on, not taking the hint.

Patsy didn't really take hints. However, she was kind and helpful and I liked her a lot. Even if she'd once almost gotten me killed.

"I don't want to talk about it," Robbie said, growing even paler.

"Sure, hon. You want your usual? It's the same as Charlotte's. Even the dessert. You want your Devil's Food Special or you want to wait for Robbie, Charlotte? You know, Robbie, you really need to get a bit more sun."

We both stared at her back as she moseyed toward the kitchen, braid swinging, Birkenstocks shuffling, tie-dyed skirt swaying with a slow cheerfulness, if there was such a thing.

"Don't worry about Patsy," I said. "She won't even remember she saw us this time tomorrow."

"Why did you say that?"

"What? About Patsy?"

"Yeah, not remembering."

"Just in case the police take an interest in it. After all—" I leaned forward and lowered my voice, a bit later than I should have. "You got that file illegally."

He shrugged. "That's the thing . . ."

I waited.

Finally I said, "What thing?"

"There was—"

"Here you go, Robbie," Patsy said.

Robbie jumped.

Patsy added, "Fresh batch of fries. Do you have the timing or what? Don't worry. There's more where that came from. Extra chicken in the club, just the way you like it."

She must say that to all the customers because there'd been no way that club had been made up especially for Robbie. I knew that the kitchen staff at Betty's went through dozens of the same favorites every day, and they managed to keep on top by preparing ahead.

Robbie just nodded. Didn't speak.

"And Charlotte, here's your dessert. I figured you need it, being involved in another murder so soon."

"Don't talk about murder, Patsy. It ruins my appetite."

"Mum's the word," she whispered and tiptoed away backward, finger to her lips. Naturally, every other customer in our section stared at her with interest. Betty's? What had I been thinking?

"I can't eat this," Robbie said. "My stomach's in knots. I might be sick."

"You're not going to be sick. Tell me what happened."

"The file was there."

"Yes." A slight edge had crept into my voice.

"But it was empty."

"What?"

"Empty. Empty. Empty."

"Actually, I heard you."

"That means someone else took it."

"Of course."

"And that means—"

I finished his sentence, "That we are not the only people who are interested in Barb's background."

"This is really bad news."

"Is there another place it could have been stored? Ready to be filed?"

He shook his head. "All the files are kept in a central filing cabinet in Fredelle's office. Fredelle never gets behind on her filing, but I did check everywhere else just in case. I even looked in the nearby files in case it was misfiled."

"Oh boy. Who else had access to her files?"

"Theoretically, no one."

"Maybe the police took it. Barb's missing. Just because they pretended not to be interested doesn't mean they weren't. I think it's a power thing."

"I don't believe it was the police," Robbie said. "When a file is removed, Fredelle makes the person sign for it, and then she places a card in the section saying who has it.

There wasn't any card there. She would have filled one out even if the police refused to sign for it. But why would they do that?"

"So it probably wasn't the police. It wasn't me. It wasn't you. So who does that leave?"

"Any one of the employees of Quovadicon, I suppose. Someone might have known how to get the keys."

I thought about Mel and Del or whatever their names really were. "Let's narrow it down. Do the warehouse people have access to the keys to Fredelle's office?"

He shook his head. "No. And I doubt if they would have been in a position to spot where she hid them. They're not in the main office that much. They even have their own lunchroom."

"Okay, that leaves the office staff and the sales force and customers."

More head shaking. "A customer would never find this key."

A thought flitted through my head. "Did Barb know where the key was?"

He frowned. "Barb?"

"Yes. Face it. She doesn't want to be found. She's an intelligent woman. She knows what kind of information is in the files."

"You think she took the files to hide personal information about herself?" His face seemed to crumble. "So that I couldn't find her? Couldn't she trust me? I'd do anything for her."

We had no time to wallow in Robbie's special pool of self-pity. I said, "She did it so no one could find her. She needed to disappear as soon as she heard the news about her friend. She knew this man was dead and I'm guessing she knew why."

Robbie blinked. "But when she got that call, it was a shock to her. She grabbed her purse and tore off out of the building. She almost knocked Autumn over on the way. I tried to follow Barb and she told me to leave her alone. I—"

I had to stop him. There would be time enough for sympathy when this was done. "You're saying she didn't have time to get the files. She just left."

"Everyone was stunned by it."

"Everyone? Who else was there?"

He closed his eyes, to concentrate, I assumed. "Fredelle. She was really nervous that day. Worse than usual. She screamed when Barb rushed by."

"I think she was nervous about the potential effect of my visit to the office. Who else?"

"Dyan. And one of the sales guys. I don't know his name."

"Dyan?"

"Yes. She was constantly snooping around. She was never at her own desk. Always pretending to be photocopying. Missy never spent much time making copies."

I wondered if he could see the lightbulb going on over my head. "Oh, right. Missy."

"Now *she's* a really nice person. She always had time for people, and she didn't stick her nose in everyone's business and try to make trouble."

"Unlike Dyan."

"Right. Everyone hated her."

"And someone hated her enough to kill her."

His eyes widened. "It wasn't me. Even though it was in my office, it wasn't me. I think I could have, but I didn't."

"I believe you, Robbie. You weren't even in the building."

"That's right."

All the same, Robbie was still not completely off my suspect list. Perhaps that's why I chose not to tell him to keep an eye out for Barb in a black Honda Civic. "One last thing, Robbie. You have a sophisticated IT system. Have any of the personnel files been maintained on that system?"

He squinted at me. "It's mostly to track orders and shipments, big customer files, that kind of data. Not so much stuff about employees. Fredelle's a bit old-fashioned about technology. She can barely use a computer. A lot of it's in her head."

"Fredelle mentioned that your father was the person who hired Barb." Not quite the truth. Missy had told me that.

He blinked. "But why?"

"I have no idea. But I suppose Fredelle wouldn't argue with him about her."

"Argue? She'd never argue with him. She worships the ground he walks on. She always has."

"Maybe she felt hurt that he took the initiative to hire the new IT person out of her hands."

He kept shaking his head while I was speaking. "No. No. No. Fredelle isn't like that. She doesn't have a big ego. It's not all about her. It's all about my dad and the company and me, too. She loves us and she loves Quovadicon. Whatever he wants is good for her."

"And if someone tried to harm you or your father or the company, do you think she could be dangerous?"

"No! Stop coming up with these crazy theories. Have you seen her? She's a sweet little lady. She's almost sixty-five. She loves puppies. She couldn't hurt anyone."

I said nothing, just thought about Fredelle lying to me. Robbie believed she was a saint, but I didn't buy it.

Patsy sauntered over again and frowned at Robbie's plate. "Want me to box that up for you? Shame to waste it."

Robbie shook his head. I knew Patsy enough to say yes. Otherwise she'd never leave us alone.

"Sure thing, Robbie. Maybe dessert's what you need."

"Box up his dessert, too," I said. "And can you do the same for mine, please, Patsy?"

Robbie looked grateful. I felt sorry for him. As Patsy drifted away to box the desserts, I said, "Now I need *you* to do something for me."

"What?"

"Check out Dyan's desktop and see if she had any information about Barb. Can you do that without getting caught?"

"I can do anything without getting caught."

I thought we'd earned our cake. Anyway, on a week like this, you never know when you'll have a chance to sit down and eat again.

Missy opened the door and wiped her hair out of her eyes. It took a couple of seconds before she recognized me. Behind her a child wailed.

"I saw you on television," she said. She didn't smile.

"Yes."

"It had to do with the company and Dyan's death. The police said they'd be questioning you."

I did my best not to appear dangerous. I had stopped at home on the way and picked up Truffle and Sweet Marie. They can be great at defusing tension. This turned out to be a waste of effort as Missy didn't pay any attention to either of them. She was interested in me and my relationship with the police.

I didn't try to explain Nick to her. I was glad I no longer needed the bandage on my head. It did give me the look of a desperado.

"That was just one officer. He changed his mind. I was injured by the killer, too."

"If you don't mind me saying, it wouldn't be hard to fake an injury."

I had to admire her. No wonder she was missed at Quovadicon. The airheaded Autumn and the late Dyan couldn't compete with this supermom. She wasn't finished though. "Honey," she called back into the house, "can you come out here, please?"

"Honey," when he rumbled through the door, had probably played fullback for the high school team. He looked like nothing had turned to fat. He also looked like he was crazy about his clever, nice, and pretty blond wife and would do anything to protect her from nasty little organizing villains like me and my dogs. He scowled at them.

I said, "Sorry. I had to have the dogs here. I hope they don't make you nervous. They're in training to be therapy dogs, and the more exposure they have to different people and situations, the better."

He scratched his head. "Therapy dogs? You mean they go to a psychiatrist?"

She bit back what seemed to be a fond smile. "No, honey. They go into hospitals and nursing homes to help people relax. It's good for the blood pressure and reduces stress. Remember Granny with her cats?"

"Huh."

I seized the opportunity. "I know you're busy with the twins and I realize that this is pretty weird, but I was hired originally to help Barb Douglas with her desk."

Missy seemed to relax a bit. Maybe because hubby was there. She chuckled. "Oh that desk! It's getting to be legendary."

"Yes, that's the point. It seemed to have been legendary almost from the moment she arrived. As if she didn't want anybody to come near it."

She met my eyes. That clicked. "I wondered," she said, "how it could get so bad so fast, but it seemed kind of mean to mention it. And Robbie was so keen for me to be nice to her."

"There's something wrong about the whole production,"

I said. "She's missing. I don't know if you are aware of that. No one can find her, and a man we believe she was associated with was found dead in the trunk of his car. I need to find out about her, and I keep hitting brick walls."

The sleeping giant took that moment to wake up and glower at me. "She's missing? And you're involved? Maybe you should just stay away from my wife and family."

Missy bit her lip.

"Thanks," I said, talking as fast as I could. "I need to know why she picked Quovadicon, how she came to be there."

He lumbered forward. "You better leave now or I'm getting the cops."

I called his bluff. "Go ahead, call them. They know I'm here."

He opened his mouth, closed it again, glowered, and thought about that.

I rattled on, "There's no information about her. Nothing. No relatives, no next of kin. No work history."

Missy snorted. "Of course there is. It's all in the personnel files."

"They're missing. I just want to know how she came to work at Quovadicon."

Luckily, Missy didn't ask me why I didn't approach Fredelle about this seemingly innocuous request. "No harm in it, I guess. It was sort of a secret, but no, with all this terrible stuff going on, perhaps you should talk to Mr. Van Zandt. I think I told you that he brought her in. He said he didn't want everyone to know that he did."

"But why the secrecy?"

She shook her head. "I have no idea."

"Didn't anyone ask?"

"He plays his cards close to his chest, as my grandpa would say."

"Well, Robbie must have known. Maybe that's why he wanted people to like her."

"Boy, for a smart lady, you're sure missing that point. Mr. Van Zandt didn't think that Robbie could tie his own shoelaces. He wouldn't consult him on bringing in a new hire."

"Not consult perhaps, but surely Robbie would know."

"Nope. Robbie never had the vaguest idea what his father's plans were. He was kept right out of the loop on everything."

"So he had no clue."

"Right."

"Fredelle would have known."

Missy frowned, perhaps because the sound of an infant crying drifted through the screen door. A look of panic fluttered over her large husband's face.

"I don't think Fredelle did know. She had some surgery around that time. I handled the paperwork and filed it. It was just before I left to have the twins, a bit earlier than I planned. I never really filled her in. So unless Mr. Van Zandt told her, there wasn't much in the files beyond a couple of references. I don't even remember seeing her résumé."

"But a new position, surely she'd be consulted on that as office manager. Was it a new position?"

"Consulted? Not so much. Mr. Van Zandt isn't so big on consultation. I think she found out after she came back and Barb was there. She'd just accept that. And I would have, too."

"Really."

She grinned and pushed her hair out of her eyes. "I can't do anything with this mop since the twins came along."

Her hubby said, "You still look good to me."

I put in my two cents' worth. "And twins would be worth a bit of extra styling products."

"For sure."

That was good. They'd both relaxed a bit.

Another wail wafted through the door, and hubby looked ready to panic. I said, "I should let you get back to them, but one more question. So you're saying Fredelle wouldn't get upset to be treated as if her opinion didn't count?"

Missy shrugged. "I've been trying to explain. We were all used to it. It's a one-man kingdom and Mr. Van Zandt is the ruler. Fredelle didn't mind. Nobody else cared. Except Robbie and Dyan, of course."

"One more thing, I need to talk to a couple of your drivers. I believe their names are Mel and Del?"

She shook her head. "I know all the drivers. No Mels or Dels."

"They may have been kidding about their names. Mel's middle-aged, oversize seventies-style mustache. Del's younger, shaved head, Celtic tattoos. Big guys, both of them. Mel wears a baseball cap."

A flicker of recognition showed in her eyes. It was replaced by a guarded expression. I wasn't sure what I'd done. "I know who you mean. But they don't work for us, I mean Quovadicon anymore. Oh boy. My husband panics when the twins cry. I have to go."

"Wait, can you tell me their names?"

But I was talking to the air. Both of them had vanished into the interior.

Not so fast, lady, I thought. I knocked on the door again. Politely, but firmly. I rang the doorbell for good measure.

The husband showed up at the door again. He was sweaty and on the verge of panic to my eye. For some reason, that made him seem even larger.

"Go away and stay away," he said.

Resist the urge to multitask.
In the long run, each activity will take longer.

17

Lucky for me, I had a savings account, because I wasn't going to make anywhere near my expenses on this particular week. If you work for yourself, you have to sock away extra during the good times. Savings account or not, I was happy to check out the teenage girl's chaotic bedroom that evening. No office politics there, no missing women, but probably plenty of mother/daughter dramatics.

The day hadn't yielded much, despite a chunk of time wasted cruising around Woodbridge to check out black Honda Civics. Eventually I drove home to drop off the dogs and try a few training tricks. They were not in the mood. "Not optional," I told them.

I managed to eat a stir-fry instead of ice cream for dinner and to gather up some materials for the client visit. I find that having some fun photos and options available can make a difference with adolescents. Even so, sometimes nothing makes the difference.

I fixed my hair and makeup, switched into dark denim dress jeans and my fitted leather jacket with a scarf, and headed out. My headache had subsided. I wasn't under arrest or under attack. Plus this client was one of the few people in Woodbridge who hadn't seen me on television during my frequent crime sprees, and I loved her for it.

The disastrous bedroom was worth the trip. As I stood with my client at the open door, I estimated an even two feet of clothing strewn on the floor. The bed was unmade. Glasses and plates covered the surfaces. Curling posters of boy bands that I didn't recognize covered the walls. Schoolbooks and papers and art supplies were strewn on top of the layer of clothing. The dominant scent was stale pizza with a hint of last week's gym clothes. A Chihuahua in a pink jeweled collar moved through tunnels under the garments, appearing occasionally to bare tiny teeth and yip at us. I am always pleased when someone else owns a naughty dog.

My client bit her lip. "I can't even catch the little monster. Sydney says we can't go in her room because it's private property and it would be a violation of her rights."

"Really?" I said.

"I suppose that's true, too."

I let it slide. Not my relationship. "Is she around?"

"She's taken over the basement and refuses to participate. I really don't know what to do. I am sorry to have dragged you all this way. Of course, I'll pay you for your time."

Excellent. That saved me from making the point to her. I said, "Let's be optimistic. I have some samples of rooms to show you. They're fun. I see a lot of art supplies. Is she artistic?"

The mother shrugged. "How would I know? She never talks to me. Do you think this disaster is her way of keeping me out?"

"My guess is she's just defining herself."

"I worry about what's she's hiding. Marijuana plants or

something. I don't even know what. I'm not a snoop, but if I were, I'd never find it anyway."

"Or she's just growing up and wanting to make her own decisions."

"What do you think I should do?"

"I'll leave the samples for you. And you can tell Sydney that if she's interested that she and I can work together and you'll—"

"Mind my own business?"

"I was going to say 'pick your battles.' "

"That's what my therapist tells me. Unlike some of my friends' children, at least Sydney stays home long enough to create and maintain this . . ."

Turbulence, I thought. "Did your therapist suggest that you stop doing her laundry?"

"How did you know?"

"Just a guess," I said with a glance at the ocean of clothing in front of us. I kept a straight face, too, as we headed for neutral territory to check out the samples. I bet myself that Sydney would show up within fifteen minutes, sit sulkily with us, and sneer at everything I brought. I won that bet. I also figured that Sydney would want to meet with me on her own, but she'd never let herself look excited about it. Right again.

—

My new client's mother stood waving from the front porch of the house as I left. It had been worth the long drive home on the interstate just to see the look on her face. Sydney and I now had an appointment booked for Monday evening. She had some fun prep work to do on the weekend, mainly identifying what she used her room for, such as studying, socializing, hobbies, music. I asked her to consider whether she wanted to see her clothing or keep it out of view. Although as most of it was on the floor, I thought I knew the answer. I waved back as I backed out and eased the Miata onto the street. I was grinning, too, as I headed for the highway. The project had taken my mind off recent events. It was positive and soothing, and there was a chance that everyone would be happy with the outcome. Now all I had to do was head home, walk the dogs again, and what? The grin faded.

Of course, being late September, it was already dark before eight. I had nothing much to do that evening, except envy my friends: Sally busy with her family, Margaret busy with her TDG man, Jack busy planning the bike race that ate the world and . . . but I didn't want to think about that.

Unfortunately, dog training can chew up only so much time. Maybe tonight would be a good time to clean out the freezer. I could relabel all the frozen foods with fresh crisp date info. Maybe I could color-code them according to contents. That would be fun. Red for meat and chicken, yellow for soups, green for vegetables, and white for ice cream, although that didn't last long enough for dates to be an issue.

Of course, labels could peel and curl. Or else be impossible to get off the tops of containers. What about color-coded containers? That would be even better than mere labels. I could get lovely square ones that would fit together and look nice and neat in the freezer. Perhaps a trip to the Container Store was in order.

These were pleasant and diverting thoughts as I motored along. And except for the number of trucks on the road, it would have been a relaxing drive back. But why are huge trucks so unnerving on the highway at night? Perhaps it's their size, or the weird way their front views simulate menacing human faces. The semi behind me was driving too close for safety. *It's just nerves*, I told myself, *they're vehicles full of sacks of sugar and plastic soda bottles and disposable diapers. There's nothing threatening about them.*

Get back to thinking about that freezer of yours. What needs to be done?

Hold on. Who was I kidding? Except for a new stash of Ben & Jerry's, two bags of stir-fry veggies, and a variety of fancy ice cubes, my freezer was a vast empty wasteland. I had absolutely no need for containers. Of course, that could change. Maybe I should make some soup, and that would allow me to label it. I could swing by Hannaford's and pick up the soup ingredients and jump-start that project. After all, I already had the labels. Of course, I had no idea what was actually in homemade soup. Onions? Celery? Chickens? Magic spells? It wasn't like my mother had ever whipped up a batch of savory stock. That's what caterers were for.

Before I started my soup campaign, it might be a good idea to actually get some soup recipes. That would be another pleasant diversion. I could print out the recipes and put them in a little binder. Or keep them in a folder on my computer. Or would it be better to get a cookbook? A soup cookbook. There was a lovely new and used bookstore uptown on the arcade. That might be the best thing. I could get advice, as I had never actually owned a cookbook. It might represent more of a commitment to this soup venture than merely printing recipes from the Web or scoring a copy of *Soup for Total Losers.*

Of course, it wouldn't take a team of shrinks long to figure out that I didn't need soup at all. My usually smooth workweek had been chaotic; I was feeling lonely; my social network seemed to be in self-destruct mode; my best friend was lost to me, perhaps forever; and I needed a new way to use my downtime. Perhaps one that wouldn't involve chopping celery.

I was still two exits away from my route, but I was fed

up with the looming truck. Time for a different route. I wanted to ditch that turkey. I signaled and moved over to the exit lane. The truck pulled over, too. He was still close enough that his headlights made it hard for me to see. Never mind. At least there wasn't much chance that he'd be going my way.

Wrong.

I turned left to head back into Woodbridge. He followed. I decided I didn't want those headlights behind me all the way into town. Easily dealt with. I swung right to take the old route into town. No truck driver in his right mind would take this route. It was peppered with stop signs, hidden driveways, and blind corners. Plus it went through Vineland Estates, which had ridiculously low speed limits.

Just what I wanted.

Apparently just what he wanted, too. *We'll see about that*, I decided, making a quick right, stopping at the second stop sign, and then managing an even quicker left. Next I turned right to get onto a long and winding road that was scenic in the day and quiet and empty at night.

So long, sucker.

My heart rate soared as the headlights followed. What the hell? He wasn't even slowing down for those stop signs. His wheels squealed as he took the turns too fast for safety.

There's never a cop around when you want one. And I really wanted one. I would even have been happy to see Nick the Stick at that point.

But come on, someone had to see this huge thuggish vehicle barreling through a residential area. But although there were lights in the houses and the flicker of televisions, no one stood on their lawn chatting, no one was conveniently pulling their car into their driveway. I was on my own.

I gunned the Miata and sped ahead. The lights got no farther behind. In fact, I thought they were getting closer. I needed to attract attention fast. I leaned on my horn, staccato beeps followed by long, loud blasts, then beeps again. Three short, three long, three short, all run together. SOS. My organized childhood badges continued to pay off.

Please someone hear me and stick your head out the door. This guy thinks he has no witnesses. Bad, bad news, because at the end of this small development was a track of parkland surrounded by woods. My heart rate spiked again. Was this where the Impala was found? Had that driver been run off the road by a truck straight out of a horror movie and then murdered? I tried not to think about the body in the trunk.

Whatever else happened, I had to stay where someone might spot me. I didn't know Vineland Estates well, but I remembered that several of the streets ended up on the route to the park. The others appeared to keep going around in circles, crescents, and possibly spirals straight to hell.

I pressed on the accelerator and rocketed around a corner. The truck stayed on my tail. In my rearview mirror I could see it wasn't hauling a trailer, just the cab. Who knew one of those could whip around like that? The Miata is easy to handle and turn. I kept making short sharp twists. I changed my direction without warning, up and down the meandering crescents of this seemingly uninhabited neighborhood. I kept leaning on the horn. Still, by the time anyone stuck their head out the front door, I would have zoomed on to the next street. Would anyone ever spot the speeding truck and call the cops?

By this time, I felt angry as well as desperate. With all those paved driveways and basketball hoops, couldn't one kid be out practicing layups? Did everything have to stop just because it was dark? What was this country coming to?

My cell phone was in my handbag, within reach, but I needed both hands to hang on to the wheel. As I shot down a relatively straight stretch of road on Malbec Crescent, I held the wheel with one hand and unzipped the purse with my other. By the time I yanked out the phone, the truck had gained. He was almost on my bumper. I floored it and flew into the next crescent. The roar behind me told me he had the same plan.

Valpolicella was the same as every other street in the area, the houses well-spaced with large lush lawns. I thought about driving straight across one of the lawns, but I worried about sinking into a backyard pool. Plus, the spaces between the houses were so wide that the truck could just follow. I pictured myself up against a fence with the cab pushing me into it. As I struggled not to panic, I shot past a house with a three-car garage that narrowed the space between it and its neighbor. I jerked the wheel and did a U-turn past the truck. I switched off my lights, then turned again sharply and careened down the side lawn and between the two houses. Luckily there was no pool, and better yet, no fence between this property and the one in back of it. I flew across the property and out onto the street behind. I needed to get out of the view of the truck for long enough to hide myself and my car.

Halfway down whatever wine street I had turned onto, luck smiled on me. A double garage door was open, one car inside. I turned sharply, hit the brakes, and slid into the garage. I hopped out of the Miata and spotted the garage door button. I pushed it and heard not only the rattle of the door closing, but also the rumble of the cab approaching.

My heart was still pounding as the garage door automatic light flicked off. I stood there in the pitch dark, disoriented. Why hadn't I looked to see where the door to the house was? At least I still had my cell phone in my hand. I managed to flick the phone open and call 911 by the dim light of the tiny screen.

"Help! I'm being chased by a crazy truck driver! I think he's trying to kill me. Get someone out here soon!"

Mona Pringle's familiar snide tone responded. "That you again, Charlotte?"

Oh boy. I guess she owns the four-to-midnight shift. "Yes."

"Well, the fun never ends."

"Mona," I whispered, "it's not fun. I don't know where he is. I am in a garage and it's dark and I don't know if he is outside. He could drive his truck through the door and crush me and maybe he's listening."

Okay, I realized how nutty that sounded, but it was all true, if a bit jumbled.

"Where are you?"

"I told you, in a garage."

"Address?"

"I don't know. Somewhere in Vincland Estates. The street's parallel to Valpolicella on the south side. I don't know the street name or the number of the house. He was chasing me and I just drove in and closed the door. I kept blowing my horn but no one heard me."

"Oh, people heard you all right. We got lots of calls about that truck chasing a Miata. I should have known you were involved. We have units on the way to the area. We'll try to find your location."

I blinked back hot tears, a response to the shock of the chase. "I'll try to find out, too."

The phone was a dim source of light, but perhaps enough to find a door. I felt my way along the garage wall.

Mona was squawking. "Charlotte?"

"I'm trying to find out where I am."

"Units are on their way."

"Tell them to watch for a big truck, just the cab."

"What color?"

"I don't really know. It was behind me shining its lights, they practically blinded me. And it's dark out, but I believe it was red."

"It'll have to do."

"Wait! It's a Volvo. I saw the name on the front."

"What about the license plate?"

I paused. I closed my eyes to recall. "There wasn't one."

"Well, there had to be one, Charlotte. That's the law."

"This guy's not so big on the law," I said. "There won't be many murderous trucks rampaging through this neighborhood. Tell them, if they see one, just stop it."

"Yeah. They figured that out already. And Charlotte?"

"What?"

"Maybe you should stay put."

"Well, I'm a sitting duck if that truck takes a run at this garage, if he saw me come in."

I picked up a rake as a weapon, not that a rake is much defense against a Volvo of any size or color. I hammered on the door to the house.

Nothing. No voices. No answer.

I tried the doorknob. To my astonishment, it opened. Lucky me, open garage door, open door to the house. Bless this family. Absentminded people went way up in my estimation. I stepped through the garage entrance and into the house. Everything was dark. No sign of anyone. At least the streetlight illuminated the interior enough to avoid tripping.

"Hello?" I said.

Nothing.

"Where are you?" Mona said.

"I'm inside someone's house. There doesn't seem to be anyone home. Mona, if I pick up the phone here and call 911, will you be able to tell where I am?"

Mona sounded miffed. "I was just going to suggest that." I could hear her calling out to someone else in the dispatch center that a call from Charlotte Adams would be coming in and to get the address. Pronto. "Don't turn off your cell, though," she said.

By this time I had stumbled into the kitchen. *Telephone, telephone, find a telephone.* At last I found the portable phone and pressed the three magic numbers. My fingers were shaking.

One of Mona's co-workers picked up immediately. "Okay, hang in there," she said, "we got you. Number forty-three Chianti Drive."

I slunk along the hallway and crawled along the living room floor. The house smelled of furniture polish and Tex-Mex leftovers that hadn't made it back to the fridge, and, unless I was mistaken, someone had been smoking an illegal substance. Were they all stoned? Was that why no one answered my knock? But I had more urgent matters to think about. I crawled through the living room and over to the large bay window. I stuck my head up and peered out onto the street. Clear. No one there, no one coming. I had just about let my guard down when the malevolent cab rumbled into view, slowly, creeping past each house. Most were in darkness, and not a human being was in sight. Were my diagonal tire tracks still on the lawn?

The truck stopped. Did I only imagine the evil hissing of the brakes? Smarten up, I told myself. There is no way he—or worse, they—can know you are here. Even if he spots your tire tracks, there's no possible way he can see you crouched here. The laws of physics don't permit it.

The truck backed up and turned toward the window where I was hiding. What had given me away? As the engine roared, I scrambled away from the window and across the hallway.

I shouted into both phones, "He's going to ram the house. Get some cars here fast. He's going to come right through the window!"

I dashed up the stairs, dropping the house phone handset.

I could hear the 911 operation squawking. In response to a truck that probably weighs eighteen tons, hurtling straight at you, flight is the only real choice. As I hit the second floor running, a door opened and a sleepy-looking teenaged boy in pajama bottoms lumbered into the hallway.

I screeched to a halt.

I believe we both screamed.

He rubbed his eyes.

I caught my breath and regained my equilibrium before he did. "He's taking a run at the house."

"What?"

"Is there a way out from the second floor? Oh no, I suppose not. This was a bad move on my part."

By this time, his adolescent jaw practically rested on his bony chest. I suppose he thought he was dreaming. He said, "Who are you?"

"I'm Charlotte. We absolutely need to get out of here right away. We're in danger, and I mean big-time."

"What?"

"Please stop saying *what*. I'll explain when we're safe. The back door might be blocked. If there are two of them in the truck."

"What? I mean two of . . . who?"

"Later. It will take too long. Is there a good hiding place here?"

"What?"

"No more *whats*. Someone is after me and they're about to ram your house with a truck."

He blinked.

Useless in a crisis. *Heaven help your future mate*, I thought.

So. Next move? Under the bed. Behind a door? Anyone who would chase an innocent person through a residential area and try to ram a house they were hiding in would not hesitate to search under a bed.

"We need a place to hide."

"Wha . . . I mean, there's the closet."

"They'll look in the closet. Is there a way out to the roof?"

"No. But I have a secret compartment in my closet. If you want to try it. There might be room for both of us. You're not too big. That is, if you're really real."

I followed him back into the bedroom. "What do you mean, if I'm really real?"

"I'm probably just dreaming you and this whole thing. I had a lot of tacos just before I went to sleep."

"You're not . . ." Wait a minute. Why was it so quiet? Shouldn't that damned semi have hit the house by now?

I headed through what must have been the parents' bedroom to the window and lifted the corner of the blind to check on the truck. A massive oak tree blocked my view of the lawn. I listened. I couldn't hear anything that sounded like an engine revving. Had they just come into the house instead?"

"Where's this hidey-hole?" I said. "Mona? We're heading into a hidey-hole in the boy's bedroom closet. They're about to ram the house with the truck."

"Never dull with you, is it?"

"Who's that?" the boy asked.

"911 operator."

"911?" he squeaked.

"Yes, the police are on their way."

"The police?"

I perked up. "Oh, hey. Is that sirens? That's great. Sounds like they're getting close already."

"Yeah. Oh shit. I better flush my stash."

"By all means," I said shakily, "we don't want to complicate an already unbelievably complicated situation."

He raced back to his room, grabbed a small bag of something, and scurried to the bathroom. As the sirens drew closer, I heard the toilet flush. One, two, three times. He wasn't a boy to take any chances.

I hurried down the stairs as the first knock sounded on the front door. I was filled with joy and relief until I heard a familiar voice.

Shorten your To Do list.
Pick the top five items for the day and sort them in priority order.
Don't add more than you can do.
Keep new tasks recorded on a master list.

18

"Charlie? Are you in there?"

What were the chances?

I opened the door. "Hello, Nick. What brings you here?"

"Hey, *you* called 911, babe."

"I figured I'd get patrol cars, not a detective. And don't call me *babe*."

"There are uniforms here, too. 911 call went out. So, like, what's this about a truck?"

Behind Nick's handsome head, a "uniform" rolled his eyes. Nick's all-around dopiness is well known inside and outside the force. Now with his wife Pepper on sick leave, he'd be on his own to figure things out.

I spoke past him to the officers on the pathway. "I was pursued by a truck. A big rig, Volvo. Red. Just the cab. No license plate. I think there were two people in it, but I can't be sure."

"Why would they chase you, Charlie? Did you cut 'em off in traffic or something?"

"No. They or maybe just he followed me from the interstate and . . ."

"Were you coming home from a club or something? Some guy figured he wanted to get a little friendly?"

Not everyone's like you, Nick, I thought. I raised my chin and stared him down. "I was at a client's home, and on the way back I noticed him on my tail. I thought he was just playing games, being a bully, trying to scare the woman in the little sports car. Having fun."

Out of the corner of my eye I could see the boy hovering nervously on the staircase.

"So what are you doing here?" Nick looked around. Sniffed the air.

The boy quivered.

I stepped outside, waving Nick along with me.

"I tried to outrun the truck. It followed me all through this subdivision. I was doubling back, blowing my horn, but he was determined."

One of the uniforms spoke up. "We got a lot of calls about that. They thought it was kids drag racing or something. So we've been driving around . . ."

The other one silenced his partner with a dirty look. "Let's let the lady tell her story."

There was hope for the force after all.

I continued. "There was a space between two houses over on Valpolicella. I thought my little car could fit in and maybe the truck wouldn't be able to, so I gave it a shot and ended up on this street."

"Chianti," the chatty one said.

The partner said, "Keep going, miss."

"So I spotted this open garage with only one car in it and I turned back and drove in."

Nick said, "Whose garage is it?"

"I don't know."

"You didn't even know them?"

"Right."

Nick would have trouble with that, a garage being a man's castle.

I preempted his next question. "I needed to hide."

Not that it worked. "You just drove into their garage, just like that?"

The smart uniform said, "She was being chased by a rig that would squash her and her Miata like a bug. So it'd be all right in that case."

I shot him a grateful look. "That's right. And I closed the door so the guy or guys who were trying to squash me wouldn't know where I had gone."

Nick's brow was furrowed. Perhaps he was trying for an intelligent and thoughtful appearance. "Hm. What happened then?"

"Well, I knocked on the door, hoping the homeowner would answer and we could call the police. And I called 911 on my cell phone."

"And did the homeowners answer and scare the guy or guys away?"

"No one answered, so I just went in to use the—"

"You unlawfully entered someone's house?" Nick shook his big beautiful empty head.

"Extenuating circumstances," the future of policing in Woodbridge said in my defense.

"I guess." Nick needed to chew on that one for a while.

"And I called 911 on the house phone so they'd know where I was, because I had no idea after that wild chase."

"But you were in someone else's house," Nick said.

I was just about to say, *Give it a rest*, when the boy stepped outside.

"I'm Jason," he said, "I live here. It's okay if she was in my house. I invited her in. It was an emergency."

Nick nodded sagely. "Okay, okay. Yep. That's good."

The smart officer's opinion of Nick seemed to be written right across his face, not that Nick would pick up on anything subtle like that.

I said, "Getting back to the issue of the truck. I peered out the window and saw it on the lawn, moving toward the house. I thought it was going to smash its way into the house and we'd be toast. I told the operator."

Not So Smart said, "Yeah, we got that one, too, but we thought—"

I didn't wait to be bailed out this time. I said, "Where is the truck? Did you spot it? It must have taken off when the patrol cars showed up."

Smarty said, "We didn't see him, but there's an APB out and—"

"That's an all-points bulletin, Charlie," Nick said. "We use them to—"

"Right. Everyone knows that. And they have the description?"

"Yes ma'am," the bright light said. "And we think we'll get a bit more from talking to some of the homeowners who called about the truck's rampage through the area. It will all help track down this guy."

"One thing I want to mention. There was a killing not far from here the other day."

All three of them nodded gravely.

The boy's eyes widened.

"I think the truck was trying to chase me into that area. It's very isolated. Maybe I would have ended up as a victim, too. Driven off the road, murdered, and then stuffed in my—"

Nick scratched his head. "Not much room in the trunk of your sports car, Charlie."

The smart officer said, "Do you have any reason to believe that this truck was connected to that?"

"While he was pursuing me, I realized where we were headed and what had happened, and I did everything I could to avoid that spot."

"Do you know anything about that murder?"

"Nothing," I said.

"You think someone is randomly targeting people on the interstate and then running them off the road? Thrill killing?"

"Yes, that could be it."

"Do you know anyone with a big rig?"

"No one. Except . . ."

"Yes, miss?"

I looked him straight in the eye while trying to appear rational. "This will sound crazy."

"Let's hear it."

"I was almost run off the road on my way to an appointment at Quovadicon on Monday; that's the day after that body was discovered."

"By a truck?"

"No. I got a look at a woman in an SUV. She was headed straight for me. I swerved and ended up on the median. My Miata got stuck on the cement planter."

Nick scratched his head again. "Try to stay on track. He's asking about trucks, Charlie."

The other officer didn't even glance at Nick. "It's okay, miss. Keep talking. You feel there's a connection?"

"First, a truck came down the road right after the SUV. There were two guys in it, and I was standing in the middle of the road by then. I guess I was just shocked by what had happened."

I was thinking fast. Finding connections I hadn't thought about.

"The woman driving the SUV was Barb Douglas. She was obviously in a panic and driving like a bat out of hell."

"Okay." He carefully made a note of that.

"The guys in the truck were really ticked off at me because they had to stop. Now I'm wondering if those truckers weren't pursuing her."

The two younger officers exchanged glances, while Detective Nick merely looked puzzled.

Smarty said, "Then?"

"They lifted the end of the Miata and I was able to get off the median. The woman in the SUV was long gone by then. I learned later that she got a call on her cell phone. I think someone called to tell her about the murder and that was why she panicked."

"You know her?"

"I hadn't met her, and she's been missing ever since."

Smarty frowned. "Are you sure? We don't have any reports on missing women in the system."

I said, "That's true. I understand your policy says you don't take info on people who might have walked away of their own accord. I didn't understand it. Her door was open at her apartment. Her cat was missing and not in its crate. Her landlord and landlady couldn't understand it. She never went back to work and—"

"Hold on. You know all this how?"

"Because I spoke to the police, to Nick's wife, in fact." To Smarty I explained, "We went to school together and I went to visit her at home. She's on sick leave because of a difficult pregnancy. When I asked, she told me they don't follow up on this kind of situation."

Nick blanched. Mention of his wife has that effect. I should have brought Pepper into the conversation earlier.

Smarty cleared his throat.

I let it all out in a torrent. "And she told me about the policy, so I followed up myself. I was supposed to meet with her, and there was a reason to believe she would be upset by that. I got this woman Barb Douglas's address and

I went to reassure her, and that's when I realized that she was really missing."

"Sorry, miss. I think you must have misinterpreted what Detective Sergeant Monahan said. We would definitely follow up on a situation like this. I know the book cold, and that's our policy."

So Pepper *had* been lying. I had sensed it and I hadn't been smart enough to do an end run around her and march into the station. Was Barb Douglas lying dead somewhere in the back of her SUV because I hadn't had the guts to follow through?

"There's more," I said.

The boy on the step said, "Awesome."

"Yes, miss." The pencil was poised.

"The men who stopped in the truck gave me their names, Mel and Del, and said they were with Quovadicon."

Scribble scribble.

"But I learned afterward that there was no one in the company by either name."

"You could have been wrong about the names?"

"I'm sure that's what they called themselves."

"Would you recognize them?"

"Sure I would. I'll never forget their faces."

"Have you seen them before or since?"

"Today I thought I saw them filling up a van at a gas station."

Our eyes locked.

Smarty said, "Do you have a description?"

"Sorry, I took off when I saw Del stop the fill-up and hop into it. Just a generic white van. Now I'm asking myself if they weren't chasing her on that road and maybe they caught up to her eventually and now . . . Oh my God."

"That could be one possible reason, miss. We don't want

to overlook it in our investigation. Detective Tierney is in charge of that case. You'll hear from him."

We both cast a glance at Nick, who appeared to be having problems following the conversation.

He frowned on cue and said, "So these guys might know who you are? And that's why they tried to run you over? Not sure . . ."

"I'm a witness, Nick."

"Oh."

The boy plunked himself down on the steps and stared at us. This was probably better than anything on his PlayStation.

"And," I said, "one more strange connection. The murder victim was found in the trunk of a blue Impala."

"Okay."

"Barb Douglas was seen in the passenger side of a blue sedan, possibly an Impala, parked outside her apartment on several occasions. Seemed like a friendly relationship. I'm just passing on what her landlord said. Someone should talk to him about all of this."

Smarty said, "Yes. Detective Tierney will follow up on that. But there are lots of blue Impalas out there. The media mentioned the body in the trunk. They didn't give a name or anything, so why would this Barb panic?"

Everyone blinked at that.

I said, "I told you that somebody called her just before she tore out of Quovadicon."

Smarty said, "We'll just have to find out who that was."

Well, that was a relief. Someone official would try to find out what the hell was going on. I would be off the hook.

Nick chose that moment to be solicitous. "Do you want to go in and sit down, Charlie?"

The boy's eyes widened yet again.

"No," I said, "I want to go home and I want to make sure I get there without being killed by a truck."

Just as Nick the Stick got a lascivious look in his eye, Smarty said, "We'll see you get home safe, miss. I'll take you in the patrol car, and my partner can drive your car."

I blurted, "I hate police cars. I'm not going in one ever again. Never."

The not-so-bright cop said, "Hey that reminds me, weren't you the one they found with that dead body? Didn't I see you get put in a squad car?"

The boy looked at me in a totally different way now.

I said, "It was an ambulance. I was injured, too. So don't try to pin that on me."

He brightened. Probably tickled that anyone could think he could pin something on them.

Smarty held up his hand. "It's for your own safety, miss."

Nick stuck out his chiseled chin. "This lady is a really good friend of mine. I can take her home. No problemo."

I refrained from using the word *fool* when I responded, but only barely. "Uno problemo. You are also driving a police car, Nick."

"Yeah, but—"

"I know there are two syllables in *never*, but try."

Smarty barely suppressed a smirk. "In the meantime, miss, while we're working out the travel arrangements, anyone you want us to call to stay with you tonight?"

Smarter and smarter.

I tried Margaret. No answer. Well, she was probably on a date. She'd have her cell phone turned off. By now, Sally would be conked out after a long day.

So that left Jack.

"Yes. My friend Jack Reilly." This time he wasn't getting off the hook. I whipped out my cell phone.

"Is this someone you know well and trust, miss?"

"Of course. He's been my friend since we were kids and

he's also my landlord. He lives downstairs. He'll do anything for me. Anything."

Nick scowled.

"I'll call him now. I don't know what's wrong with me," I muttered.

"Shock," Smarty said. "Anyone would find it hard to think clearly after that traumatic experience."

Jack is number 1 on my speed dial.

"Hello?" A woman's voice.

"Sorry," I said. "I must have the wrong number."

I didn't bother to add, *I must have pressed the wrong something-or-other because I've just narrowly escaped an attempt on my life.* She didn't bother to say, *Don't worry about it*, before she hung up.

I pressed 1 again. The same woman answered. I said, "Oh."

Before she hung up, she snapped, "Try to have a little consideration."

Something had obviously gone awry with my new cell phone. Had I programmed the numbers incorrectly? Was I losing my grip? On the third attempt, I dialed Jack's number from memory. By now, I recognized the voice.

"I do *not* have the wrong number," I said firmly.

The exasperation was clear in her voice. "Oh, for heaven's sake. Exactly who were you looking for?"

"Jack Reilly. And please don't tell me that this isn't Jack's number, because it is."

"You want to speak to Jack? Why didn't you say so?"

I refrained from saying, *Because he usually answers, and I don't have to tell him that I'm calling to speak to him.*

"He's not available," she said.

"What do you mean? Has something happened to him?"

"He's busy. He can't come to the phone right now."

"Well, please tell him it's Charlotte and I've had a . . ." I hesitated because I wasn't sure how to describe what I'd just had. "Tell him it's an emergency."

Her sigh conveyed the absolute burden this put on her. "I can't interrupt his meeting."

"Let him decide whether it's important enough to interrupt his meeting," I said.

"Whatever," she muttered. "Hang on."

I hung on for at least three minutes while trying to avoid Nick's eye. I heard her voice come back on the line. "Sorry. Jack said he'd try to find time to talk to you tomorrow afternoon."

I snapped the phone shut.

"Something wrong, miss?"

I pulled myself together. "No. Nothing. I guess my friend is still in his meeting. It's for the bike race to raise funds for WAG'D, that's a dog rescue group."

"Don't worry about it, Charlie. I'll follow you home if you want to take your own car. Make sure you're all right."

I sort of imagined Nick's brain to be like the inside of a Victoria's Secret catalog, with all the bra models whispering *Oh, Nick, baby* after running their tongues over their already glossy lips. I shuddered. I never wanted to be part of that nightmare vision.

Smarty raised a thick eyebrow. "I know that group, miss. They do great work. Where's the meeting?"

I blinked. "I don't know."

Smarty said, "Tell you what. I'll drive you home. My partner will follow with Sergeant Monahan in case this truck shows up."

Although I often fear for the future of the Woodbridge police, this young officer and Detective Tierney gave me faith. At least they were smart. Pepper was probably smarter than both of them put together and multiplied by four, but for some reason she'd started lying about missing women.

"Thank you," I said.

He nodded gravely. "I want to be sure that everything's under control."

I was pretty sure he meant Nick.

Back in my apartment, Nick leaned against the doorjamb in what he probably thought was a macho pose. The world's greatest lover was scared of Truffle and Sweet Marie. They didn't care for him, either. Probably remembered his last visit.

"How is Pepper getting along?" I said. Before he could answer, I added, "Does she mind you working nights? Must be hard on her."

Smarty was looking around my apartment with interest. "Detective Tierney said he'd put a car on you. He wants to talk to you later. Okay?"

I nodded.

The dogs sniffed him and decided he was okay. Mostly they wanted to cuddle with me. That suited me just fine. I wasn't crazy about having the three cops in the house, especially as they kept looking around. The not-so-bright one actually opened the fridge. I felt too tired to suggest that my appliances were off-limits for casual pointless snooping.

"You eat out a lot, eh?" he said.

Smarty shot him a dirty look, saving me the trouble. "Check the backyard," he said. "Might be someone out there. You want to make sure it's secure."

"The backyard?" his partner said.

"Yup."

"But we're on the second floor."

"Just do it. It's on you if someone climbs up here and . . ."

I didn't like the sound of that. Maybe that's why I jumped when I heard people on the staircase. Jack was a vision in his Hawaiian shirt and baggy shorts, as usual, immune to the weather. I felt my throat constrict. With Jack home, life would return to normal. I wanted to fling myself into his arms and say, *Make these cops leave. Keep the evil trucks away. Walk the dogs. Bring me ice cream.* Of course, when I looked past his shoulder, I spotted Blair. She managed to look cool and impossibly beautiful with her snug Lycra gear and that enviable mane of blond hair. At least Jack still reserved his Lycra duds for races and not street wear, and his hairstyle was the familiar spiky bed head that I loved. Blair laid a proprietary hand on Jack's Hawaiian shoulder and cooed, "Hi, Charlotte, looks like everything's under control here. We're *so* glad you're all right. Let's give Charlotte her privacy, Jack. She has lots of protectors."

Trouble getting ready for work in the mornings?
Set up your coffeepot the night before,
so it's ready to go with the click of a button.
Or better yet, get a coffeemaker with a timer.

19

"That Blair creature clung to him like six feet of Virginia Creeper," I whined to Margaret when she finally answered. She sounded tousled, if that's possible over the phone.

"Get over it, Charlotte. It's midnight and tomorrow's a workday and I'm so not in the mood."

Where was the sympathy? The warmth and understanding you'd expect from a friend?

"And what is this 'we' all about?" I whined. "She said *we*, almost like she and Jack were a couple. As if."

"What is your problem? You never let your relationship with Jack proceed past the good-buddy stage. You know he wants to get married and have children. So if that's what he wants, let him go. Why should it bother you?"

I fought back my feelings of outrage and countered. "Why do you always answer a question with a question?"

"Why do you care?"

"Because I'm upset. I'm upset about everything. I'm upset that a woman is missing and may be dead. I'm upset that another woman is dead and I was hit by a stapler and practically framed for her murder. I'm upset that I was chased by a killer truck."

"You were chased by a killer truck?"

"There you go again, answering a question with a question."

"If you don't mind me saying so, you're not sounding like yourself, Charlotte. You seem . . . unhinged."

"You'd be unhinged, too, if you thought you were going to end up in the trunk of your car in the same area where that man's body was found. Not that the police made any connection between that murder and the missing woman until tonight."

I waited for a response. I thought I heard Margaret muttering. "Killer truck. Trunk. Murder. Missing woman." That kind of thing.

"Can you talk into the phone? I can hardly hear you," I said peevishly.

More mutters.

"Margaret?"

Mutter.

A horrible thought washed over me. "You're not alone, are you?"

"That is correct. Not that it's any of your business."

I seized the moment. "It's that cop, isn't it? He's supposed to be chasing stolen cars. Why is he wasting time on dates?"

"Because, as I've mentioned already, it's midnight. Tell me, Charlotte, do you want to be on the executive committee that decides who Margaret gets to have a relationship with? Because if so, you'll have to take a number after my mother, my father, my grandmother, and every other Tang relative."

"I'm sorry."

"I thought you were my friend."

Low blow. "I am. It just took me by surprise, that's all. I'm . . . very happy for you."

"Humph."

"By the way, Margaret, I think you are my friend, too. But you don't seem very interested in my life-or-death experiences tonight."

"Well," she said, finally. "I suppose you'd better tell me about the killer truck."

"What about Jack and—"

"The killer truck. That sounded more life-and-death somehow."

"But the thing with Jack and that woman is more upsetting."

"Let it go, Charlotte."

"And Nick managed to get into my apartment again, too. He showed up after the truck incident."

"Really? Ew."

"And I feel bad for Pepper."

"Not as bad as you'll feel if she ever finds out."

"Anyway, Pepper's involved in this, too. She knew who the missing woman was. She told me she didn't but she did. So maybe this person's in a witness protection program or something. Margaret? Are you there?"

Mutter mutter.

"Margaret?"

"My colleague doesn't know anything about this woman. And in his opinion, there's no chance she's in witness protection."

"Give me one good reason why not."

"The feds would never tell the local cops. End of story."

"And that's because?"

"It seems they're the biggest gossips on the planet."

I thought I heard a protesting mutter in the background.

After I hung up, I flounced around the apartment alarming the dogs. I set out my clothes for the next day, sorted out my handbag, prepared my briefcase, straightened my desk, made my prioritized To Do list, and set up the coffeemaker for the morning. Next I tossed in a load of laundry, exfoliated my face, and put on night cream. I slid into my flannel jammies and curled up on the sofa with one entire box of Kristee's black-and-white fudge. Some people would call that a luxury.

I called it a medical necessity.

I spent the night tossing and turning, dodging flying trucks and broccoli bullets. Mel and Del were driving the trucks and firing the bullets. I dragged myself out of bed, flicked on the coffeemaker, and waddled out with the dogs. There was no sign of life at Jack's place. The door was closed. His bike was gone. Apparently this race planning was a twenty-four-hour-a-day business.

We stomped back five minutes later. I was afraid to look in the mirror in case I spotted a black cloud over my head. I sipped my coffee and revised my To Do list.

- *Det. Tierney re Mel and Del*
- *Robbie re info on Dyan's computer*
- *Fredelle re Barb's references*
- *Practice for Therapy Dogs orientation meeting*
- *Prepare strategy for working with teenage daughter before next meeting*

It didn't escape my notice that work was forming a smaller and smaller part of my To Do lists. Further down the priority list, too.

I started with a call to Detective Tierney before I even took my shower. He must have been out detecting because it went straight to voice mail. I left a message and said I'd be home until ten a.m. and I urgently needed to talk to him. I was thinking more clearly now. I wondered if the information I'd unloaded on the three police officers the night before had reached the detective's ear.

Robbie was next. Surprisingly he answered.

I filled him in on the events of the night before. "I am absolutely certain the driver was trying to kill me. I think it's those guys I told you about, and I'm pretty sure Fredelle was lying about them. I plan to tell the police."

"That's really hard to believe."

"She's holding back lots of stuff. I'm out of sympathy for her. Missy might know, too. I'll tell the police to talk to her."

Robbie squeaked. "Missy! But Missy's really nice. I don't want the police hassling her."

"They won't hassle her. She'll tell them what they need to know. Remember, all this is connected to Barb in some way. We have to do whatever's necessary to find out what's going on with her."

"That's right," he said. "We're in this together."

"Any luck with Dyan's computer?"

"Nothing. It's actually been wiped clean."

"Really? Then there must have been something that incriminated someone at Quovadicon."

"Good point. I'll try to recover the files. I've already substituted another hard drive so no one will notice I've taken hers."

"Good thinking. And speaking of hard drives, we should see what's on Barb's."

"I'm ahead of you there. Lots of files, but I combed through it and I couldn't find anything strange."

"Keep at it."

"I will. You be careful."

I wasn't sure at what point Robbie and I had become allies, but whatever works, I decided. We did have a common goal.

—••—

When I hopped out of the shower, the message light was flashing. Life's like that. Ramona's instructions were crisp and to the point. "I might have a bit of joy on your Barbara Douglas question. I got a few hits on the business databases. She wrote several articles on business applications for new technologies a few years back, seems to have been working at tech start-ups in Silicon Valley. The latest article I can find shows her working in San Raphael at a place called, let's see, oh right, Vector Vici, five years ago. I'll see if I can turn up a photo. In the meantime, I've printed out the articles and citations. They're here for you. Pick them up when you come for your orientation. Wish I could do more."

I imagined Ramona was up to her patootie with her regular demanding library patrons. As usual, she'd bailed me out. And I had an idea. I picked up my new cell phone and blocked the number before I made my call.

Fredelle answered somewhat breathlessly, as though she'd run halfway across the office to catch the call in time. "Quovadicon. Fredelle Newhouse speaking."

I plowed on before she could extricate herself from the call. "Charlotte Adams here. I am willing to avoid going to your employer to tell him how you lied about being involved with Therapy Dogs in order to trick me into working on Barb's desk, provided you answer one quick question." Before she could respond, I asked, "Do you know where Barb worked in between Vector Vici and Quovadicon?"

"I'm sorry?"

I repeated the question, adding, "It would give me a jumping-off point. Did you get a reference from Vector Vici?"

"Mr. Van Zandt did, but . . ." She paused. This confirmed

that the Barb Douglas who'd worked at Vector Vici was the one I needed to find.

"Charlotte?" The quaver was back in Fredelle's voice. Maybe she just trotted it out when she needed to manipulate someone.

"Hmm?"

"I think we should leave Barb alone. Let her get back on her feet."

I said, "Sure. Gotta go. Places to go, people to see. Calls to make."

But more accurately, I had to work on my fibbing technique. And I had to Google Vector Vici.

"Bruce here."

The voice was middle-aged but casual. A nice voice, but with the kind of confidence that befits an entrepreneurial CEO. I believe in starting at the top. More efficient.

I liked the fact that Bruce was answering his own phone at seven a.m. California time.

I said, "Hey, Bruce. This is Joanie Roadhouse. I'm trying to track down my old friend Barb Douglas. I want to reconnect and I don't have any way to get in touch with her. She called me not long ago, but I lost the message and I've hit a wall. I know she doesn't work with you anymore, but I thought you guys might be able to help. Any idea where she is now? If you have an e-mail address, that would be great. Or even a city."

"Is this a sick joke?" The casual good humor dropped out of Bruce's booming voice.

"What?" One more thing to catch me by surprise.

He shouted into the phone. "That is disgusting."

"What do you mean, disgusting? I'm just asking where she is."

"She's dead, that's where she is. And I don't know what kind of scam this is, but you have sunk about as low as you can go. Rot in hell."

"What do you mean she's dead? How do you know?"

What was going on? I was in New York State searching for Barb while people across the country were a jump ahead of me. Of course, I really really didn't want her to be dead.

There was a significant pause. "I know she's dead because I went to her goddamn funeral five years ago, and not one day goes by that I don't think about her and miss her because she was a wonderful human being. And you are a freak. Did I already say, rot in hell?"

"You did, but—"

I heard a click and then the dial tone. So much for explaining myself.

"So," I said in a whisper. I didn't want to attract the attention of Ramona's more formidable reference room regulars, who were just hitting their stride for a day of shushing the other patrons and the library staff, too. "If Barb Douglas is dead, who is the person we thought she was?"

Ramona shook her silver earrings. "Who knows? Some identity thief. Happens all the time."

"Seems like a very dangerous game for identity theft. Barb is missing, Dyan is dead, and I was attacked in Quovadicon and chased by a pair of homicidal truckers. Not to mention the dead guy in the trunk of the Impala."

"A good point, Charlotte. Maybe you should just leave it to the cops."

"They're not doing anything. I need to find out for my own protection. Maybe I should be afraid of Barb instead of fearing for her safety. Maybe she's behind the truck attack. Maybe she thinks I'm in the way. I must have misinterpreted the fact that the truckers seemed to be chasing her. Maybe they were leaving together. Part of a gang."

"Spectacularly conspiratorial. But even so, you should be careful."

I kept my voice down. "I'll do my best. But this fake Barb really fooled a lot of people."

"Not hard to do. You usually assume that the person you are talking to is really who they say they are, especially in the workplace."

"So if she's not Barb, we don't have any way to find out who she is. It's a dead end."

"Maybe not so dead an end. I wonder if this person, whoever she was, knew Barb back in San Raphael or through work in some way. Barb Douglas must have died young. Her colleagues would all know and talk about it."

I nodded. "That's genius, Ramona. I don't think I can call Vector Vici again, but do you think you can get me an obit?"

"Please, I'm a reference librarian. We live for such tasks."

Item 4 on the To Do list was work on the dog training. I could have done a bit of work on the disastrous-bedroom project, but everything in its own time.

"Listen, you turkeys. Get off that bed and get practicing. You won't be any kind of therapy dogs if you can't even pass the evaluation."

I had slipped out of my business clothes and into a soft old black T-shirt and a pair of baggy yoga pants for our training session. One nice thing about dogs: They don't judge you by how you look. Of course, they don't do what they're told either, but you can't have everything.

I ignored their yawns and placed them on the floor. We

were working on the DOWN command. I had the door open so that I would hear Jack in case he came home. He had more of a gift for dog training than I did. Truffle and Sweet Marie had been working on the DOWN command for a long time, even before the evaluation criteria sheet showed up in our lives. Let's just say it wasn't going all that well. We got SIT. We got WAIT. We even got LEAVE IT. But we were not down with DOWN.

I knelt on the floor. "SIT," I said, seductively.

They sat.

Easy as pie.

They gazed at me expectantly.

"Now, DOWN," I said in what I hoped was a compelling tone.

They continued to gaze.

"DOWN."

No reaction.

Of course, you are supposed to use their names when issuing commands. "Truffle, DOWN."

Truffle cocked his head. I could tell he was wondering if I had lost my marbles. Sweet Marie looked on, perplexed.

"Like this," I instructed, lying on the carpet so they could see how it was done.

Truffle leaned over and licked my nose.

Sweet Marie barked.

"Look. How hard can it be? You want the treat, you have to DOWN. This is how you do it."

Four beady eyes regarded me. I think if they could have picked up the phone to call for assistance, they might have done it.

"You like to play games and you're very good at it. So this is like a game. Just try it. It's easy."

Stare.

"DOWN."

Truffle turned away, more in sorrow than anger.

"Come back here. I know you're short and you don't want to get any closer to the floor, but . . ."

I'm not sure when I became conscious of the pair of glossy black loafers, but when I looked up, they were attached to a pair of long legs in casual pants. The pants were topped with a nice-looking charcoal shirt, a silk blend if my instincts were still good, open at the neck. The whole outfit was very stylish on Detective Connor Tierney. If you'd asked me to guess, I would have said he looked like a man on his way to a serious date.

He just smiled and jingled that silver key chain. I wondered if that would get annoying after a while.

There are times where there's just nothing you can say, really, so it's best to keep your mouth closed. I stood up with what infinitesimal amount of dignity remained to me.

"Good dogs," I said. "That went well. We'll polish the rough spots tomorrow. So, Officer Tierney, I'm glad you turned up."

Luckily for me, he was still looking just past my left ear. Maybe he wouldn't see that blush spreading up my neck.

He said languidly, "Maybe I should lie down."

"No need. Training session's over."

"Too bad. I'm really good at sitting."

I gestured toward the sofa.

"Impressive," I said as he sat.

"Years of practice."

The dogs ignored the banter and headed for his lap. They were getting altogether too cozy with the fuzz.

"Would you like something? Coffee?" I stopped myself from saying *Doughnuts?* For one thing, Connor Tierney didn't look like the kind of person who would eat doughnuts. He didn't look like the kind of man who would be a police officer, either, but what do I know.

"Excellent," he said.

"Regular? Decaf? Espresso? Shade grown? Fair trade?" I had no idea why I was prepared to ramble on with choices.

Luckily, he said "Espresso" before I could continue on to tea, herbal tea, sparkling water, or red wine.

I headed to the kitchen and reached for the espresso maker. That gave me a chance to pull myself together. I ran a hand over my hair, which probably had dog drool in it. I brushed the rug lint off the front of my black T-shirt and yoga pants. There wasn't much I could do about my bare feet. At least my pedicure was still in good condition.

I arrived back with two tiny espresso cups that my mother had sent from Italy on her fourth or possibly her fifth honeymoon. For my part, I buy the best espresso I can find.

"Nice," he said.

I perched on the chair across from the sofa and waited. The dogs stayed with him.

"So," I said, after a while. "I want to tell you about what happened to me last night and what I think it might mean."

He said, "First, I have big news. That's why I came over."

Big news. Since when did the Woodbridge police send detectives wearing silk shirts over to update occasional suspects on the latest scoop?

"Really. What's happening?"

"This is great coffee."

"Espresso blend. And the news? Because if you don't have any, I want to talk about a pair of truck drivers."

"Let me finish. Well, you know the truck that terrorized you?"

"Of course I know it." This dragging it out was getting old fast.

He grinned. "Sorry. I guess I'm . . ."

I managed not to say *being a jerk.*

He said, “We found it.”

“You did? That’s amazing. You didn’t have a license number or anything but the make and color.”

He stared at his hands for a minute. “An alert citizen on a hike phoned in that he’d sighted a truck in a ravine and a couple of officers checked it out. Red Volvo rig. New one, too.”

“And who owned it? Why were they chasing me? Did you find out what that was about? Did they say anything about Barb Douglas? Which reminds me—”

He lifted his espresso cup again, took a sip. “That’s the thing. The rig itself was stolen from the Troy area a couple of days back.”

“Stolen.”

He nodded, assessing me.

I said, “Were you able to arrest the—”

He shook his head, made a face.

I blurted, “So that means you don’t know anything about the guys who tried to kill me. They sure made it look like they were serious about that little game.”

He took another slow sip, swallowed, and said, “We know something about them. They were serious, all right.”

His attitude was beginning to get under my skin. “And there were two of them? Because that’s—”

“It looks that way.”

“I believe they worked for Quovadicon. You can get more information about them from Fredelle Newhouse, the office manager at the company, or from Missy Manderly, who used to work there. Both of them are being very secretive about these two men, if you ask me. But I can give you a good description of them. It’s weird that I was pursued the same day I saw them at a gas station. They must have found out where I lived after I gave them the slip. I'm easy to find. I think they'd been following me, waiting for their chance to finish me off. Wait a minute. How do you know they were serious if they didn't get arrested? What's to stop them from stealing another truck and running me down with that, for whatever bizarre reason?"

He paused as if making a major career decision, flicked an invisible bit of lint from his silk shirt, and then said, "Mainly because they're dead."

If there's only one clutter-free zone in your home, it should be your bedroom. Work materials, bills, and clutter in this space can prevent you from getting a good night's sleep and being happy and productive during the day. Naturally, books are not clutter.

20

Ramona handed me a copy of the obituary for the real Barb Douglas. Before I could glance at it, she said, "Two more people dead? I heard that on the news. We're up to our patooties in cadavers. But if they're looking for more candidates, I can offer up some names."

I didn't want to ask what the reference prima donnas had been up to that day. I guess she was glad I was there to cheer her up.

"It was the same guys who tried to run me off the road."

"The homicidal truckers? So what happened?" she said merrily. "Did they run themselves off the road?"

I shrugged. "I don't know exactly what happened. The driver was definitely reckless, but even so, he seemed to have amazing control. You should have seen him making those tight corners when I was trying to escape. Do you think they were on drugs or something to make them act so . . . ?"

Ramona shook her head. "You'll probably never know, if the cop couldn't tell you."

I said, "Well, this will sound like a terrible thing to say and I really don't wish a violent death on anyone, but I'm glad they're not out on the roads waiting for me or anyone else again."

Ramona said, "I hear you. So just how hot is this guy?"

"What guy? The cop?"

"Of course, the cop. Who else?" She rolled her eyes.

"Did I say he was hot?"

"You didn't have to. I'm a reference librarian. We read between the lines. It's a magical trait we use to find answers to vague rambling questions that don't indicate what the person actually wants to know."

"Huh. Well, that must come in real handy. I'd say this officer is prime-time-television-one-hour-police-drama-with-detective-with-mysterious-past-and-troubled-present-and-good-wardrobe hot."

"Yum."

"You're welcome to him. He's not my type and he never really makes eye contact. Plus he showed up at my apartment, but he wouldn't listen to me."

"This is just a guess, Charlotte, but he showed up because you left him a message. And maybe he doesn't listen and tell you much because when there's something to investigate, you barge in and next thing there's trouble. Bang bang guns. Dead people."

I scowled at her. "Well, *I* didn't kill them."

A few of the library regulars shot me dirty looks.

"There you go again," Ramona said. "Bellowing in the reference department."

"They have to be connected with Barb. They were on the road behind her when she almost ran me off the road. If they worked at Quovadicon, they'd have access to the building. Maybe they made the call, got in there, and killed Dyan. And knocked me out."

"But why?"

"I don't know why. You have to admit, it's too coincidental to have these things happen. They must be connected. The police, or at least Pepper and Nick and now this new guy . . ."

"Tierney," Ramona said helpfully. "The police don't want civilians involved in something like this, especially you, Charlotte, with your tendency to make waves."

"But I *am* involved. Not that I want to be. You'd think they'd want to talk to me when I have something to say. They always drag me in when I don't want to go, and when I tried to tell Tierney about Barb, all of a sudden he had to leave."

"Makes for good TV, though, you have to admit that. Especially when you're in your pajamas."

"Yoga gear. There's something weird about the police behavior. I'm convinced Pepper Monahan recognized Barb Douglas. And knows something about what happened to her."

She said, "I hear the green-eyed monster is under control with impending motherhood. I suppose Nick is still fooling around."

"He is. Not much I can do about that. I have to take my chances and visit Pepper again."

"Well, good luck with that, and remember, I'll be here to help you pick up the pieces. And you have other friends, too. You might need 'em."

"By the way, speaking of friends, you told me that you knew Robbie. You didn't seem too fond of his father, the great hero. In fact, you seemed quite ambivalent about Reg Van Zandt every time we talked about him."

"Yeah, well," Ramona said. "I've known Robbie since he was a kid."

"And?"

"And he was a sweet guy. Very shy, very sensitive."

"Let me guess. Bullied."

"For sure. It was like he was born with a *KICK ME*

sign. I had to stand up for him more than once or he would have been beaten to a pulp outside the community pool."

Robbie Van Zandt would have been lucky to have the young Ramona in his corner when he was a kid. I sure liked having her fortysomething self in mine. "So weren't these bullies afraid of his father the war hero?"

She snorted. "No way. He would have cut his tongue out before he ever told his father he was being picked on. Imagine how hard it must have been to be the geeky smart kid with the glasses and a little stutter and arms and legs like twigs. He idolized his father, and the father overprotected him, I think. Robbie always felt he was such a disappointment. And he takes life so seriously. That's how it seemed to me. I was just a teenager myself, but I really liked Robbie and, of course, I was a lot bigger and tougher than he was."

"I guess he's still under his father's wing, working for Quovadicon."

"He'd be an asset. Give him a number or a theorem or a law and he was first-rate. He might have been able to flourish somewhere else, but . . ." She shrugged. "We don't see that much of each other any more, maybe that's my fault, but I always felt he had a tragic story."

"Why would he have stayed?"

"He tried to get off on his own. He had some great opportunities in California in the tech boom, but Mrs. Newhouse talked him out of it. She convinced him it would kill his father."

"What? Why would it kill Mr. Van Zandt?"

"Well, not having Robbie there to take over the family company if something happened to the great war hero. The strain on his father's heart worrying about him. So Robbie did his degree and tech training in the area."

"You mean he's been groomed as a successor? Really? I can't see him in the boardroom or the bank."

"Exactly. It was all bull hooey. Some people think they'll live forever, and they want to keep other people under their thumb. No wonder he had a breakdown."

"Breakdown?"

Ramona caught herself. "I shouldn't have said that. It's no one's business, and I was out of line."

"What kind of breakdown?"

"As I just said, Charlotte, no one's business but Robbie's."

I felt a surge of anger on behalf of poor trapped Robbie, even though I still wouldn't choose to walk down a dark alley with him. I knew Ramona wouldn't give me any more information. But I could tell by her reaction that whatever had happened, she didn't think Robbie was a danger to anyone. I backtracked. "Agreed. He sure doesn't seem like the CEO type."

She relaxed. "And he doesn't want to be a CEO. His father just can't let up on the control. I wonder what he thought about the relationship with Barb."

Well, now, I wondered that, too.

When I settled in at home, I asked myself: Had Reg Van Zandt discovered that Barb was a fraud? Or had he known it all along? Had the game changed when she became involved with Robbie? Did he think the relationship would lead to another breakdown? Had he decided to kill her to keep her from luring his son into a relationship or even a marriage? Was Fredelle in on whatever he might have done?

I shook my head at this. How did the man in the trunk of the blue Impala fit in? What about the truck drivers? Did they work for him? Did they pursue Barb and try to kill me on his orders? What did I really know about that anyway?

It was just circumstantial. Whatever was going on, Barb Douglas seemed to be at the heart of it.

The dogs lay on my feet as I read her obit. A list of accomplishments and volunteer commitments: Big Sisters, UNICEF. Predeceased by her parents. No siblings identified. Fondly remembered by her friends Hugo Speigl and Jim Smith and many others, unfortunately not named.

If I remembered correctly, there were so many Jim Smiths in the country that they had their own society. I pinned my hopes on Hugo Speigl and Googled him.

Jackpot.

Within a couple of minutes, I had a phone number, but no e-mail. Of course, the phone call got me voice mail. When doesn't it?

I left a pleasant and upbeat message for Hugo, saying I had an inquiry about the late Barb Douglas, and I understood he'd been a friend and could help me. I left my number if he wanted to call back, but also said I'd try again later on my own dime.

Well, that left one more thing I had to do, and I didn't plan to do it on my own. I called for reinforcements: Sally claimed her neighbor owed her big-time because Benjamin had treated her sprained ankle. She planned to call in the favor. Margaret succumbed to a serious guilt trip focusing on the nature of friendship. She asked if by any chance I'd been hanging out with her parents. Naturally, Jack didn't answer his phone.

The Van Zandt place was situated on a multiacre spread that ran down to the Hudson. The property was surrounded by a wrought-iron fence, with a phalanx of security cameras at the entrance. I figured he had plenty to protect. It might not have been convenient to Woodbridge, but this home and surroundings seemed pretty close to paradise. I gazed around as the gates opened and our three cars drove through. The lawn swept up to woods at the crest of a long gently sloping hill. It rolled down to the water and the rocky beach below. The home was sprawling and modern, with various additions and outbuildings in tasteful materials, blending into the surroundings.

"That's nice," Sally said, pointing to the wildflower garden meandering by the side of the long drive. I sniffed to show that I wasn't fooled by a few purple coneflowers.

I also refused to be charmed by the idyllic pond near the side of the house.

"Look at the ducks!" Sally said.

I ignored the comments and the ducks. I was here to confront a man about actions that had led to death, disappearance, and disaster.

At the front of the house, I was faced with a wheelchair ramp with switchbacks up to the house. Window boxes with late-season marigolds lit up the long rails. I gave the thumbs-up to Sally and to Margaret, who had followed in her car.

Sally called out, "Say the word and we'll be there in a second."

Margaret said, "This is such a bad idea, I can't believe I let you blackmail me into it."

"Try to live a life above reproach, Margaret, and I'll have nothing to hang over your head."

"Yeah, you wait until you meet someone. I'll have fun then."

"What are you two talking about?" Sally called.

"Surprise endings," I said.

"Don't ask," Margaret said.

"Why isn't Jack here?" Sally asked.

"He has more important stuff to do," I said.

Reg Van Zandt opened the door himself. I had been expecting a team of servants. Instead, I gazed down at an aging man in a wheelchair. If you formed your opinion of him based on the silver hair, the weathered face, or the twinkling dark eyes, you might think this was a gentle man, easily deceived. I thought the truth might be different.

"Welcome," he said. "You must be Charlotte Adams. Come in. I've heard a lot about you."

He pivoted, obviously expert in handling the wheelchair, and I followed him into the interior. It was simple and comfortable. More about hobbies and comfort than making the trend magazines.

No point in beating around the bush. "You need to—"

"Is that fudge?" he said, pointing to the gift-wrapped package in my hand.

I nodded. "Black-and-white fudge from Kristee's Kandees. I'm intruding and I thought you might like some."

"I'm willing to share," he said. "What about your friends?"

"My friends?"

"The two who are parked outside." He gestured toward the front window.

"They're just waiting to see that everything's all right," I said.

He swiveled back to me. "Why wouldn't everything be all right?"

"Well, because people are dead or missing. I've been attacked and pursued, and all that makes a person cautious. Don't you think all that should stop?"

He chuckled, a low pleasant boom. "So you brought reinforcements. Full marks for resourcefulness. All right. Go ahead. You've got the floor."

"I'll cut to the chase. What happened to Barb Douglas?"

"I have no idea. Why are you asking me?"

"Because I think you know what's going on. You hired Barb, no one is really sure why. You did the reference checks, I heard. You're an astute businessman and I think you would have thoroughly vetted a new hire. In which case you'd have discovered that Barb Douglas died a few years ago."

I had dropped Fredelle and perhaps Missy into the deep end, but what choice did I have?

"Is that so?" he said, frowning.

"That's where it started. Then someone killed a friend of hers and she panicked and fled. I thought she was running for her life, but now I don't know."

"I really have no idea what you are talking about."

"Sure you do. You knew about her friend and his death. You didn't even blink when I mentioned him."

"Well, it *has* been all over the news."

"The connection with Barb and the dead man wasn't. It wasn't anywhere. Not at the office."

"Surely Fredelle wouldn't breach confidences."

"She didn't. There are ways of checking things out."

"Legal ways to get the information, I hope, Miss Adams."

I continued on the offense. "You went over everyone's head and caused bad feelings in the office to bring in a woman who wasn't who she claimed to be."

He shrugged. "She's an exceptional woman."

"What did you have her doing? Were you running some kind of scam and she was part of it?"

"That's nonsense. You don't know what you're talking about."

"Here's what I do know. I know that the guy's dead in the trunk. I know that Barb is gone, dead, hiding, kidnapped, or otherwise connected with the killers. I don't know which. But I do know she has to be at the center of this. I know that Dyan is dead because of something she found out. I'm lucky I looked like a good person to frame for her death, or I would be dead, too. I also know that two truckers who seem to have a connection to you tried to kill me last night. And I know that they're in the morgue now. Everything comes back to Quovadicon."

The dark, intelligent eyes lit up with amusement. "You think I created all this death and destruction from the vantage point of this wheelchair?"

Is that what Robbie believed? "You're involved somehow. And you must be aware that your son is devastated. He cares deeply for Barb Douglas or whoever she really is. Fredelle is having some kind of breakdown. One of your employees is dead, killed in your offices. Three other men are dead. It's time to come clean."

He met my eyes, and I felt a chill down my bones. "Perhaps you're right, Miss Adams. Some people may need to know. But you're not one of them."

"I think I have a right to know. Dyan died because she wanted to meet with me to tell me something."

"You were in the wrong place at the wrong time meddling in things you have no knowledge of. That does not convey rights. You are lucky you weren't killed. As you said, the men who chased you in the truck are now dead. You don't need to worry about them anymore, but I suggest you stick to what you do best. What is it? Yes, closets. So turn your talents to helping the ladies keep their shoes in good order and keep away from my business."

"I think *you* made the call to clear out the office the day Dyan was killed."

"That I did not do. Why would I? Do you think I got where I am by wasting time and money?"

"Maybe it was worth it to frame me."

"I don't need to frame you, Miss Adams. You seem to be on a self-destruct course all on your own. People can get caught in your wreckage. Please stay away from my family. Robbie doesn't need anyone to push him further over the edge."

"Just tell me what's going on."

He smiled. "Thank you for bringing the fudge, Miss Adams. If you have concerns about what has been happening, I suggest you take your intrusive questions and bizarre accusations to the police."

My phone vibrated. I answered.

"Chill. I'll be right out. Don't dial 911 yet," I said and snapped it shut before making the best of a bad situation and leaving with my head high. "Keep in mind that several people know I was here to talk to you, and we'll make sure others learn about it, too, including the police, as you suggested. And I don't want to be followed, threatened, or otherwise bothered again."

"Now you have your own black-and-white fudge," I said, as my team of bodyguards settled back in my living room. "It's your bribe for being there."

Sally said, "Excellent choice of bribe. There's nothing a box of black-and-white fudge can't fix." Sally has her goals in life, and they are unwavering. She added, "The fudge is fantastic, but I do feel let down in the drama department. After all, no desperate rescues were required."

"That was fine by me," I said. "I had been thinking more along the lines of a 911 call rather than having you storm the castle."

"The biggest problem," Margaret said, "was that we all looked like gold-plated wingnuts."

I was glad she hadn't mentioned the lost billable hours from her law practice.

"I know you both dropped everything to come out there

and it turned out to be for nothing, but it might have been serious and it means a lot to have my friends with me when I need them."

Sally and Margaret exchanged glances.

Sally said, "That reminds me, where exactly was Jack?"

More glances. Did they think I'd lost my sight?

I said, "Jack's busy with the race fund-raiser for WAG'D. You know that."

Sally said, "Right. All meetings, all the time. What's that about? No wonder you're upset."

"I am not upset. I know there are lots and lots of organizational activities to make sure it runs smoothly. So it can be hard to reach him." I lifted my chin. Who wants to be cast in the role of the dumped friend?

Sally's right eyebrow was raised, and Margaret was looking even more inscrutable than usual. However, they did take the time to exchange glances once more.

"Will you two stop doing that? He has a life, that's all. He doesn't owe any of us attendance twenty-four-seven, last I looked."

I thought that sounded credible for a complete and utter lie. Maybe I fooled some of the people this one time.

Sally said, "Oh, well. A bigger problem is Reg Van Zandt."

"That's the thing. I saw his face. He wasn't surprised by my information. I'm convinced he already knew Barb wasn't who she said she was. But I don't believe he knows where she is now and I think he's worried."

Sally got to her feet. "But where does that leave us? Or I should say leave you, because I have to get home."

Margaret stood up, too. "I'd better hit the road, too."

As she opened the door, Sally called out. "Watch the news. Todd Tyrell might be on to something."

I said, "Oh, don't be ridic—"

But Margaret had already clicked the remote. "Todd gives me the creeps, but he always seems to be ahead of the cops. Can't argue with that."

I blinked to avoid the flash of teeth. Todd was on location, on a grassy stretch near a ravine. Although the trees behind him were swaying in the wind, his gelled hair remained unmoved. Naturally, he was in full verbal flight.

The citizens of Woodbridge are on high alert today after the confirmation of two more murders in our formerly peaceful town.

Margaret said, "Whoa."

I crossed my arms and glowered at the screen. "Two more murders? Look at him. He can scarcely contain his glee."

Sally delayed her departure and stepped back into the room and said, "Shhh."

An anonymous source close to the Woodbridge police force has revealed that both truck drivers killed in yesterday's fiery crash in a lonely ravine on the outskirts of the city had been shot at close range prior to the crash. Police have not confirmed that these latest murders are connected with the death of a still unidentified man found in the trunk of a car on Sunday.

A shot of the blue Impala flashed across the screen before the camera returned to Todd.

The dead truckers are the third and fourth victims of what appears to be a murderous crime wave in Woodbridge. On Wednesday, forty-nine-year-old Dyan

George was found battered to death in the offices of Quovadicon, in Patterson Business Park.

The Quovadicon office appeared behind Todd's head this time. Like magic. While the very photogenic Autumn stared teary-eyed and Mr. Halliday scowled at the cameras, poor Fredelle could be seen gesturing for the camera crew to leave. Her neat silvery hair stood on end, and she had the look of a small, trapped pet. The image behind Todd switched. Of course it did. WINY no longer had to rely on last year's stock footage of me being hauled into the cop shop wearing my pajamas and pink fuzzy slippers. Now they had new material: I was being hauled out on a stretcher, but it certainly looked like I was being grilled by Nick. He looked like an action adventure hero. I managed to convey the impression that I was drug-addled and possibly inebriated. My head was bleeding, but I figured most people watching this clip would assume it was splatter from one of my many victims.

Further unconfirmed reports indicate that Charlotte Adams, shown here following the murder of Dyan George, was involved in an altercation with the dead truckers in the Vineland Estates last night.

"*What?*" I squeaked.

Stay tuned to WINY for updates on this breaking news. This is Todd Tyrell keeping an eye out for you.

"An *altercation*?" I shouted at the television. "I was *pursued*, you pointy-headed orange mutant. I thought they were going to kill me."

I stared at the television, ignoring the blatant character

trashing that Todd usually generated. The shot of Fredelle brought to mind another apparent fact that had been bothering me. Fredelle knew Reg Van Zandt's voice. They talked all the time. Yet she hadn't recognized that the call was a prank. So which was it? Had Reg really made that call, or had Fredelle lied about that to implicate me?

Leave your prioritized To Do list on your desk when you finish work at the end of the day. Have the number-one priority file ready to tackle first thing in the morning.

21

Sally and Margaret left me stewing over that problem and the broadcast as a whole. When the phone rang, I was pacing irritably, trying to figure out a way to interrogate Fredelle. I considered letting it go to message. Todd's broadcasts often lead to a flurry of bizarre calls. But there was no point in procrastinating. Just get it over with. I snatched up the phone and said, "Charlotte Adams."

"Hello. This is Hugo Speigl returning your call. You wanted to talk about Barbara?" He had a nice voice, slightly formal and elegant, European perhaps.

I inhaled. "I did."

"May I ask why?"

"This will sound very strange, but someone seems to have assumed her identity, and that person is involved in some dangerous business."

"Heavens," he said. "Really? Who would do such a thing?"

"That's just it. I don't know. But there's a chance it was

someone who knew her. If I e-mailed you a photo, could you tell me if you know this person?"

He paused. "I suppose that would be all right."

"It's just a name. Probably it's no one you know. But this woman is in grave danger, so if you do have information, you may help save her life."

Another pause, longer this time. "Yes, I will do that."

I thanked him, jotted down his e-mail address and told him I'd get it to him as soon as possible.

"I am just going out for a few hours," he said. "I will look for it when I return."

Robbie answered his phone on the first ring. Maybe he didn't get that many calls. Maybe he was hoping it was Barb.

"I have a lead," I said.

"What kind of lead?"

"Can you meet me at Jumping Java in twenty minutes? Bring me that memory stick with a selection of photos. I'll fill you in when you get there."

When he blew into Jumping Java, Robbie had an array of printed candid shots of Barb as well as a CD. I'd scored a table and picked up two cappuccinos and some biscotti just before he got there.

"What kind of lead?" Never mind *hello.*

"It's a long story."

He dangled the CD under my nose. "I'm trusting you. You have to trust me. What kind of lead?"

"Okay. This may be a shock."

He stiffened.

"The woman you know as Barb Douglas is really someone else."

"What?"

"The real Barb Douglas is dead."

"It's not such an unusual name. There could be lots of people . . ." He slumped in his seat.

"Accept it, Robbie."

He nodded. "It explains a lot. But why would she hide that from me? Why wouldn't she trust me? I would have kept her secret."

I didn't bother to suggest fraud or other criminal activity. "We'll find out. I am sending a couple of these photos to a colleague of the real Barb Douglas to see if he recognizes her."

"Will she get in trouble?"

"She's already in trouble, Robbie. We're trying to save her life." *Or save ourselves*, I thought, as I took the CD from his hand. "I'll let you know if I find out anything."

Robbie jumped to his feet, creating a cappuccino puddle. "I'm coming with you. I want to talk to this guy."

"Forget it. He's in California."

"I'll fly out there."

"If you want to help, ask your father what he's hiding. He hired Barb. I think he knows who she is."

He slumped back into his chair. "He won't tell me anything. He treats me like I'm a wayward teenager. You really think he knows?"

"Yes. And if you don't think he'll cave, work on Fredelle."

"Even Fredelle knows something?"

"Pretty sure. She said that your father called and told everyone to leave Quovadicon the afternoon that Dyan was murdered."

"Yes."

"But he didn't call. Someone used my cell phone to call the office. Figure it out."

He frowned as the implication dawned on him. "But Fredelle knows my father's voice. She'd never make a mistake like that."

"Exactly."

Robbie stared at the puddle of coffee on the tabletop. "Fredelle's been in my life since I was born. She's like family. What's going on?"

"I don't know. Maybe you can find out."

At home, I inserted the CD and sent the best of the photos to Hugo Speigl. Nothing to do but wait on that front. I decided to keep busy until I heard back. I practiced SIT and STAY with Truffle and Sweet Marie until I ran out of dog treats. Still no e-mail.

I took their dog bedding and tossed it into the washing machine to freshen it up. I fluffed my pillows.

Nothing from Hugo.

I know, I know, people actually have to make a living. But this wasn't turning out to be that kind of week. When people try to kill you, you deserve time out for a while. I figured it would take months if not years to get the dogs up to speed. Even though the evaluation might be months away, I hadn't been so worried about a test since high school algebra, which in retrospect was a cakewalk compared to getting Truffle and Sweet Marie to SIT and STAY for longer than a nanosecond.

Two minutes later: nothing from Hugo. A walk would help. I attached the leashes and we headed down the stairs and around the block five times at full speed. That was enough to blow off steam. We were all panting when we returned, and I picked up Truffle and Sweet Marie and staggered up the stairs.

I squeaked in distress as a vision descended, blocking access to my apartment.

"Oh," Blair said, sounding slightly put out. "There you are."

I was so not in the mood for people with long legs and big mouths and other attributes too annoying to mention suggesting that I hadn't been exactly where I should have been.

"What's that supposed to mean?"

"Doesn't matter. Don't panic. Jack just asked me to fill you in on his situation."

I resented the hint that I might panic. I mean, really, who did this woman think she was?

"Jack has a situation? Well, that's an improvement. Congratulate him from me if you run into him, please."

"Try to be mature about this." She smirked.

Now why did that comment make me want to feed her to the fishes? I shook myself. What kind of thoughts were taking over my brain? I have never done anything violent in my life. But the veneer of civilization is thin, and now I had motivation.

"Would you mind not blocking my access?" I said icily.

She stepped aside. "What will I tell Jack?"

"Anything you like. I'm quite busy, and I can't stand on the stairs all day talking to you. You might mention that."

She shrugged. "He said to remind you about the pledge form." She reached into some mysteriously hidden pocket. "I have an extra one in case you have lost yours."

I stepped farther up the stairs so I could look her in the eyes. They were my stairs, after all. Why not use them to my advantage?

"I do not lose things."

Her smirk returned. I knew what she was thinking. I'd lost Jack and she'd found him.

I slammed around the apartment afterward, bothered by this ridiculously perfect golden vision. I ate two Mars bars and checked my messages, but I had none. Nothing from

Jack, despite the urgent messages I'd left him even before my trip to Reg Van Zandt. And still nothing from Hugo.

I ate the last tub of Ben & Jerry's New York Super Fudge Chunk. It just seemed right. As a rule, I would have split it with Jack, but that wasn't going to be happening.

The dogs regarded me with their intelligent and beady little eyes, assessing their chances of getting the empty B & J's container to rip apart.

"Forget it," I said.

Again with the looks.

"I am *not* jealous," I added. "Not even a little bit. What's more, I have never been a jealous or envious person. Everyone who knows me is well aware of that. So don't bother trying to make me feel bad."

Sweet Marie yawned. Truffle turned his back to me and curled up for a nap in a strip of late-afternoon sunshine.

"We'll be training again in a minute, and you'd better get everything right or you can kiss treats good-bye."

They cocked their little heads and studied me. Maybe this time they'd have to try a bit harder.

In the meantime, I kept busy rearranging the items on my desk and re-rearranging them. Everything looked wrong. Everything. Even my cozy little apartment seemed wrong, the dogs seemed wrong, and I seemed really wrong.

What was the matter with me? Jack was an independent person. At one time I would have also added *loyal*, but it seemed that people change. Even so, there was not a single good reason why he couldn't have a relationship with a woman who looked like a genetic triumph. He was a big boy. Why shouldn't he spend all his time with a manipulative, tall, totally-devoid-of-humor person?

I could always find someone else to tell my troubles to, someone to watch loser flicks with, someone who would always show up when I needed help, someone to bring sandwiches to and share ice cream and laughs. Someone who loved animals. Someone funny and intelligent and kind and generous, who didn't mind coming to the rescue when required—well, until recently.

How hard could that be?

I checked my e-mail and picked up the phone. I did my best to be polite when Hugo answered.

"Did you get the photos?" I asked evenly.

"Yes, yes. I did."

I rubbed my temple. "And do you know her?"

"I did, but there must be some mistake."

"Mistake? What mistake?"

"She wouldn't pretend to be Barb. I can't imagine that. Especially because—"

"Who wouldn't? Especially because what?" I tried to keep my voice level. Hugo knew this person and, unless I was wrong, liked her a lot.

"I don't want to say."

"Suit yourself. But her life's in danger."

"I am sure it is not. Angie could always look after herself. She was strong and independent. That's why she decided to become a police officer. I haven't heard from her in a long time."

"What? Angie was a police officer?"

"That's right."

"Can you tell me her last name?"

"I don't think that would be wise. I would need her permission, and I haven't seen her in years. Not since Barbara's funeral."

As Pepper answered her door, my cell phone vibrated. I let it go. Pepper looked worse than the last time I'd seen her. Had she been crying? Pepper never cried. Didn't even believe in it. That was one of several legacies from her father, some good, some not so.

"What now?" she said, leaning against the doorjamb.

I blurted out, "You're really pale. Is everything all right?"

"I'm all right," she snapped. "You're kind of pale yourself, but without a good excuse."

"In that case," I said with a weak grin, "maybe we should both sit down."

"Make it short. It's my predinner nap time."

"No problem. I'm in kind of a rush, myself."

She lowered herself onto the sofa and glowered at me.

I waited until she got comfortable. "So, do you want to tell me what Angie was up to? It would sure make my life easier."

Her jaw dropped. "Angie who?" she said unconvincingly.

Of course, I had no idea Angie who. "You know Angie who," I said.

"If I do, it doesn't make it your business."

"It's my business when she disappeared after almost running me down. It's my business when a woman is killed and I'm attacked. It's my business when trucks try to run me down."

"Angie has nothing to do with that."

"Yes, she does, Pepper. You know it and I know it."

She took a deep breath, flinched, and put her hand on her belly. I wanted to say, *Don't play the baby card*, but for once I didn't think she was playing at anything. I said, "Is she working undercover? Is that why you can't tell me?"

She shook her head. "Angie is not your business."

"Did you go to the academy together? Is that it? You don't want to expose another cop? You have to tell me."

"I don't have to tell you anything. Get that through your thick head." Pepper glowered.

I refused to be sidetracked by insults. I knew that Pepper grew up with verbal slings and arrows, and they were one way to keep control. I'd consoled her often enough when we were kids.

"I need to know if she's dangerous or if she's in danger."

There was a long silence from the sofa.

"You know why that's important, Pepper."

"I don't want you to make the situation worse."

"What is the situation?"

She curled her lip. Not a good look for someone in madonna mode. I decided I wasn't leaving without the information.

"Fine," I said. "I'll ask Connor Tierney. I believe you mentioned he was at the police academy with you. If you knew Angie, I bet he did, too."

She sat up straight and winced. "Don't tell him anything. He's the most ambitious SOB I ever met. I wouldn't trust him not to . . ."

I refrained from mentioning that Pepper was the most ambitious person that I'd ever met. For a woman, she could still manage to be an SOB. I said, "Well, you talk or I will. What the hell is going on?"

"She never became a cop. She didn't finish. She had a fling with one of our instructors, a married guy. Didn't go well and she left. Last I heard she was doing security work, talking about getting her PI license."

"So she wasn't working with the police."

"Not that I know."

"What about the guy who died in the car? Do you know anything about him?" When it started to look like she didn't plan to answer, I said, "Was he a cop? They must have an ID by now. There must be some reason why they haven't released his name or that information."

I could tell by her expression that I was right and that she knew who it was. One more push. "So I'm guessing it was the same guy she was having the fling with."

"Look, you got enough out of me. I don't know any more. I recognized her picture, and I didn't want to cause her any grief. I really liked Angie."

I kept my cool. "Did you tell her anything about me?"

"Read my lips: I haven't been in touch. I wouldn't know how to reach her if I wanted to. She didn't contact me. Nothing."

"And the guy who died?"

"I had no reason to talk to him." She scowled, something left unsaid.

"Because?"

"Well for one thing, he was an instructor; for another, he left shortly after she did. I heard he set up a corporate security business. I don't know anything else. Do you mind leaving? I feel like crap. I need to call Nick."

Nick, true to form, didn't answer. She left a message that probably would have blistered his manly ear. Pepper's white face got whiter as she spoke. You didn't have to be a doctor to know she was in pain. She tried his pager next. It must have been hard to have me watching.

"I'm clueless about all this stuff," I said, "but I have started to ask myself, who needs men? Why don't we take a run over to Woodbridge General?"

"I'll never squeeze into that tiny car of yours," she said.

"Then let me drive yours. I can pick up the Miata later."

She shook her head.

"Lots of cabs at the hospital," I said, to eliminate any suspicion that I'd cadge a lift from Nick. "Better safe than sorry. Or I'll just dial 911, and don't think I wouldn't."

"Okay, but don't ask me another single damn question. I mean it," she said.

I knew it was serious.

Forty-five minutes later, Nick finally showed up. I backed out of the hospital room and left him to his fate. "I hope everything's all right," I said. "Please keep me in the loop, Pepper. I'll take your car home and pick up mine."

Once I got back to the Miata, I took a minute to check my cell phone for messages. One from Robbie, two from Fredelle, one from Connor Tierney.

"Charlotte?" Robbie's disembodied voice said. "Now I understand about the phone call to clear the building. And I think I'm going to have some great news for you. Please get back to me as soon as you can. I'm heading over to the office."

Naturally, his cell phone went to message. "I was at the hospital with a friend. My cell phone was off. I'm available now," I said. "Dying of curiosity. Next time, give the whole story, not vague hints."

As a precaution, I called Quovadicon. Robbie hadn't shown up yet. I asked Autumn to have Robbie call me the minute he arrived.

She breathed, "Sure thing, Caroline. I'll let Fredelle know, too."

Protect your work investment with a safe environment and a good-quality, well-maintained fire extinguisher.

22

"Charlotte?" Fredelle's quavering tones said. "I need your help. I have worked out what happened to Dyan. I can't trust anyone. Can you meet me here after the office closes?"

I said, "Would that be the same office where Dyan was killed and I was knocked out and left looking like a murderer? Because you must be kidding."

"I'm desperate."

"Still not happening."

"Together we can help save Barb. Please come soon."

I snorted. "Right, and while I'm doing that why don't I rip off my clothes and run into the graveyard at midnight?"

Of course, I was talking back to a voice mail message, something I'd done far too often in recent days.

"Please don't let me down, Charlotte. I beg of you. Barb's life is at—"

I listened to the dial tone and rolled my eyes.

Now I had a ridiculous choice: race off to a place where one murder had already taken place, prodded by a woman

I no longer trusted, or sit home and chew my nails because I had promised all my friends that I'd avoid rash and dangerous activities.

I'd promised myself the same thing.

What to do?

The dogs cocked their heads, meaning, Let's practice commands and you can give us lots of treats and we may even cooperate.

"I doubt that," I said, picking up the phone.

I got Margaret's voice mail and Sally's voice mail. I swallowed my pride and called Jack, too. Voice mail. I left messages detailing what was happening, describing Robbie's call and Fredelle's.

There was just one person left.

Connor Tierney was not too important to answer his phone. And even better, he was not too busy to join me at Quovadicon. Apparently, that was the most excellent idea I'd had in a long time.

"I'm on the far side of town," he said. "Give me a chance to get over to the site first. Don't go in without me."

"Do I look crazy?"

"No comment. Although I can't actually see you."

"Very funny."

"I need you to give me a fifteen-minute head start and then you'll wait until I'm there."

"You already said that. And may I remind you that I'm the person who let you know about this. I don't really trust Fredelle, but I don't think she's capable of killing anyone. And as for Robbie, well . . ."

"Hold that thought. I'm getting into the car."

"I have to be back here in time to go to a meeting tonight." I didn't mention it had to do with the dogs. He already thought I was nuts.

He said, "Fifteen minutes won't make a difference to Fredelle. So don't go early! Bye now."

I used the head start time to do one more run through SIT, LIE DOWN, STAY, LEAVE IT, and COME. I was amazed at how much improvement there had been in a few days. Meaning that they did COME and SIT once each. Perhaps they could become therapy dogs after all. Unless a whole new set of challenges was thrown at me at the orientation meeting.

I changed quickly into the clothes I would need for that session: crisp chinos, a white T-shirt, my fuchsia cashmere hoodie, and casual flats. I grabbed my umbrella because the sky had clouded over alarmingly. I tossed the dogs a couple of treats and told them they were in charge.

By the time I slid the Miata into the visitors' parking area at Quovadicon, the trees on the fringe of the property were swaying alarmingly. There was no sign of Robbie's silver Camry, but I spotted Fredelle's shiny red Ford Focus parked near the loading docks rather than the front door. The bright yellow Volkswagen convertible was parked next to a Mercedes SUV. And an unmarked white Ford Taurus of the type favored by the Woodbridge police department was angled in that way that says cops own the world. It almost blocked a battered black Civic with dusty plates. The door to the Civic was ajar. I crept over to it, expecting to find Barb Douglas. I still wasn't used to thinking about her as Angie. But the car was empty. Had she gone inside? I couldn't imagine why.

I was supposed to wait for Tierney, but he must have figured that didn't work both ways. Nice. I just love that whole two-sets-of-rules attitude. Because he had a gun and a sense of his own importance, he could just waltz in anywhere.

Well, Fredelle had called *me*, and I was pretty sure she'd talk to me. I stepped out of the Miata just as the first large heavy drops splashed on the car roof. A rumble of thunder followed, and then the rain began to sluice down. I grabbed my umbrella, but it flipped inside out as I opened it. By the time I could adjust my hoodie to cover my hair, it was plastered to my head. Not that my hair was so important, but I knew that if anything in the slightest bit newsworthy was to happen here, Connor Tierney would appear crisp and chisel-jawed and generally heroic on WINY news. I was equally sure that if the cameras were rolling, I would be soaking wet and windblown with just a hint of homicidal mania tossed in for the viewers' appreciation.

The front door opened and Autumn appeared, absent-mindedly stepping out and squealing as her long hair swirled around her in the gale winds.

She ducked back into the building, peered, and spotted me with a start of recognition. She waved and called. "Oh, hi, Caroline! Hurry up! You'll drown."

I staggered up to the entrance, fighting the wind and rain. Autumn and I struggled to open the front door and pull it shut behind us.

"Awesome," Autumn said. "This is really something." Her keys dangled in her hand as she assessed her chances of getting to her vehicle. "I don't even have an umbrella."

"Wouldn't do you any good," I said. "It would blow inside out in a minute. Do you have a raincoat?"

She shook her head. "I'm glad you got here. Fredelle's been really worried about you."

I'd been worried about her, too, but I had no idea why she'd be worried about me. "Because of the storm?"

Autumn blanked. "Wow. I have no idea. I'm sorry."

Being Autumn, she'd never think to ask, either. But of course, why was I even surprised?

"Don't worry about it, Autumn. Did Robbie ever show up?"

"I didn't see him. And I have to leave now."

"So where is Fredelle now? In her office?"

"No, she's over in the loading dock. I don't know what she's doing there. She told me to get lost." Autumn's face fell. "That's not really cool, is it? I don't know what it is about this place, but everyone seems to be really nasty lately."

"I hear you."

"Do you need me to show you the way? I have this sort of date with a guy I met and I'm like really late. I wasn't even supposed to be here this evening, but Fredelle called me back in. That was before she told me to get lost. Do you think that's fair?" She bit her lip.

"That's okay," I said. "Don't miss out on your date. I know the way to the dock. I'll find her."

Her pretty, vacant face lit up again. "Awesome. Wow. Thanks, Caroline. I'm sure glad I put the top up on my Bug or I'd be really soaked."

As she leaned hard to open the door in the face of the wind, I said, "I'll bet. By the way, did you see the police officer come in yet?"

She turned, braced against the door to open it into the wind. "Police officer?" She frowned. "Red hair?"

"Yes."

"Really hot?"

"I suppose. Depends on your taste."

She laughed and licked her lips. "He's to my taste." The laugh stopped midgurgle. "Oh, sorry, Caroline. Is he your boyfriend?"

"Definitely not. His car seems to be here. Have you seen him?"

"Earlier. Maybe he went straight to the warehouse. Could be that's why Fredelle was acting so weird."

"Could be."

"But I have seen him before."

"Right. Okay, thanks. I'll find Fredelle."

Perhaps Connor Tierney had chosen to sneak up on Fredelle. But at least he was there. And he was smart enough to avoid the spectacular airhead Autumn. In fact, I was starting to hope she'd vanish into the storm, because a conversation with her could bring on a headache in less than five minutes. Autumn twirled her hair into a neat twist and stuck a pen through it to hold it in place against the wind and rain. On her, even that looked good.

"Bye!" She waved, the keys dangling from one hand and her cell in the other. She gave the door a serious shove with her shoulder.

Something twirled in my mind, too. What was it? Something wrong. Really really wrong.

As she approached her car, I ducked back inside, making sure I could see where she was going, without being noticed. I couldn't think of a single good reason why airy Autumn would have been carrying the silver key chain that Detective Connor Tierney liked to juggle.

Luckily, she wasn't the only one with a cell phone. I hugged the nearest wall and whipped along through the darkened central office space. I ducked into Fredelle's office and peered out the window. Autumn unlocked the door to Tierney's car and climbed in.

I decided only two things were possible: Either they were working together and conspiring to get me into the loading docks for some unknown reason. Perhaps they were holding Fredelle? Or Autumn and Fredelle were working together, again for unknown reasons, and they had Tierney in the docks and didn't want me to know about it.

Of course, by the time I'd articulated these two possibilities, I'd realized there were others. But the main thing was, people were lying and cars were being moved by people who shouldn't be moving them. Whatever was going on, it wasn't good. I'd found myself in a tight situation without a trusted police officer or, better yet, officers. There was a good chance that Fredelle or Tierney was in danger, although possibly from each other. To say nothing of Robbie.

I stopped again. The red Ford Focus was Fredelle's, and then there had been Tierney's unmarked white Taurus, now parked by the warehouse, and Autumn's yellow Bug. But who owned the SUV? It wasn't Robbie, for sure. Could someone from the warehouse afford a Mercedes SUV? Did that mean there was someone else in the building as well? I hurtled along the hallway toward the staff room and the door that led to the loading docks. Before I got there, I stopped outside the IT area and glanced behind the baffle Fredelle had placed there on my instructions. I needed to call for help and fast. I hurled myself into the IT area and scrambled behind Robbie's desk. I shivered as I thought of Dyan dying behind the next desk. At least the room had been cleaned up since, including the legendary desk surface. No sign of the stinky sardine can or the ripe sneakers, although it was hard to forget those aromas. Except for a cotton scarf forgotten on the coat rack and a few files on Robbie's desk, it was spotless. The tangle of cables had been sorted and stacked in a cardboard box behind Barb's (as I still thought of her) newly neat desk. I figured Barb had gone to a lot of trouble to create that messy desk, most likely to keep people away from her while she investigated, but it sure hadn't worked out for her. As I crouched there, I decided against speaking out loud on my cell phone. I sent a text to my misfit group, asking them to alert the police to trouble at Quovadicon. I added Pepper to that list. I had just finished when a low rumble filled the air. I took a chance, climbed on a chair, and stared out the window. A big rig rolled slowly, ominously toward the building.

I found myself shaking, catapulted back to my terrifying encounter with the late Mel and Del. It would be a long time before I could see a truck like that without reacting. *They're dead*, I told myself. But what did this mean? Was it just business as usual? A trucker arriving to unload or load cargo? In which case, could I count on him to help?

I decided against trusting. A good thing. The rig stopped and the driver's door swung open. It took me a second to recognize Autumn's father as he jumped down and came around to the near side and let down a long ramp from the back of the trailer. While my jaw was still hanging, Autumn arrived in Tierney's Taurus and deftly drove the car up the ramp. I heard the rumble of a door opening into the docks.

They knew I was there. Was I going to be the next person whose car was driven away? A terrible thought hit me: What if Tierney was in the trunk of his own car? Would he just be delivered to some death site? Or was he part of the welcoming committee for me and I had foolishly invited him to the party?

Who was watching the show in the loading dock? If Fredelle or Tierney was being held prisoner, they couldn't be left unguarded. Was a third person involved? Was it Robbie?

I slipped my cell phone into my hand and crawled under the desk. If Robbie was involved in whatever was going on, I didn't want him to sit in his chair and spot me cowering there. I didn't dare make a phone call, but my fingers got busy with a new text:

Update: Prisoners @ loading dock Quovdcn. Tierney in danger. Brng pollce asap! Before I sent it to my misfits, including Pepper, I added: Hiding cars. Maybe bodies.

My phone vibrated back quickly.

I squinted at it. Under a desk in a room with no lights on

at dusk isn't the ideal reading space. Pepper's text read: Officers on way. U hav no idea. Danger. GO.

GO? *Get out.* Easy for her. She must have been out of the hospital, but she wasn't stuck under a desk. Of course, she wouldn't have fit under the desk.

I texted: Trapped.

My legs were cramping from hunkering down. I thought hard. Whatever was happening to Fredelle and Tierney would need more than me to stop. If I opened the door to the loading dock, Autumn and her father would see me and presto, I'd probably find myself in a remote wooded area in the trunk of my car. I'd be no use to anyone.

On the other hand, if I could just get out of the building, I could call 911 and direct police to what was happening. I wondered if Mona Pringle had an address for text. I decided if I survived this time, I'd make a point of getting it.

I took a chance and crawled out from under the desk and stood up. I climbed on the chair and peered out the windows over the bookcases. With the slope of the surface in front of the building, there was a good ten-foot drop there. I glanced around. Could anything break my fall if I leaped? A chair cushion? Anything.

I came up empty. I checked around for rope. Perhaps I could lower myself. Pepper and I had done that from her bedroom window often enough at the tender age of fourteen. I probably still had the knack. Just needed the equipment. I stared at the many coils of cable in the box. Could I join some together to make a rope substitute? If I used the chair to break the window, would they hear?

At the sound of voices, I ducked back again.

"I don't know where she is. She didn't go out the front door, I'm sure of that. Don't worry. She won't get away." Autumn's voice, but where was the airy attitude, the spoiled dozy failed college girl who couldn't get through a minute without saying *awesome*? This person sounded totally in charge.

"She can't be far," the male voice said. I recognized the commanding tones of Autumn's father. "I've got the other bitch. At least that's over."

Bad, bad news for me.

Be prepared for wardrobe malfunctions:
Keep a compact sewing kit with decent scissors in your handbag.

23

"You're right. Her Miata's still there," Autumn said.

The deeper voice. "Won't help her much. She's a long way from anywhere."

"Yeah, and I disabled it, just in case."

"Good, let's deal with those other jackasses and get the hell out of here before anyone else shows up."

Very bad. I wasn't crazy about this new version of Autumn. Or her father. And who were the jackasses? Fredelle? Robbie? Tierney? Was one of them a collaborator?

"Okay, baby, I'll check around outside to be sure. You cover in here."

Gee, thanks, Daddy.

Autumn said, "She's probably cowering under one of the desks. Shouldn't take long. Nowhere to hide once I peek under. Bang bang."

"No bang bang yet. Bring her back with the others when you find her."

"What for?"

"The cops already suspected her of murder. This time

we'll do a better job of making sure it sticks. We have to get rid of the rest of them anyway. We can't let them out of here now."

"Good thinking. That snoopy bitch has it coming."

Oh double crap. Even if Autumn started at the front and made the rounds of the cubicles and the desks, it still couldn't take her more than a couple of minutes to check out the entire office. I hoped she'd try Barb's desk last. I thought about dialing 911, but I knew that the sound of the operator's voice might be enough to attract Autumn and her weapon.

I needed to do something fast before Sally and Margaret showed up. I'd thought their presence would deter any violence. Now I realized anyone in the way of Halliday and Autumn was out of luck. I opened my phone. Luckily the phone offered just enough light for me to text them a warning to stay away and call the police again.

I would have liked a weapon, even though I wouldn't know how to use one. I closed my eyes and thought hard. They popped open. I knew where there was a weapon and I did know how to use it. Robbie and Barb's space was close to the staff room, and the baffle in front of IT meant there was a small blind spot. If I played it right, I could get out of the office area and into the staff room without being seen.

I peeked into the corridor and saw no sign of Autumn, although I could hear her taunting me from what I thought was Fredelle's office.

"Might as well come out, Charlotte. I'll go easy on you if you don't make me work too hard. Remember, I'm the one with the gun."

Like I could forget that. I scooted along the hallway and into the staff room. The large glossy red fire extinguisher was right where it should have been. My office fire warden experience had just paid off. Big-time. I also knew that if it had been properly filled, it would have a force like a cannon. Knowing Fredelle and Missy, it had been properly filled.

I snatched it off the wall and crept back toward the IT area. Autumn was standing on the other side of the baffle, facing Barb's desk and calling my name. She said, "I'll huff and I'll puff and . . ."

My heart was pounding, but not enough to drown out her voice.

"Well, Charlotte. This is the last room. The last two desks. I guess I'll just have to fire into both of them."

I said from around the corner, "I may be able to blow your house down. So I have a deal to propose to you."

She snorted. "Don't make me laugh. What kind of deal could you have to offer me?"

"You want to hear it or not?"

The hardest thing was keeping the shake out of my voice. *Sound strong. Sound confident.* My mother always said, *Fake it until you make it.*

"You're not in much of a bargaining position," she said. "I have plenty of ammo."

"I'm sure you do. But if you kill me, then you'll never know what I have to say."

"What if I don't care what you say?"

"You're the one looking at life in prison."

"Make it good."

"On my terms."

"Get real. You don't have any terms. You're a perfect target. I'm here ready to fire."

In the past year or so, stalling has become one of my best talents. So have guessing and filling in the blanks.

"Here goes: The police now know you stole my phone; you had access to it. They also know that you told Fredelle the call came from Reg and that he'd called the meeting, so you could clear out the place and deal with Dyan. You needed to get rid of her because she'd been snooping around. She was getting close to uncovering your secret."

I didn't tell Autumn I didn't know what the secret was, because I was faking it. I gave it my best guess. Logically it had to be connected with the fact that Quovadicon was a shipping company and that Daddy must have found a way to use the facility for his advantage. No wonder he'd planted Autumn where she'd have access to schedules and equipment. Who would ever suspect that dimwit?

"What did she do? Figure how the shipments were working? Just a matter of time until she worked out who was behind—"

"Dyan was a nosy bitch, just like you. Found some info when she was peeking at Barb's desk."

"So she was getting closer."

"You know, I don't think you really do have any useful information, and you haven't persuaded me not to shoot you."

I took a chance. "Here's another argument in favor of cooperation: Tierney had it all figured out. And it doesn't matter if you have him here. He doesn't work alone."

"That cop? He's another pretty boy who likes to get the glory for himself."

After my wave of relief that Tierney wasn't involved in this conspiracy, I prayed that my instincts were right and Barb Douglas, who was really Angie, wasn't also a conspirator. "All right, but it has to do with where Barb would have hidden her information. She'd spent months documenting and building a case."

An intake of breath.

Jackpot.

"And you would know this how?"

"Because I have been investigating. Surely you must have noticed, when you weren't monitoring people's phone calls and checking out their desks. Everyone in the office but Robbie forgot about Barb. But I haven't, and neither have the police. So if you want to know what I have, you have to put your gun down."

"I think I'll just shoot you instead."

"Your call. But Barb's information will come to light, so you'll have one more thing to go down for."

Silence.

I held my breath. I wondered if she would conclude that she didn't have much to lose by killing me.

"All right. I'll lay the gun on Robbie's desk, but I'll be able to reach it, so don't try anything or you will definitely be dead. That clear?"

"Perfectly. Thank you."

"Get moving. You're not really in charge, you know."

"Oh, I know that," I said. Anything to get her off her guard while I got the proper grip on the fire extinguisher.

I ducked to the far side of the baffle. I wasn't really expecting her gun to be on the desk and I was right. She was waiting for me to enter on the right side. I whipped into the room from the left.

I shouted, "Autumn!"

As she turned to face me, I angled the extinguisher, squeezed the handles together, and held steady as the cloud of pressurized yellow powder shot into her mocking face. Autumn collapsed to her knees, clawing at her eyes. Her head connected to Robbie's desk with a *thwack*. Her head snapped back, and she crumpled in slow motion to the floor.

Was she dead?

Even if she'd come at me with a gun, even if she was tied to Dyan's murder and Mel and Del's deaths and the man in the trunk of the car, even then, I wasn't trying to kill her. I just needed to stop her. Coughing from powder, I felt the pulse at her neck. Her pulse was strong. I glanced around for something to secure her. But who ever finds rope in an office?

Her eyes were still closed. I had no idea how long she'd be out. I prayed I'd have enough time as I snatched some of the cables from the box. I bound her hands and feet and considered the next hurdle. The minute she opened her eyes, she'd open her mouth and scream. Then I'd get to meet Daddy and his gun. And he'd really have something to be mad at.

Not so good.

I grabbed the scarf from the coat rack and fashioned a gag out of it. I tucked Autumn's gun into the back waistband of my chinos. What did I know? It always seemed to work on television. I hoped it had a safety, even if I didn't know exactly what a safety did. I was thoroughly out of breath by the time I rolled a hundred and twenty pounds of Autumn's limp form under the desk. Were the keys to one of the vehicles in her handbag? I picked up her bag as well as my own and scrambled to my feet.

I checked out the window again. Still no police. But I did see Autumn's father climbing into a Quovadicon truck. Who was in the warehouse with Tierney, Robbie, and Fredelle? One good thing, whoever was guarding was short one mean girl and one bad daddy.

I dashed to the staff room again. I stood in front of the door to the warehouse loading dock for a couple of heartbeats, calming myself, getting my breath under control. I tried to imagine what the warehouse and loading dock would look like. Where would a bad-guy guard be standing? No way to know that, but I assumed he wouldn't be guarding this door, as the newly in-charge Autumn was taking care of matters on this side. I slid the gun from my waistband, held on to my handbags, and carefully opened the door. Naturally, in a well-maintained building, it did not squeak. I stared into a vast cavernous space with containers stacked on skids, forklifts parked, and tractor-trailers waiting to be filled. I stared down a set of concrete stairs. I took a while to believe the image: Fredelle, Robbie, and Connor Tierney were leaned against a container, several feet from each other. All three were bound and gagged. They were restrained properly, by someone who had taken the time to learn how. I recognized the duct tape. I'd had problems with duct tape in the past and it's something I cannot look at without gagging. I turned at the sound of a low moan. In the far corner near the exterior doors, a woman lay sprawled on the floor, unmoving. At least the moan meant that Barb, or more accurately, Angie, wasn't dead.

I still had my cell, but I reached into my handbag for my sewing kit and took out the scissors. I hurried down the stairs and with shaking fingers cut away the gag from Tierney's mouth. I dialed the three magic numbers. As Tierney barked instructions to the 911 operator, I snipped the duct tape binding his wrists and moved to the ankles.

"My hero," he said.

"Believe it." I couldn't bring myself to grin. "Autumn's tied up inside the IT office."

When he stopped rubbing his wrists, I handed him Autumn's gun. At least one of us knew how to use it. Then I turned to Fredelle. Tears streaked her pale, plump face. Her aqua sweater was rumpled and dusty. She shook as I snipped through the bonds.

When the gag came off, she gripped my hand and blurted, "I am so sorry, Charlotte. Autumn had a gun. She made me say that Barb's life was in danger. She said she'd kill Robbie if I didn't."

I took care of Robbie next. He was wheezing as I got the gag off. I moved behind the forklift on my way to see how badly injured the woman I still thought of as Barb was. Just as well, because I heard the loud beep of a truck backing up. I ducked out of sight as the overhead door from the parking lot slowly opened. Halliday jumped down from the cab of a Quovadicon rig. The pricey business suit was gone. But even in dark jeans and a waterproof jacket, he was confident, menacing, and deadly.

"Well, what do we have here? The kids are not behaving, I see." He turned and trained his weapon on the unconscious Barb. "Let's fix that."

Tierney stood up and leveled the gun at him. At least he knew what he was doing.

Halliday sneered. "Give it up. I'll take this nosy bitch with me for the hell of it. Put the gun down or I'll shoot her right in front of you. I've got nothing to lose."

Tierney slowly lowered the gun, bent, and placed it on the cement floor. Halliday smirked, his weapon still trained on the still form on the floor. He glanced around. Was it possible that he didn't realize that Robbie and Fredelle were no longer tied up? My heart fluttered when he spotted me.

Tierney tried a distraction, his voice remarkably calm. "You know you can't get away with this. You'd better quit while you're ahead. I am a police officer. At this point you can still make a deal, give us information about the car theft ring, purchasers. It will go easier on you."

"I think we will get away with it. You're the guy with the problem." He gestured to me. "You. Snoop sister. Get over here."

I shook my head. I knew he would shoot me if I got within shooting distance.

Tierney said, "The place will be surrounded. You start shooting and it's the end for you and your daughter. Keep that in mind."

Perhaps Halliday was distracted by that and didn't hear Robbie utter a low growling sound, hardly human. Or perhaps he was caught off guard when the door to the office banged open and a vision in a wet Hawaiian shirt appeared.

Jack stared wildly around at the frozen tableau. "Charlotte? What's going on?"

Halliday raised his weapon and fired. Jack's eyes widened. He opened his mouth, but nothing came out as he tumbled down the concrete stairs. I screamed and started to rush forward. Halliday stood between Jack and me.

Halliday said, "You too, lady." He turned his weapon in my direction. Behind him, Robbie launched himself at Halliday, roaring like a wild boar. As Robbie knocked his knees out from under him, I raised my handbag and Autumn's and whacked Halliday on the head.

Not-so-lucky Halliday dropped. Robbie leaped on him, punching wildly, a cartoon character held back too long. I raced toward Jack as Tierney took over. Robbie was still roaring. I heard Fredelle sob. "Robbie! Stop, you'll be killed."

Tierney said, "Move away, Robbie. I don't mind shooting him, but you're off limits."

As I knelt by Jack, blood spread through the yellow starfish on his shirt and pooled onto the floor. He whispered, "I should have come earlier."

I took off my hoodie and pressed it against the wound. "Tierney! Call for an ambulance," I yelled as I fumbled for my own phone. But of course, the wailing sirens were getting closer, almost upon us.

My whole body shook. "Jack, please don't die because of me."

I lowered my head to hear his whispered words. "I'm sorry."

I said, "Don't be sorry."

Jack's voice cracked as he struggled to speak. "Sally showed up at our meeting. She told me what's been happening. I feel like such a doofus. I am so sorry, Charlotte, that I wasn't there for you. Blair said she was helping me focus by handling my calls. She must have deleted your calls. She didn't pass on any of your messages. Not a single one of them. You know I would have been there for you. I had no idea Blair would be so—" He gasped for breath.

I said, "Shhh. It doesn't matter. Don't try to talk."

Jack's eyes closed. He was still breathing, shallowly, but for how long?

Through the open door, I saw a team of uniformed police officers advancing, weapons drawn, and, moving up behind them, the tall, dark, and granite-faced Frank D'Angelo. I was thrilled to see the detective, but how had he known to show up? Of course, Margaret must have called him when she picked up my voice mail. I could always count on her to take action.

"Jeez, Tierney, you astound me. How pushy can you get?" Frank said, glancing around. "If you had to ruin my dinner date, couldn't you at least have left something for me to do?"

The emergency workers bent over to check Jack. I was still shaking. I did my best to calm myself to ask, "Is he going to be all right?"

After what seemed like an eternity, one of the paramedics flashed me a grin. "Looking good for this guy. He's lost some blood, but it seems the bullet missed all the important parts."

Jack whispered again, "Of course I'm going to be all right. I have some making up to do."

I predicted a long, long night at the hospital, but that would all be well worth it.

Detective D'Angelo stepped toward us to see how things were going with Jack. Jack's eyes were closed, but he was breathing well, and I could feel the strength in the hand I held. I managed a smile. "They say he's going to be okay. And don't worry, Frank, I think that's one dinner date that will wait for you. And there's a nice surprise inside. The other half of the Halliday team, all tied up as a special gift. Whatever you do, don't let your guard down with sweet little Autumn. She's as much a killer as her father and she plays dirty."

He said, "Guess it's game over for both of them."

Make time for friends and social events.
It will boost your productivity, and you'll gain in ways
that are far more important than work in the long run.

24

Inside the Casa di Mario, wall sconces reflected soft light on the Tuscan murals. The white tablecloths, the flickering candles, the clink of glasses, and the laughter of the guests gathered around the huge table testified to a great party. It was the first time we misfits and other key players had been together since all hell broke loose at Quovadicon two weeks earlier.

"Are you going to eat the rest of your *ravioli al burro e salvia*?" Attaboy. Jack knew how to bounce back. He was sporting a new Hawaiian shirt with bright blue and orange parrots and even wore long pants in honor of the occasion.

I said, "Help yourself. You earned it."

Pepper, more pregnant than ever, leaned forward to catch Jack's eye from her seat at the end of the large table. For reasons I didn't fully understand, Jack and I were sitting next to Pepper and Nick, with Sally and Benjamin at right angles to us at the other end.

Pepper said, "I suppose you'll be taking advantage of that flesh wound for the rest of your life."

Jack said, "It seems to be working for me. How about you? Are you going to finish your ravioli, Pepper?"

"You bet your dumb Hawaiian shirt I am," Pepper said.

Margaret called across the table. "Relax, Jack. The next of several courses will be served soon. You might want to save room for the *pollo al limone* and the risotto, among many other things."

Frank D'Angelo stood and raised a glass of red wine to Margaret, at his side and gorgeous in an ivory silk cocktail suit, with her hair twisted into a glamorous updo.

He said, "A toast to my beautiful bride."

As we rose to join in the toast, Margaret produced an unlawyerly blush. That encouraged a loud clinking of forks on water glasses, and Frank dipped Margaret into an adults-only clinch.

Next to me, Sally sighed and whispered, "I don't remember the last time I saw her in anything but a navy blue suit. But I suppose you can't really buy a navy blue two-piece wedding dress in a wool blend. And even though she cheated us out of a big wedding, you have to admit an elopement is very romantic. It did keep her parents off her back." Sally's husband glared at her, as he so often does, not that she noticed.

Next to the surprise bride, Mr. and Mrs. Tang sat, smiling for once. Perhaps it was the constant glass clinking. Or more likely the new Italian son-in-law who looked like he could make tall, dark babies.

Sally said, "Margaret thinks her parents are planning a giant Korean celebration after this."

Jack said, "Cool. I love Korean food."

People took advantage of the lull between courses. As Pepper got up and walked around the table to chat with Margaret and Frank, Nick nudged me and said, "You know, Charlie, I never figured out everything that was going on. Did you?"

"Eventually," I said.

"Pepper flips if I ask her about it. She's real touchy lately. I can't really ask any of the guys at work, because I'm supposed to know this stuff. But you're my friend, so I figure you'll tell me. So this Barb person was undercover?"

"Private security and her real name was Angie something," I said, hoping Pepper didn't react to this cozy conversation. "She was hired by Reg Van Zandt to find out whether someone inside the company was using his fleet and logistics systems for criminal purposes. He didn't know who, or what they were doing, and he didn't know who he could trust, but his foreman figured out that something funny seemed to be going on. Numbers weren't quite matching up. They thought maybe they were shipping counterfeit goods or even drugs using the fleet, but it turned out that the Quovadicon system was being used to transport stolen high-end vehicles with fake documentation. That was the same case that Frank had been working on and I guess Tierney had some involvement in that investigation, too, not that he confided in me."

Connor Tierney took that moment to leave his seat and pull up his chair between Nick and me. I'd been surprised to see him show up at the celebration dinner, but apparently he and Frank were the best of pals. He said, "They supplied the cars and fitted them up with false vehicle information numbers. With the fake VINs, no one could trace them. A big business. Halliday used the Quovadicon rigs, and he arranged to have the drivers you knew as Mel and Del hired on at the company. Autumn was in charge of fake documentation that didn't make the official records. After all, Halliday was an old friend of the big boss. As far as the Hallidays knew, no one was the wiser, until Barb showed up. She was able to pass on information to her partner, and they thought they would be able to report fairly soon, but he got too close to one of the dummy rigs one night and—"

"So long, sucker." Nick chuckled, not reacting to the looks he got from me and from Tierney. "So that receptionist was in on it from the start? The hot one?"

Tierney said, "Don't be fooled. Autumn Halliday was more than a pretty face. She was a lot smarter than she looked. She made sure that the shipments were coordinated and invisible with false shipping documentation. She learned it all from Daddy. Halliday was a businessman himself. Just not an honest one."

Nick bristled. "I wasn't fooled."

I said, "I was. In fact, no one suspected her, and she had the run of the office. She often stayed late. She didn't like me showing up, for sure. She stole my cell phone and used it to place the call to clear out the building; Fredelle fell for the message, and for a while you suspected me."

Nick looked puzzled. "But why did she do that again?"

Tierney answered with admirable restraint. "So she could deal with Dyan, who had been spying on Barb. Dyan knew something. She just didn't have time to figure out what she knew, and Autumn made sure she didn't find out."

Nick's voice rose. "Well, then who killed the guy in the trunk?"

I said, "The guy in the trunk was Barb's partner. I should really say Angie's partner, because that was her real name. She kept in close touch with Van Zandt. I think she even called him from the crime scene and told him her partner was dead and she was taking off."

Ramona, regal in blue shantung silk and twinkling silver earrings, had followed Tierney over and joined us. She butted in at that point. "No kidding. I think this Angie and her partner were the ones who took the library files on Quovadicon when they were researching. Should be a hanging offense. You all keep that in mind."

Margaret glanced over and said, "Don't worry. We want to keep on your good side, Ramona. We'll play by the rules."

Nick said, "But why did they kill him like that?"

I said, "They wanted to stop his investigation. They would have killed Angie, too, and she knew it. She panicked and fled, just ahead of them. I'm guessing that someone in the Woodbridge police told her he was dead and warned her to get away from the office fast. I wonder who that was."

Tierney had the grace to look sheepish. I said, "At least you don't need to lie about it any more."

He said, "I knew Angie from school, and I knew her partner, too. I didn't like him quite as much. She got in touch when she came to town and let me know what she was doing. So sure, I passed on the information when we found the first body. She was vulnerable, and Frank here kept me in the loop. Frank and I started to suspect that there might be a connection with his car theft project. Big money in that game. We knew that the people running this car theft ring were high-stakes players with a lot to lose. After her partner's murder, I told her to stay out of sight, but she kept in touch. That's why we stalled you, Charlotte."

Sally said, "It makes my head hurt, it's so complicated. So who killed the so-called Mel and Del?"

Tierney said, "We'll probably never prove it, but we're sure one of the Hallidays disposed of them. Mel and Del were great as muscle, but they weren't bright enough to withstand questioning. And Charlotte had recognized them. They became a liability. We've tied that killing to Autumn's weapon, although it will be hard to know which Halliday pulled the trigger. That's why conspiracy is so useful."

Sally interjected, "So Angie was on the run, afraid for her life. Whatever made her come back to Quovadicon?"

I said, "Apparently, love makes women do crazy things. It seems she was just as smitten as Robbie was. He fell for her despite that disgusting desk, and she fell for him despite his lack of social finesse. She decided to see him one more time to say good-bye and explain what had happened. She called on the office phone and foolishly set up a meeting on a side road near Quovadicon. Autumn eavesdropped on that call as she had on so many others. Autumn sent her father to collect Angie, while she took care of Robbie. He told Angie they would kill Robbie if she didn't play along. She must have realized that the Hallidays meant to murder them both."

Ramona said, "Good thing it didn't work. I think they're made for each other."

I nodded. "I guess those wedding magazines I spotted in her apartment were more than just décor."

Ramona said, "I told you he was sweet. I'm glad they met up. Too bad it led to all this turmoil and danger."

I nodded. "No kidding. A lot could have been avoided if Reg Van Zandt hadn't tried to control the investigation, not that he suspected Robbie or Fredelle, but he didn't trust their judgment."

Ramona had an update on that. "At least it was the turning point for Robbie to get out from under his father's thumb. Robbie has tons of money squirreled away. As you can tell from his wardrobe and car, he never spends a cent. Now he's taken Angie off to a resort in the Caribbean to rest and recover."

Sally said, "What does Robbie's father think about that relationship?"

"I think Robbie's past caring. He has a reason to be his own man now. I, for one, am glad. I think they'll end up at the altar before too long," Ramona predicted.

Pepper, edging back to her seat, overheard. A small smirk hovered on her lips. "I guess they'll find out in time what that's worth."

Nick looked up at her with big sad puppy eyes. "Aw, come on, babe. You don't mean that."

Sally said, "I hope the Van Zandts appreciated how many people were endangered."

I said, "Well, Robbie apologized for getting me out to Quovadicon that day. He'd called me, being so mysterious, because he'd figured out that Autumn had fooled Fredelle. I let the cat further out of the bag by telling Autumn he was meeting me, too. I didn't even suspect her at that point. I thought I was being sensible calling Tierney. Who could have predicted what was going on?"

Sally had been unusually quiet. "So why did Fredelle show up?"

"She'd left for the day and when she spotted Robbie rac ing back, she circled back and followed him. She's always been a mother hen to him and she just wanted to apologize, but she found herself facing Autumn and her weapon. Then Tierney showed up waving his badge, I bet. Is that right, Connor?"

Jack said, "Those chicken cutlets are taking a while. What about your rosemary bread? Are you going to eat that?"

Tierney had returned to his seat at the other end of the table, opposite Sally and Benjamin, but he was close enough to hear most of our conversation. "At that point, they were between a rock and a hard place."

I said, "Perhaps that's when they hatched the plan to kill everyone and make it look like I had done it, because I'm widely known as a danger to Woodbridge. That might have kept the investigation from leading to them."

Pepper said, "Well, they're locked up now, and they're not getting bail."

"It all worked out all right, except that Charlotte missed her Therapy Dogs orientation meeting," Sally added.

I said, "That was okay, too. The pooches still need a lot of work. The spring session seems more realistic."

Jack stood and said, "You're right. And since we're toasting, here's to happy endings. And hey, look, here comes the *pollo al limone*."

The wineglasses were lifted. "To happy endings."

Pepper raised her water glass. "Yeah, sometimes they happen."

The bride stood and added her own toast. "To friendships. And to new beginnings."

Jack gave me a nudge.

From the end of the table, Tierney winked.

Mary Jane Maffini is a lapsed librarian, a former mystery bookseller, and a previous president of Crime Writers of Canada. In addition to creating the Charlotte Adams series, she is the author of the Camilla MacPhee Mysteries, the Fiona Silk series, and nearly two dozen mystery short stories. She has won two Arthur Ellis awards for short fiction, and *The Dead Don't Get Out Much*, her latest Camilla MacPhee Mystery, was nominated for a Barry Award in 2006. She lives in Ottawa, Ontario, with her long-suffering husband and two miniature dachshunds.